William Bradshaw, King of the Goblins

by

Arthur Daigle

Publication Information

This novel is entirely a work of fiction. The names characters and places portrayed in it are the work of the author's imagination or are used fictitiously. Any resemblance to actual persons living or dead, events or locales is entirely coincidental.

William Bradshaw, King of the Goblins

by

Arthur Daigle

Cover illustration by Aaron Williams

This book is dedicated to my father, Edward Henry Daigle.

About the author:

Arthur Daigle was born and raised in the suburbs of Chicago, Illinois. He received a biology degree from the University of Illinois Urbana-Champaign, and has worked in such diverse fields as testing water quality and grading high school essay tests. In addition to his writing, Arthur is an avid gardener and an amateur artist and photographer. This book was almost inevitable given that the author was fan of fantasy and science fiction since he was old enough to walk. This is his first published novel, with more on the way.

Acknowledgements:

There are many people who deserve credit for helping me with this novel. Much of the inspiration came from the works of the puppeteer and filmmaker Jim Henson and the British artist Brian Froud. I hold these men in the highest regard for their great humor and creativity. I also owe a debt to the Millennium Writers' Group, which I was a part of for many years until it folded in 2009. I received a great deal of feedback from the members of the group, and I greatly miss their company.

Lastly, I owe a tremendous debt to my family for their support, especially my brother David. David helped edit the novel and offered many suggestions.

William Bradshaw, King of the Goblins

by

Arthur Daigle

Chapter One

Trespassers will be shot;
survivors will be sued, kicked
in the shin, and shot again.

Puzzled, Will studied the sign on the door. It struck him as being a bit antisocial for the front door of a law office. He wasn't sure what he expected a law firm to be like, but this didn't look right. The building itself was nothing special, just a big brick box near a busy intersection. But the glass door in front had that message etched into it.

William Bradshaw was a young man, six feet tall and lean, with short brown hair and gray eyes. He wore an old suit that itched and wasn't good enough to make the right impression with people.

Normally Will had nothing to do with lawyers, but this bunch had recently advertised for a manager's position to oversee one of their projects. The advertisement had almost no details besides the firm's address and phone number. Out of desperation he'd applied, and to his surprise they agreed to interview him for the position.

Looking at the message on the door, he wondered if coming here was a good move.

In the end he had no choice in the matter. His efforts to find work had all been dismal failures. Worse, he still had student loans to pay off, and the bank was getting impatient. Their last letter described (in friendly terms) how large men with baseball bats would visit him to discuss repayment of his loans if he didn't start sending money soon.

Cautiously, he tried the door. It opened smoothly, with no alarms or signs of armed guards appearing. He stuck his head inside and looked around.

The building's lobby could double as a rain forest. With the exception of a trail leading from the front door to the offices, there wasn't a square inch of space not covered in potted plants. They were big plants, too, some reaching up to the vaulted ceiling. Thick vines clung to the taller plants and connected them together in a single tangled mass. Along the trail was a desk half-covered with blooming orchids, and a lady secretary hammering away at a computer keyboard. She was pretty and wore black business attire and a machete on her belt. She glanced up from her work when he entered.

"If this is about the plants, we're working on it," she said.

"No, this is about the interview for the manager position," Will replied.

"Oh good," the secretary said in relief. "I thought you were with the health department. Those guys have been on us like white on rice! I mean, seriously, one person gets a tropical disease and they have to make a federal case out of it. If you see anything move, don't touch it."

"Right," he said as something scurried through the undergrowth. "Why so many plants?"

She shrugged. "You know, I'm not sure. It started with an African violet and kind of got out of hand from there."

Will took a piece of paper from his pocket and checked it. "I'm supposed to meet with someone named Twain. I'd appreciate it if you could point me in the right direction."

A door behind Will opened and an older man stepped out. "Jennifer, I need some coffee, all the documents we have on the Palmer case and a bear trap, preferably steel."

"That's him," the secretary said sourly.

The man standing in the doorway looked wrong to Will, but he wasn't sure why. Twain stood around six-foot-four and was of average build. He had gray hair and a gray mustache. He was dressed in a conservative gray business suit, black shoes and necktie. That said, there was still something slightly odd about him. Something about his eyes, or maybe the way he walked.

"Ah hello, you would be Mr. Bradshaw. My name is Mr. Twain, do come in." He smiled at his secretary and said, "Now Jennifer, don't go frightening our friend Mr. Bradshaw. You know that's my job."

"I'm very glad you're here," Twain said cheerfully as he shook William's hand and showed him into his office. "And ten minutes early. Is that because you're impatient, you're nervous, or you need to use the bathroom?"

"Uh, none of the above," William said.

Twain smiled. "That's good, because we don't like impatient people or nervous people. And we have no public bathrooms."

William walked into Twain's office, a large room with a wood table, five padded chairs and a steel door at the back of the room. There were three bizarre paintings hanging on the white walls. The first picture showed giant squids playing poker, while the second showed a bar where Twain was sharing a drink with a shambling plant-thing that looked like a cross between a man and a compost heap. The last painting was of Kermit the Frog as President of the United States. Come to think of it, Kermit would be better than most of the yahoos who'd ever held the job.

"Do sit down, Mr. Bradshaw," Twain said pleasantly.

"Thank you. I have some questions about the position you're offering."

Twain smiled condescendingly. "Mr. Bradshaw, we here at Cickam, Wender and Downe are very busy, frightfully busy, really, and this is taking up time I could be golfing and billing a client. Now are you going to sit or do I need to club you with that chair?"

"I'll sit," Will said nervously as he sat in the chair opposite Twain.

"First good move you've made, Mr. Bradshaw," Twain said, still smiling. "There's no time for rational thought or common sense in business. That's where ninety percent of questions come from."

Puzzled, Will asked, "Where do the other ten percent come from?"

"People asking to use the bathroom. That's why we make it a policy not to have one."

Before Will could say anything else, he heard a loud snap. Twain shouted in triumph and dove out of his chair. He got up off the floor with a confused look and a mousetrap bent out of shape. The lawyer took a tiny piece of paper stained with cheese crumbs off the trap. "Blast it, the writing's too small. Can you read this?"

Will took the scrap of paper and saw tiny words written on it. "It says, 'next time, make it cheddar'?"

Twain stood up and boldly pointed at a mouse hole low on the wall of his office. "Your luck can't hold out forever, you infernal rodent! One of these days you'll slip up and I'll send you back to the fiery realm that spawned you!"

"Mouse trouble?" Will asked. Nervous, he scooted his chair away from Twain.

Twain scowled and sat back down. "Of the worst kind! I told that miserable rodent I wouldn't take his case and he threw a fit. He's holed up in here and refuses to leave until I say yes."

"Why don't you hire an exterminator?" Will asked.

"I tried that," Twain said. "The man was here for three days. In the end we had to have an ambulance take him home. Poor man's been traumatized for life. I seem to recall hearing he'd changed jobs and become a turnip farmer. Oh well, my problem, not yours. Back to the business at hand."

Twain opened a folder and took out a copy of Will's resume. Smiling again, he took out a red pen.

"Cickam, Wender and Downe was founded in 1851 by three lawyers who wanted someone else to do their work for them," Twain said. "They decided to only accept men of great intellect, unsurpassed integrity and a firm understanding of the law. They gave that up after five years when no one fit the bill. This led them to hire any fool who could manage to open a door without hurting himself, which produced a slightly higher number of successful applicants. But there are only so many jobs and too many idiots trying to get them! It's been my experience that people will lie, cheat and steal to get a job here. So far no one has tried killing someone to get hired, but give it time." Twain's eyes narrowed. "You don't have a gun, do you?"

"No," Will told him.

"A knife?"

"No."

"A spatula?"

A bit exasperated, Will replied, "That's not a deadly weapon."

"You wouldn't say that if you met my second or fourth wife," Twain retorted.

"Mr. Bradshaw," Twain began, "when we advertised this job we received over seven hundred resumes. None of them were even remotely qualified. You, however, are less unqualified than the other candidates. In fact it came down to you and an organ grinder's monkey in Florida."

"For a job as a manager?" Will asked quizzically.

Twain nodded. "It was a close one, but the monkey refused to relocate. Now then, Mr. Bradshaw, you say you have managerial experience?"

"Yes, at my first job."

That was stretching the truth until it broke. His first job was at a petting zoo where he 'managed' seven guinea fowl, two foul tempered geese that attacked children on sight and a border collie. The job lasted three weeks and ended when the border collie decided dry dog food wasn't going to be good enough anymore. Will felt very bad about what had happened to the guinea fowl, but those geese had it coming.

"Good, good," Twain said and wrote on the resume with exaggerated strokes of his pen. "And you have no problem working outdoors?"

"No problem at all."

That was less of a lie. His second job involved spending three months scooping road kill off highways. Will had learned how to identify many small animals native to North America during that job, provided they were two-dimensional.

"Working with people from other cultures isn't a problem for you?" Twain asked.

"Oh no."

"Then everything looks good." Twain wrote on the resume, smiled at Will, then crumpled the resume up and threw it in a trash can.

"What did you do that for?" Will demanded.

"Mr. Bradshaw," Twain said pleasantly, "I have been instructed to ask prospective employees a series of questions, a few of which actually make sense. I'll need you to answer them as truthfully as possible, and remember, there are wrong answers and you're probably going to give them to me."

"Are you sure you're doing this right?" Will asked timidly.

"Don't know, I've never done this before," Twain replied. "Question number one, have you ever committed a felony or serious crime?"

"No."

Leaning forward, Twain asked, "Have you thought about committing a felony?"

"Does that count?"

"It does in Canada. Question two, have you ever thought about defrauding your employer of all of his money, fleeing the country and spending the rest of your life living in luxury in Jamaica?"

"Uh, no."

"Hmm, wouldn't last a day working here," Twain said bluntly as he scribbled something down on a sheet of paper. "Question three, have you ever eaten an entire block of cheese in one meal?"

"No," Will said. "What does this have to do with a job as a manager?"

"Excuse me, but I'm the one with the list of questions," Twain said peevishly. "Question five—"

Confused, Will asked, "What happened to question four?"

"Broke both legs while skiing. Silly fool went and ran into a tree. Question five, in the event of a nuclear disaster, would you pray to the Almighty God, run and hide, or blame a coworker for causing it?"

Exasperated and more than a bit confused, Will said, "I don't know. What sort of a question is that?"

"Apparently a good one."

Will didn't think the interview was going well at all. Twain wasn't making any sense, and when he did he was abusive. Will figured Twain was nuts, or drunk, or he used to teach gym class in high school.

The questions kept coming. "Question six, were you born under the astrological sign Pisces, Virgo, Sagittarius, tiger, dragon, ox, banana slug, tree sloth or Ford Pinto?"

Will opened his mouth, then paused to collect his thoughts. "Wait, some of those are western zodiac, some are eastern zodiac and the rest don't make sense."

"Very little in life does make sense, Mr. Bradshaw, and then only because it's lying. Question seven, how many people have you eaten?"

"What? Wait just a minute!"

"I'd love to, but I have a pressing appointment later today. Come on, how many?"

Will stood up and folded his arms across his chest. "I haven't eaten anybody! What kind of a question is that?"

Twain gave him an exasperated look. "Mr. Bradshaw, I'm sure someone told you it's perfectly all right to lie during an interview, but it's simply not true. You are most certainly a cannibal. It's written all over your face."

"I am not!"

"Fine, if you're going to play games with me I'm going to have to make an educated guess. I'm putting down five."

"Give me that!" Will said as he tried to snatch the paper from Twain. Twain slapped his hand away.

"No!" Twain shouted. He grabbed a rolled-up newspaper off his desk and swatted Will with it again and again. "Bad applicant! Bad! Bad!"

"Stop that!"

"Question eight!" Twain shouted as he climbed up onto the table and leaned forward into Will's face. Will stumbled back into his chair. "Have you ever found yourself in an abandoned warehouse in Sydney, Australia, only two bullets left in your gun and no less than three rabid mountain gorillas armed with wiffle bats coming right at you!"

"No!"

"Thank God for that," Twain said and got back into his seat. "Happened to me once and I barely made it out alive. All right then, I think you'll do just fine."

"Fine?" William demanded. He was trying to keep his temper and failing. "Fine for what? I still don't know what I'm supposed to be doing for you!"

"Oh the job isn't with us," Twain said and stood up. "Cickam, Wender and Downe is acting as a headhunter for a special client with very specific needs. You'll be working for them."

"Oh," William said, feeling very relieved he wouldn't be near Twain ever again. "How long does the job last?"

"You're young and reasonably healthy. I think you'll last a few weeks."

"What?" William asked. Twain walked around the table and helped Will up, then wrapped an arm around his shoulder. Still smiling, he walked Will to the steel door.

"It's been a pleasure meeting you, Mr. Bradshaw, and I'm sure you'll be exactly what our client is looking for. If you ever find yourself in need of legal help, remember that our law firm wants absolutely nothing to do with you whatsoever and may send hired goons after you if you try to contact us. Now, if you'll walk through this door, our client is eagerly awaiting your arrival."

Twain grabbed the doorknob with his free hand, stopped, then leaned over close to Will and whispered, "Mr. Bradshaw, a word of advice?"

"Yes?"

"Don't scream. It doesn't help."

With that, Twain opened the door to reveal a chamber with rough cut rock walls and a pit easily ten feet across. Tree roots grew into the sides of the pit and small unwholesome squirming things with lots of legs crawled around the edge. The pit seemed to go on forever, its bottom so far down Will couldn't hope to see it.

And then Twain pushed him in.

Chapter Two

Will screamed. He plummeted down the shaft, going faster with each passing second, the wind whistling in his ears. After he screamed, he took a deep breath and screamed again. By the time scream number two was done he still hadn't hit bottom.

"He's right, it doesn't help," Will said. He looked around helplessly as he kept falling. Torches were placed on the sides of the shaft and provided plenty of light. Pity was, there was so little to look at, just an assortment of rocks and roots and a few blank white panels with the words 'AD SPACE FOR SALE, CALL 555-CASH'.

Will continued falling. He checked his watch and shrugged. Falling down the pit wasn't hard at all, but it was boring. "I didn't think this would take so long. I should have brought a lunch."

Finally he could see a bright light far below him and the bottom of the shaft. It looked like he'd be landing soon, which was probably going to hurt a lot. Will grabbed at the roots growing into the pit, only to have them crumble apart in his hands. The bottom of the pit was getting closer.

Whump!

* * * * *

"Hey there," a squeaky voice said.

Will was laying down on what seemed to be cold, hard rock. He was sore, but not in nearly as much pain as he'd figured he'd be. His eyes were still closed. His must have passed out when he landed. Will felt someone shake his shoulder.

"Hmm," Will grumbled. For a change his horoscope was right. Falling down a pit certainly qualified as a big change in his life, and surviving it was a surprise.

"Come on, I know you're alive," the squeaky voice said.

Will rubbed his head and managed to sit up. "That part about me being alive is open to debate. Shouldn't I be kind of dead?"

"No, you should be extremely dead, but Cickam, Wender and Downe filed a cease and desist order against gravity. I've seen them do it before. It's always funny."

"Twain," Will said angrily. He was sore but still alive. He struggled to his feet and opened his eyes.

"Yeah, Twain's with them."

Will looked at the person speaking to him. Looked down at him, to be more precise. The person he was talking to stood three and a half feet tall and had wrinkly gray skin and ratty black hair. The little man (or whatever he was) wore yellow flowing robes and held a gnarled walking stick. He didn't look frightening so much as he looked bizarre. He smiled at Will.

"Ah, I'm hallucinating," Will said.

The gray-skinned man smiled and nodded. "Good time to have one. These trips are always rough."

"No, you see, I think I'm talking to a little man in yellow robes."

"That's really happening, but calling me a man is either generous or insulting. I'm not sure which."

Will looked around. He was in a limestone cave, poorly lit by torches. The floor was covered in pebbles and broken rocks, plus a generous helping of trash. The air was cool and moist and smelly. A tunnel led out of the cave, apparently to the surface judging by the faint light coming from it. Will looked up and didn't see the shaft he'd fallen down.

Will pointed and waved his hand vaguely at the cave ceiling where the shaft should have been. "Uh—"

"Oh that," the little man said. "It was a temporary gate, only enough power in it to stay open a few minutes. Now that you're through it closed down."

"How do I get it back?"

The little man shrugged. "No idea. That's not the kind of magic my people know how to work."

"Your people? Okay, stupid question—"

"That's my favorite kind!" the little man said cheerfully.

"Who are you, who are your people, and why am I here?"

The little man counted off fingers as he answered each question. "I am Domo, reasonably loyal servant. My people are goblins. You're here because you got the job."

Will stared at the little goblin. "Job? Are we talking about a job advertised by a law firm for a manager?"

Domo nodded. "We *are* talking about the job as manager, and Cickam, Wender and Downe did advertise for it."

"They didn't say anything about being thrown down a pit with goblins in it!" Will shouted.

"Of course not," Domo replied. "I mean, they would never get anyone if they said that. So they decided to lie like a cheap rug to get you here. It works more often than you'd think."

"Oh no. I don't want anything to do with this," Will said as he backed away.

Domo followed him and laughed. "Yeah, we get that a lot."

Will looked down the tunnel. There was light coming that way, so it was an obvious way out. The first order of business involved getting out of here. After that, finding Twain and beating him silly seemed like a good idea.

"This has been a...unique experience and, uh, you've been really helpful," he told Domo as he slowly edged toward the tunnel.

"You're too kind," Domo said.

"But I really need to be going. Tell you what, I'll write you a thank you letter the second I get home." With that Will turned and ran down the tunnel as fast as he could. Behind him he heard Domo shouting, but he was already too far away to hear it. Within seconds he was in the open air.

Which really didn't improve things any.

The tunnel opened on a courtyard several hundred feet across and paved with cobblestones. In most places the cobblestones were covered in dirt and wiry grass, and elsewhere there were piles of garbage. Around the courtyard were dozens of buildings, all wrecked. At the very least the buildings had the windows and doors knocked out. Some of them were also missing walls and roofs, while the better kept ones simply had holes knocked in them. The tallest building was three stories high, and in the distance he could see what looked like a gatehouse and wall standing a good six stories tall. A network of thick creeping vines with broad leaves and white flowers covered every building.

Filling the courtyard and the buildings and the gatehouse in the distance were goblins, hundreds or even thousands of the little creatures. They looked only a bit like Domo, some being a foot taller or shorter, others much heavier or thinner. Their skin color ranged from light blue, to gray, to red, to green, and some were light-skinned like Will. Unlike Domo, most of them wore simple leather clothes or rags. Even in large numbers they looked goofy instead of frightening.

The assembled crowd of goblins saw him and cheered. Some held up banners with a black spiral on a green background, while other goblins threw confetti. A band got going on drums and horns with what might charitably be called music. The crowd stomped their feet in time with the musicians. Above all the noise was the sound of hundreds of voices chanting.

"Will-i-am! Will-i-am! Will-i-am!"

Will staggered back against the tunnel entrance, wholly confused. Domo walked out of the tunnel and stepped in front of him. The little goblin raised his hands and the crowd quieted.

"Brothers, friends, hangers on! We have been without leadership for an entire year since King Vickers the Cunning escaped. But those hard times are over!" The crowd cheered. Domo pointed his walking stick at William and shouted, "Behold our new king, William Bradshaw, moniker to be determined later!"

The crowd cheered again. William staggered back. He felt lightheaded and his stomach was getting queasy.

"Speech! Speech!" the crowd bellowed.

"I, I don't feel well," Will muttered before he passed out and fell over backwards. The nearest goblins grabbed him before he hit the ground.

"Short and to the point," Domo said. "He'll do well."

* * * * *

"Don't feel bad," Domo told Will after he regained consciousness. "This was a lot to take in, and nobody prepared you for it."

"Exactly how could anyone prepare me for this?" Will asked. He was awake now but still felt lightheaded and his stomach was unsettled. After Will passed out, the goblins had taken him into a tunnel and left him in what they called the throne room. The name was misleading, since there was no throne, just benches, a footstool and a couple of wooden crates used as desks. Domo and a few other goblins stayed with him as he recovered.

Domo stroked his chin while he considered the question. "I don't know, maybe stuff you in a garbage can with rabid chipmunks and then hit the can with a sledgehammer. A few days of that would have helped."

Will tried desperately to keep that image out of his mind. "What do you want me for anyway?

"Kind of slow, isn't he?" a furry goblin said.

"Did you miss that part about you being our new king?" Domo asked.

"Heard it, yes. Understood it, no."

Domo took a deep breath and sat down on the footstool. "It goes like this. You are in the Kingdom of the Goblins. If you have a kingdom, you have to have somebody as king. Right?"

"And exactly where are we?" Will asked. "Getting here was pretty confusing, and it doesn't look like I'm in Kansas anymore."

"Depends on what part of Kansas you're referring to, I suppose," Domo said. "The Kingdom of the Goblins is on the world of Other Place. You came from your world, now you're on ours."

"And I got here how exactly?"

"Magic."

Will frowned. "Magic?"

"You asked for an explanation, you're getting one. If you want one that makes sense, you're in the wrong place."

Will waved his hand. "Okay, keep talking."

Domo continued. "There are dozens of kingdoms on Other Place. Most tend to cater to one species or another. There are two kingdoms for dwarves, one for elves, a troll kingdom and something like twenty human kingdoms. That's just counting the big ones. Each one has a king. You are our king."

"Why me? Why have a human in charge of a kingdom of goblins?"

Domo shrugged. "Somebody had to get stuck with the job."

"That doesn't make any sense," Will protested. "I'm no king. Why put me in charge? Listen, if you think I'm qualified because Twain showed you my resume, you're in for a big disappointment. Everything on there is a lie except my name!"

"And you spelled that wrong," Domo said with a smirk. He held up the copy of Will's resume that Twain had crumpled up. Will snatched it from him, unfolded it and studied it carefully.

"By golly, you're right."

"Twain already told us about you, the parts you didn't write down," Domo said. "As we see it, you're uniquely qualified. Maybe you haven't figured it out yet, but we're pretty screwed up. Nobody takes anything seriously here, including orders from our king. If somebody came here with their head full of ideas about making this a better place, making us efficient or smart, he'd go nuts. No, we've found our best kings are like us; complete and total losers."

"There has to be a way out of this," Will said. "Why don't *you* rule them, or one of these other guys?"

It took half a minute for the goblins to stop laughing. Domo actually fell off his footstool, he laughed so hard. Once they stopped, Domo wiped tears away from his eyes and said, "Oh, it's always fun breaking in a new king."

"What's so funny?" Will demanded.

"Nobody takes orders from goblins," Domo told him. "Even goblins don't take orders from goblins. We're losers, morons, two steps above duckweed. We don't lead anyone and we barely follow. We wouldn't even have our own kingdom except a bunch of kings and wizards gave it to us so we'd stay out of their way."

"It can't be that bad."

"Watch," he said. Domo looked outside the throne room, where five goblins were milling around in the tunnel. "You there! Stand on your head, stick out your tongue and stuff your fingers in your ears."

This was met with derisive laughter.

"You see, it just doesn't work," Domo said.

"Maybe people would listen to you if your orders made sense," Will suggested.

"Hmm, there's a first time for everything." Domo pointed to a different goblin and said, "You there, stop eating dirt!"

"Make me!" the goblin shouted, specks of dirt flying out of his mouth.

"That's why we need a king from another species," Domo continued. "I mean, if you're not a goblin, then by definition you can't possibly be as screwed up as the rest of us."

Will wasn't panicking anymore. This was weird, but he wasn't in any immediate danger. He still didn't want to be here, but that was something he could take care of. "There were other kings before me, and you said one escaped. How did he do it?"

"Oh that's easy," Domo said. "When you accepted the job to be our new king, Cickam, Wender and Downe made a king contract for you. It became valid once you shook their agent's hand. It should be around here somewhere."

Domo shuffled through the debris in the throne room until he found a single sheet of paper covered in writing and with gold leaf on the borders. On the top of the page were written the words: CONTRACT FOR KING OF THE GOBLINS, YOU POOR FOOL. Domo handed it to Will.

"Vickers had a contract like this. He—"

Will tore the page to shreds and scattered the bits. "Got you!"

"Not really," Domo said, and handed back the contract, intact.

"What? How did…no, hold on a minute." Will looked down at the floor. The bits of torn paper were gone. "How?"

"Magic," Domo said. "Come on, if it was that easy we'd never have a king. Vickers escaped because he found a loophole in his contract. It allowed him to go home for weddings, funerals and if the Chicago Cubs ever get to the World Series. He went home for a wedding and before he came back he got another law firm to argue his case. One year later he won the case and was gone. If you're wondering, Twain said he closed that loophole and you can't go within two hundred feet of a lawyer if you go home."

Will looked at the page, with line after line of incredibly small print. "If I can find a way out of this I can just go home?"

"Yeah, if there's a loophole you can exploit, you're free to go. Twain and the other lawyers can't stop you from looking, and by law they can't make you come back if you escape."

Will wiped panic-induced sweat off his brow. “Okay, good, that’s good. Thanks, Domo.”

“Don’t mention it,” Domo said amiably. “Of course, until that happens you are expected to lead us as our king.”

“Domo, listen to me very carefully. I can’t be your leader. If you put me in charge I will screw things up so badly you might get hurt. Do you want that?”

Domo smiled. “You *might* get us hurt? My dear boy, anyone else on this entire planet would actively *try* to get us hurt, maybe even kill us. *Might* get us hurt is a big improvement over that.”

With that Domo pointed to the door. “Your subjects await, Oh King.”

“I need some fresh air,” Will said. With Domo acting as a guide he headed through the tunnels. He felt confused and nauseous, in large part because the tunnels and city above smelled like sweaty gym clothes. He had to find some way to get a handle on the situation he was in. Hopefully Domo could help him.

“Okay, I’m king until I can find a way out of it, so what am I supposed to do?” he asked.

“I think you’ll find not doing your job takes up all your time,” Domo said as they walked. “Ruling goblins is like herding cats. You can do it for a while, but it won’t last and they’ll fight you every step of the way. Your average goblin is stupid and a bit crazy. His idea of a good time is causing confusion and chaos on as large a scale as possible to as many people as possible. That includes other goblins.”

Domo stopped and held out his walking stick to block Will’s path. He pointed the stick at a tripwire running across the floor. It was as tight as a guitar string and vibrated when Domo plucked it. A thin goblin came running down the tunnel toward Will, and Domo stepped away from the tripwire.

"Hey, it's the King!" the thin goblin shouted and ran toward them. Before Will could shout a warning, the goblin stepped on the tripwire. The wire connected to a rock hanging from the ceiling, which swung towards the thin goblin. The thin goblin dropped to the floor and dodged the rock, then got up and said, "Nice try, Floyd!"

"Look out!" Will called. Too late, the rock swung back the other way and hit the thin goblin in the back, sending him flying through the air. Will heard laughter echo through the tunnel.

"That," Domo said, "was an example of our national pastime."

"Great." Will helped the thin goblin up. The goblin seemed little worse for setting off the trap and wandered off. Keeping an eye out for more tripwires, Will and Domo continued on their way.

"There has to be more to this than not being hit by rocks," Will said.

"You'd think so, but no."

"Come on, Domo, there have to be laws or rules or customs, something like that. If I'm supposed to rule this place I need some idea where to start from."

Domo deftly avoided another tripwire. "There are no laws or rules or customs, my King. King Bob the Fool tried to establish written laws, and the goblins broke them all the first day, on purpose, mind you. He called a meeting of all the goblins to try to get them to write their own laws in the mistaken belief they'd be more willing to follow them. That disaster started with a pie fight and ended with a riot over whether or not clams fart. My King, there are no rules, there never were any, and if you plan on staying sane you won't try to make any."

Will exited the tunnel and came out into the courtyard where the crowd of goblins had greeted him on his arrival. Most of them had wandered away, according to Domo, because the show was over. The few who remained showed him no particular interest.

Gazing at the ruined buildings, Will asked, "Why is everything such a mess? I mean, most of the buildings are barely standing."

"Not our fault," Domo said. "The dwarfs who built the city abandoned it just over ninety years ago. When they left we moved in, and it didn't look much better back then. We actually patched it up a bit and fix things if they really need it."

Will pointed to a house with no roof. "That doesn't need it?"

"A home with a skylight is hot property," Domo told him.

"Why was the city abandoned, anyway?"

"Two hundred years ago, dwarfs discovered iron nearby," Domo said. "They started a mine and the city grew up to house the workers and provide goods and services for them. Then the iron deposits were depleted and there was nothing else to earn a living off of. With no money coming in, everybody moved out."

Will walked through the city. It was big enough to house thirty thousand people, and had plenty of buildings that must have been stores or workshops. The city was built for people as tall as he was and looked too big for its stubby inhabitants. It appeared as if the goblins had heavily altered the city. He saw that some places had been fixed up with bricks taken from other buildings. Every so often there was a pillar or brick chimney jutting up from the ground, the only sign that a house or store once stood there.

All the buildings had vines clinging to them, and in some cases that was the only thing holding them together. There was graffiti scratched into the sides of buildings, including the message, *If swords are outlawed, we'll have to go back to clubbing people with rocks*.

"It's funny," Will said. "All the buildings look like big boxes, like something out of Soviet Russia."

Domo chuckled. "That's dwarfs for you. No statues, no cutting edge architecture, just stone boxes. They won't spend a single coin on anything unless they get ten back. Of course we don't do anything special either, but that's because we can't."

"There's so much damage. Is everything like this?"

"Oh no, not everybody lives this well. A lot of guys live in old tunnels, and some of our diggers are making new tunnels and houses underground. Hey, you have got to see what we did to the old part of town!"

Afraid what the answer might be, Will asked, "Why?"

"We turned it into a maze," Domo said excitedly. "It's a bit worse for wear, but we're real proud of it."

"Yeah, that's something to look into," Will said as he walked between two ruined buildings. "You seem more interested in me than the rest of the goblins."

"It's too early in the morning. Most of the guys are asleep, and the ones who are awake are already causing trouble and too busy to bother with you. Don't worry, once more goblins get up you'll be thoroughly and constantly annoyed."

"You said something about a digger. What's that?"

Domo snorted. "Diggers are a guild of goblins. There are a couple of guilds. You've got warriors, diggers, builders and lab rats. Each one is a group that spends most of its time doing just one thing and doing it badly. To make things even more confusing there are specialist groups within each guild. I stay above all that."

"Do they have any leaders? Anyone I can get advice from?" Will asked.

Domo rubbed his chin. "Hmm, sort of. There are a couple of guys a bit smarter and more directed than the rest. Calling them leaders is exaggerating, and getting worthwhile advice out of them is out of the question."

"It can't be that bad," Will said. "You can't have a civilization where everyone's stupid and crazy."

"We have a civilization? When did that happen, and why wasn't I warned?" Domo asked. Will gave him a stern look, and the little goblin laughed. "Be fair, the crazy part gets us into trouble now and again, but there's nothing wrong with being stupid. Most people are dumb as a bag of hammers, and being dumb and easily swayed is a prerequisite to winning an election."

"It certainly seems that way." Will was going to say more when he stopped and sniffed. He was still wearing the same suit he came here in, and in the short time he'd spent in the goblin's filthy city it needed a good cleaning. Well, that or be put to the torch. "Is there somebody I can see about getting something to wear? This is the only set of clothes I brought with me."

"Now that I can help you with," Domo said. He led Will back through the maze of tunnels beneath the ruined city until they came to a large chamber dug into the rock.

"Your bedchamber, Oh King," Domo said with exaggerated politeness.

"Gee, nice. Wouldn't it help if my bedchamber had a bed in it?"

Domo shrugged. "I can't see why that would matter."

The bedchamber was deep underground and accessible only by tunnels. It had a pile of rags for a bed, some wooden crates and a stool for furniture, a full-length mirror, and clothes laid out on the rag pile. There were torches on the walls, and a huge scorch-mark on the ceiling nowhere near the torches.

Goblins may dress in rags and castoff clothes, but somehow they had decided their kings needed better. Will's new clothes were impressive. They included black pants and a black vest, a dark green shirt, black boots and a cape that was black on the outside with a dark green inner lining. Next to those were black gloves with dark green fingers. Topping off the uniform was a black hat with a broad brim and a dark green ribbon sewn into the base. All of it was comfortable, made from good quality material and fit like a tailor had measured him for it.

Will finished putting the clothes on and marveled at them. "This is more like it. Where did you get this stuff?"

"We make it," Domo said. "Your king contract has a clause in it that we can't give you ruined clothes or make you dress like a clown or an accountant. Enjoy it, because that's about the only help you'll get from it. There are spare sets if this one gets damaged."

"If I asked for something different—" Will began.

"We'd laugh at you," Domo told him. "Twain rewrote the contract a couple of times to prevent us from giving you clothes sized for a doll or that could fit an elephant. If you ask for a special order you're just begging for trouble."

Domo dug through the rag pile and unearthed a bronze scepter. He presented it to Will and hastily stepped back. "And here is you scepter, the sign of your kingship. It's the closest thing we have to imperial regalia, and it came with the kingdom."

"Nice," Will said. The scepter was well made, with spiral symbols etched into the metal and a small, blunt hook on the end to hang from a belt loop. There were fire opals set in the scepter, including one on the end that was as big as a hen's egg. Actually, that large gem seemed to have a tiny white lizard flickering inside it.

"It's magic," Domo said as he edged away. "The scepter contains a fire salamander and can shoot waves of fire out. Just think about how big a fire you want and press the smallest gem on the handle. But—"

FOOM! The left side of the room was swallowed up in fire so intense it burned white instead of red. The crates and rag pile disappeared in the cloud of fire, and little besides soot and a second scorch mark on the wall was left behind. Will scrambled back from the fire so fast that he fell to his knees.

Domo helped Will off the floor and said, "You have to understand, if goblins have something then it's crazy or screwed up or both. The salamander in this scepter is a real overachiever. He doesn't make small fires."

"Thank, thank you for telling me," Will managed between coughing bouts.

"If the scepter worked properly somebody would have come in and stolen it by now," Domo said. "Probably one of our kings while they were leaving. I understand that's what happened to all the towels and silverware."

Will dusted himself off and made sure he wasn't on fire. "Are there any other surprises I should know about?"

"Hundreds of them, but most are small and relatively harmless." Domo gestured to the mirror. "This is the only other important thing you'll find here."

Will approached the mirror hesitantly. It was pretty, but so was the scepter and he wasn't going to be fooled twice. The mirror was free-standing, six feet tall and had a bronze frame. The frame was covered in bird carvings, including two large eagle feet holding it on the floor. It cast a good reflection.

"What's this one going to do to me?"

"Fear not, Oh King, it doesn't blow up or anything. This is your very own magic mirror. It comes with the kingdom, sort of a consolation prize really. Mind you, it doesn't work properly."

"Because if it did someone would have stolen it by now," Will replied.

"You're catching on fast. The mirror is defective and can only see places if your followers set up a scarecrow there first. Sorry, no using it to discover bank vault combinations."

Domo waddled over to the mirror and tapped it. Nothing happened. He tapped again to no effect. The third time, he grabbed it by the frame and shook hard. "Wake up, you crazy broad!"

"Ah!" The mirror screamed as the image of a woman appeared on its surface. The mirror leaned back and kicked Domo with one of the eagle feet, sending him sprawling on the floor. Will got a good look at the woman and wished he hadn't. She looked to be in her forties, five and a half feet tall and seriously overweight. She had blond hair, blue eyes and so much eye shadow on that she looked like a circus clown. Her clothes were garishly bright yellow with orange dots. Red shoes completed the ensemble.

"All right you creep, you know better than that! If there's no king then I get to sleep." Her voice was as harsh as her looks. She spotted Will, his mouth gaping. She snorted. "Oh."

"Uh, hi," Will managed to say.

The woman in the mirror frowned. The mirror walked toward him on its eagle feet and settled down an arm's length away from him. "Hey, the name's Gladys. Listen, I know there's a speech I'm supposed to do right now, the whole bit about serving you loyally and all that. But let's be honest, you want out of here and you'll run for it the first chance you get. Am I right?"

"Yes, and if you know any shortcuts home I'd appreciate it."

"Sorry. If there's a way back to your world I don't know about it. Anyway, you'll be leaving as soon as you can, so can we forget the whole vow of servitude? I mean, you don't want to be here and nobody blames you for that. So you go run off and we'll get along fine."

Indignantly he asked Domo, "Does she get to talk to me like that?"

Domo rubbed his knee and sat up. "No, she doesn't. Gladys has to show you whatever you want, assuming she can. You won't get polite service out of her, but unlike the rest of us she has to follow orders."

Gladys tried to kick Domo again, but the little goblin scurried out of the way. "Thanks a lot, you creep! I got half the kings to leave me alone with that speech and you go and tell him different."

"You kicked me, you paid for it," Domo said and stuck out his tongue. Gladys tried to kick him again, but he scooted back.

Will frowned and approached the mirror. "Uh, Gladys, listen, I'm sure we can get along just fine—"

"Liar," she said.

"—And if any problems should come up I'm sure I can count on your support to solve them."

Gladys gave Domo a skeptical glare. "Where did you find this moron?"

"Okay, let's try this again," Will said through clenched teeth. "You'll help me when I need you or you're not going to get any sleep. I'll make sure there are goblins around you twenty-four hours a day; bored goblins that won't leave you alone. Do we have a deal?"

"Do I have a choice?" she asked with a voice as harsh as battery acid.

"Yes, it's just not a good choice." Will sat down on the stool and took out his contract. "I'm going to get to work on finding a way out of here and I need the two of you to keep an eye out for me. If the goblins show up I'd like some advanced warning."

"They're coming," Gladys said sourly.

Shocked, he asked, "What, already?"

Gladys nodded. "They're on their way now and they'll be here in a few minutes. There's twenty of them in this bunch, and I can see at least five other groups wandering around the kingdom looking for their king."

Sure enough, Will could hear the sound of approaching goblins babbling and hooting as they made their way down the tunnel toward him. Gladys walked back to the edge of the room as her image faded from the mirror. "They're bored and they've got a new king to play with. Good luck dealing with them."

Chapter Three

Will sat in his bedchamber and carefully studied his contract under the light of a torch. There was line after line of print, much of it tiny and confusing. It didn't help that the letters were flowery and hard to read. And it was weird. *Article 9, subsection 3, paragraph 10, line 5: The King cannot escape his position by means of killing off all his followers by clubbing them with a stale loaf of French bread or other baked goods.*

"So what are you going to do, boss?" a goblin asked in a squawking frog-like voice.

"Yeah, boss," another squealed.

"Will you be quiet!" Will shouted. The assembled goblins laughed. Now that he was fitted out with the king's uniform, he was being besieged by goblins. There were no less than a dozen of the buck-toothed creatures following him around at all times. He couldn't focus on the contract with them jabbering away.

"What does chalk taste like?"

"Why are woodchucks called woodchucks?"

"Who would win in a fight, Beethoven or Bach?"

"Shut up already!" Will bellowed. Roars of laughter rose up from the goblins. "Don't you people have anything to do?"

"Nope," a potbellied goblin with tangled hair said. "That's why we're here. You look kind of interesting."

Snarling, Will looked around until he saw Domo at the edge of the crowd. He grabbed him by the shoulders and set him down in the middle of the group. "Domo, I want these guys out of here."

"What do you expect me to do about it?" Domo asked. "You know they won't take orders from me."

Will's mind raced. There was no way he was going to escape his contract with these goblins pestering him. That meant he had to get rid of them, at least for a little while. "Wait! You said you guys made a maze somewhere around here?"

"Oh yeah, we built it under the direction of King Horace the Confused. Very nice, and it's holding up really well, uh, sort of well." Domo looked down. "Mind you, it was built by goblins."

"Is there any chance I can find a place in there to hide? A dead end or somewhere they couldn't find me right away?" he asked desperately.

Domo brightened up. "Sure, the place is huge. There are all sorts of hiding places you could use."

"Lead the way."

Will followed Domo and the goblins followed Will. They walked through the city, where, to Will's disgust, three more goblins spotted him and joined the group. During the entire trip the goblins chatted away, kicked rocks and asked stupid questions.

Domo led them out past the gatehouse, the first time Will had left the city. Next to the gatehouse was an enormous walled-in area Will presumed was the maze. It was as big as the rest of the city, and its walls were crumbling and full of holes. Beyond the city and maze were hills with scrub trees, weeds and large rocks. Tiny white pixies flew by, dodging rocks the goblins threw at them. There were more goblins scurrying around outside. Two of them ran over and joined Will.

"There it is," Domo said proudly as he pointed at the maze's entrance. "500,000 square feet of twists and turns and dead ends. It's the biggest maze in all of Other Place."

Will stuck his head inside and looked around. What had once been a part of the city was now an enormous maze. The walls were fifteen feet high and two feet thick, with nooks and side passages. The goblins had connected some buildings together to make walls, so it was possible to see where one house had been merged with another. Most of the doors and windows were bricked over, while cutting through existing walls made new doors. In places the maze was made from scratch with bricks specifically made for the job.

It was also a mess. There were piles of dirt in the corners, loose bricks on the ground, weeds growing up between bricks and various slimy things crawling around. As he watched, a goblin grabbed one of the squirming insects off the ground and ate it. There were holes in most of the walls. Maybe the holes were made by people trying to get out, or by bad weather, or by the plants growing in the maze pulling the bricks apart.

"Good God," he said.

"Yeah, we like it too," Domo replied.

"Oh yes, very nice. It's too bad about the condition."

The entire mob of goblins quieted down, disappointment clear to see on their faces. They didn't have anything to be proud of except this maze, and it was falling apart. At once Will saw a golden opportunity to get his followers off his back.

"You know," Will said carefully, "I bet we can fix this place up like it was before."

That did it. The goblins gave him their full attention.

"Can't be too hard," he said as he inspected a hole in the maze. "We'd need bricks to fill in the holes, cement of some kind to hold them in place, maybe some timbers to shore the walls up while you're working. Yeah, a few shovels and buckets to get rid of the dirt, a knife or axe to cut away the plants. I think we can do it."

The goblins smiled and chattered excitedly among themselves. "You think we can?" one asked.

"Oh I'm sure of it! Domo told me some of you guys are good at building things."

"Well, kind of good," a large-eared goblin said.

Will nodded. "That's great. The goblins that are good at building things can fill the holes while the rest of you get rid of the dirt and plants. I'll go get some more goblins to help with the work."

The crowd cheered and ran off. Half the goblins headed into the maze and started pulling up weeds while the rest scattered to get tools and building supplies. Satisfied that he'd gotten rid of them, Will started back toward the city. He was almost there when he saw three more goblins heading his way.

"We're fixing up the maze," Will told them. "Why don't you go help while I get some more guys to do the work?"

"Really?" one asked, seemingly surprised.

"You bet," he said. The goblins looked at each other and hurried off toward the maze, leaving Will to continue on to his throne room.

"Pretty neat work back there." Will looked around and saw Domo following him. "That'll keep them busy for a while."

"Why aren't you helping them?"

Domo laughed. “Like that was going to happen. Their job is digging and building. My job is making sure you don’t get yourself killed on your first day.”

“If I’m supposed to be your king, aren’t you supposed to follow my orders?” Will asked.

“I think of them more as well-intended suggestions than orders. Besides, you’ve barely seen your kingdom. There’s so much more to it.”

“I don’t want to see any more of it,” Will said. “I want to leave it.”

“Think of it this way,” Domo said as another band of goblins saw Will and came running. “You can deal with them or you can take a tour of your lands and property. Don’t you want to see the marvels and wonders that are now all yours?”

Will stood his ground and stared hard at Domo until the little goblin burst out laughing. “Oh boy, I thought I could keep a straight face! Yeah, the whole kingdom is a dump, but it’s your dump.”

“If I say yes, will you help me get rid of them?” Will asked.

“Deal,” Domo said. He gestured for Will to bend down and then whispered in his ear.

Once he was finished, Will said, “You’re joking.”

“I kid you not.”

The goblins surrounded Will and Domo. This group was bigger than the last, and if anything louder and more annoying. Will got them to quiet down with difficulty. “Okay guys, uh, I’m glad to see you all,” a statement that got them laughing. “No, really, I am. Your friend and fellow goblin Domo said we could use a bottomless pit.”

“We haven’t had one of those in a while,” a skinny goblin said.

“Not since a wizard sealed the last one,” replied another goblin.

"Yeah," Will said nervously. "So, uh, I was wondering if I could count on you guys to find an out of-the-way place and, uh, dig a bottomless pit."

The goblins stared at him in amazement. Will expected a stream of lame jokes if not outright derision. But instead their jaws dropped, their eyes opened wide, and when one goblin spoke it was with reverence.

"You want *us* to do a job for you?" a skinny goblin asked.

"Uh, well, yes."

The goblins looked shocked. They huddled together and began talking. All of them spoke at once and so quickly it was impossible to follow what any one of them was saying. The skinny goblin reached out and grabbed Will's hand, shaking it fiercely.

"You got it, boss! You can count on us! Come on, guys!" With that the goblins ran off, shouting excitedly.

"They seem all fired up," Will said. He couldn't help but sound surprised.

"Goblins are never happier than when headed straight for disaster," Domo replied.

* * * * *

Will spent the next few hours touring the city. It turned out to be far larger than he first thought. There was the old quarter that had been turned into a maze, the main city, and a network of tunnels running underneath them both. According to Domo, the goblin inhabitants made most of the tunnels while the miners who once lived here dug the rest. Many of the tunnels connected together, making them almost as confusing to navigate as the maze must be. The tunnels were twenty feet wide and ten feet high, many still with tracks for mining carts. From these tunnels the goblins had dug hundreds of side rooms that ranged in size from as small as a walk-in closet to as big as a school gymnasium. Guttering torches set in the walls provided some light and a lot of smoke.

"And you've got guys living down here?" Will asked as they wandered through the tunnels.

"Sure," Domo said. "It stays warm here no matter how cold it gets on the surface. There's no more room in the city, but digger goblins can always carve out new homes and shops down here."

Sure enough, some of the side rooms were businesses and workshops. Goblins were busy making rope, furniture and other goods, all of it low quality. Goblins haggled for the newly made goods, trading snails, bugs and small green frogs for the cheap goods the workshops turned out.

Will watched a steady stream of goblins hurry around him. "Exactly how many goblins live here?"

"Nobody knows, or cares. Frankly I'm surprised you asked."

"Well, if I'm their king, it would be helpful to know things like how many of them I have to deal with. I don't know how many more I can distract, or for how long."

Domo nodded. "I see your point. To be honest, most of them will be too busy fooling around to bother you. It's only the bored ones you have to worry about."

Ahead of them was a room with an open door and light streaming from it. Will looked inside and saw what appeared to be a chemistry lab, with oak tables, stools and glass bottles filled with bubbling chemicals. A few goblins scurried around, these ones wearing small white lab coats and rubber gloves.

"What's this bunch up to?" Will asked.

"They're lab rats," Domo said. "They make all our stink bombs, glue and explosives."

Alarmed, Will asked, "Goblins make bombs?"

"Not all of us," Domo said. "Only these guys blow stuff up."

An explosion rocked the lab, sending glassware, furniture and two goblins flying through the air. Will caught one before he hit a wall, while the second one hit the ground rolling and quickly got up. As smoke billowed from the room, Will set down the goblin and waved the smoke away.

"Thank you," the goblin said in a placid voice. Unlike other goblins, this one was covered head to toe in short red fur. He wore a lab coat, black pants and a white shirt. The goblin wiped soot from a pair of tiny wire rimmed glasses and put them back on. "Oh excuse me, I wasn't expecting a royal visit. Everybody, it's the King!"

In seconds goblins piled out of the lab and gathered around Will while the goblin shook his hand. "It is a pleasure to see you, Your Majesty. I am sorry I wasn't present for your arrival, but we had a most disagreeable accident involving my coat, a llama, a large kite and a batch of glue. It was definitely a learning experience."

"No offence taken," Will said.

"I lost a new lab coat in that incident," the goblin said. "Oh where are my manners. I am Vial, that's spelled with an 'a', not an 'e'. I am the head and founder of the lab rat guild. My fellow researchers and I study alchemy and related sciences."

Fearing the answer, Will asked, "And, uh, what exactly is alchemy?"

Vial dusted himself off and said, "Alchemy is equal parts chemistry and guesswork. Most alchemists try to turn lead into gold. Why they would want to do that I couldn't say, but I far prefer experimenting with explosives. Gold is common enough, but who can honestly say they can blow up a house?"

"This is surprising. I didn't know you guys had scientists," Will said.

Vial's chest puffed out with pride. "To be honest I was originally trying to get into magic, but I couldn't get apprenticed to anyone to learn the trade. Fortunately, people don't guard alchemy books the way they do spell books. I am the first self-taught goblin alchemist."

Curious, Will asked, "And how many lab rats are there?"

"Oh, anywhere from four to twelve, depending on how many accidents we have in a week," Vial replied. "It turns out alchemy isn't an exact science, and we're not doing it exactly right. But every day is a learning experience, and one day we'll figure it out. There's another forty or so of my colleagues who gather ingredients. They're an essential part of our organization, but sadly they miss most of the truly exciting work we do."

"Is it a good idea for them to, ah, practice down here where they could cause a cave-in?" Will asked Domo.

Vial waved his hand like he was shooing smoke away. "No fear, Your Majesty, we are professionals. If I even *think* an experiment is a danger to the community I do it in the open air."

"More guys can watch the fun that way," Domo added.

Worried, Will asked, "Fun?"

Domo nodded eagerly. "Yeah, Vial's experiments are one of the finest forms of entertainment around! At the very least you get to see him blow a crater in the ground. On a really good day the blast will send him airborne."

Vial took a bottle off a lab bench and handed it to Will. "I believe you will find my associates and I a valuable resource, Your Majesty. Why, the last king often used explosives just like this to get rid of all sorts of problems."

Will handed the bottle back to him. "How?"

"By throwing them at goblins, naturally. Mind you, his targets did heal eventually, so it's not a perfect system."

Will nervously eyed the vast collection of bottles. "These are all explosives?"

Vial's eyes lit up and he smiled. "Oh yes, Your Majesty! I can meet all your explosive needs. I have small bombs, large bombs, camouflaged bombs, anything you could ask for."

"Camouflaged bombs?" Will asked Vial. He didn't like the sound of that.

"They're a specialty of mine. It is a bomb that looks like a common household item. I have an entire series of exploding outhouses that have been field-tested. And then there are exploding cigars, exploding hats, exploding milk pails—"

Will pointed to a chair he was leaning against. "Does this blow up?"

Vial studied it closely. "No, but if you give me a few minutes I can fix that problem."

"No," he said firmly. "Vial, I have some guys fixing up the maze. Can you and your gang whip up some cement for them to hold the bricks together?"

"Hmm, it would be a departure from our more exciting work," Vial said. He turned to his followers and asked, "What say you?"

"Sounds good to me," a still-smoldering goblin replied. The others nodded in agreement.

"Very well, I'll hunt down the recipe and get started," Vial said. "We should have a few hundred pounds ready by the end of the day and more by morning. However, if you should decide on a more aggressive course of action—"

Will shook Vial's hand. "If anything needs to be blasted to tiny bits, I'll call you."

Vial clapped his hands together. "Splendid!"

Domo and Will left Vial to his work and continued down the tunnel. "What was that about?" Domo asked.

"Hmm?"

"Having him make cement for you, why did you do it?" Domo sounded genuinely curious.

"Because I want to live long enough to get out of here," Will said. "If he's making cement he probably won't blow me up by accident."

Will stopped and looked at Domo. "Dear God, this place is screwed up! I've been put in charge of a city that looks like an earthquake hit it, there's garbage everywhere, and I'm surrounded by goblins that act like preschoolers on a sugar high. It's almost like I've been asked to rule a nation of idiots!"

"There's no 'almost' about it," Domo said. "We *are* a nation of idiots. Look on the bright side. There are some parts of Other Place that are downright scary, with rogue golems, walking skeletons and people more dangerous than either of those. Here, we're just annoying."

As they continued through the tunnels they came upon a large natural cave. The ceiling was thick with long stalactites dripping water onto the floor. The ground was clear of rubble and stalagmites, and instead held a teeming mass of goblins. The crowd was the largest Will had seen since his introduction to Other Place. All of the goblins carried pots or bowls, and most were shouting and banging spoons against their containers.

"What's going on here?" Will shouted over the noise.

"It's the mess hall!" Domo shouted back. "If anyone doesn't want to cook for himself he comes here to get fed. There's a staff of fifty cooks who work morning, noon and night to feed everyone who comes. Warriors bring them the ingredients and they cook them."

Will studied the scene more carefully. Since he was taller than his subjects he could easily see over their heads. In the back of the cave were ten iron caldrons, each the size of a fifty-gallon oil drum. Some goblins tended fires under the vats, others stirred the vats' contents, while still more added ingredients.

And the things they threw in would make a vulture flee for its life. Will saw deer antlers and old shoes go in the vats, followed by rocks and unidentifiable squirmy things. The vats' contents looked like a thick brown stew with lumps of doubtful origin floating on the surface. It must not have smelled any better than it looked, because all the cooks were wearing what looked like vintage World War I army gas masks.

"I am not eating that," Will said firmly and folded his arms across his chest. "Look, up until now I've gone along with this farce, but I draw the line here!"

"A wise choice," Domo said. "Don't worry, your king contract includes the right to eat free at any tavern or restaurant you want."

"Really?" Will asked in surprise.

"You bet. Cickam, Wender and Downe know what goblin stew is like. Even they aren't cruel enough to make a non-goblin eat it."

Will glanced back at the stew pots as the goblins broke up a wagon wheel and added it in. "You can eat that stuff?"

"Goblins can eat almost anything," Domo said proudly. "Oh sure, the so called 'more civilized' races need spices and salt and fifty different kinds of mustard, but we goblins can stomach whatever is put in front of us. Put a goblin anywhere on Other Place and he'll survive. For all their boasting, the men and elves wouldn't last a day here."

The cooks tossed a plateful of clamshells into a bubbling vat. "I doubt they'd make it through breakfast," Will said. "Uh, about that free food?"

"The nearest inn is on the outskirts of goblin lands. I'll take you there."

Domo led Will out of the mess hall and into another tunnel. After twenty minutes of walking they came out onto the surface. It was getting late and Will was looking forward to some real food. Domo led him away from the city and into the scrub forest to the south. Scattered among the trees were scarecrows through which Gladys the magic mirror could see. The scarecrows were nothing more that copies of Will's uniform hanging from a wooden post. As they walked on the forest grew in size until it came close to looking healthy.

"It's pretty here," Will commented.

"It's coming along nicely, more in spite of us than because of us, mind you," Domo said. "When we first got the kingdom this place was a mess. Those miners left nothing behind but thistles and scrub grass. But that was a long time ago, and the land is getting back to normal."

"Well look here," a rumbling voice behind Will said. He whirled around to face the speaker, and instead of a goblin saw two creatures as tall as he was. They had green skin with fine scales, ears that looked like fish fins and serious underbites. The pair had no hair, gleaming white eyes, and wore cotton pants.

They looked strong, with long powerful arms and legs, and chest muscles that looked like they belonged on weight lifters.

"The little runts have gone and tricked another poor fool into being King," one of the creatures grunted.

"Uh, Domo, who are these two?" Will asked as he backed away from them.

"The name's London the troll," the creature said in a deep, friendly voice. With two long strides he came up to Will and grabbed his hand with a vice-like grip. The troll shook it hard enough to almost throw Will to his knees. "Good to see you! This is my brother, Brooklyn. It's a real pleasure to meet you, isn't it, Brooklyn?"

"Nice to make your acquaintance," the other troll said. Brooklyn was slightly shorter than his brother, and his scales were a lighter shade of green, but otherwise the two were identical. Brooklyn lumbered over to Will and slapped him on the shoulder. The blow would have knocked him down except London was still holding onto Will's hand and kept him upright.

"Little help here?" Will asked Domo.

"But they already introduced themselves."

London released Will's hand and went on. "You're not from Other Place, are you? No, of course not, the lawyers always get some poor slob from outside to take the fall for them. Don't you worry about the little runts! My brother and I have volunteered to keep the goblins in line for years, and we're good at it."

"Real good," Brooklyn added.

"Yes sir, when the old king was on his last nerve, he'd say, 'London, Brooklyn, get these guys out of here,' and we did it. Course you can't keep goblins out of a room for long. It's like keeping water out of a leaky boat. But we kept them out long enough that he could get some peace and quiet."

"Really," Will said as he rubbed some sensation back into his hand.

London nodded. "Yes sir, if you want to establish a little order around here, provided you don't expect it to last long, we're the right trolls for the job."

"Get your scaly behinds away from the King!" It was another goblin. This one had blue skin and wore black clothes and a cape. The beady-eyed goblin had short blue hair and pointed ears, and was armed with a Swiss army knife, the first weapon Will had seen any goblin use.

London nodded to the goblin, not at all annoyed by the order. "Here's one of the little guys now. This here is Mr. Niff, the best warrior goblin you've got. Course, saying best goblin is like saying jumbo shrimp, but he's what you've got to work with. You want me to rough him up?"

"Uh, no, let's keep the violence down to a minimum," Will said.

The troll brothers looked at each other and shrugged. Brooklyn said, "I ought to tell you, we just charge room and board for roughing people up. That's very reasonable rates for arm twisting."

Mr. Niff trotted up to Will and shook the hand that London hadn't. "Sorry about these two. They think they know what they're doing. They wandered in here ten years ago and we haven't found a way to get rid of them yet." Mr. Niff gave the trolls a fierce stare and added, "They think they can come here and use our king just because they don't have one of their own."

"We do too have a king!" Brooklyn said hotly. "It's a filthy lie to say we don't have a king when you know we do."

"Did your king send you here?" Will asked London.

London looked down at his feet. “Uh, no, it’s just, he took a fishing vacation and we got bored, so we came over here and decided to make ourselves useful. But just because he went fishing doesn’t mean we don’t have a king!”

“He’s been fishing for ten years?” Will asked.

“Uh, actually, he’s been fishing for seventeen years,” Brooklyn said. “But that’s nothing. One of our kings went fishing for 31 years. It’s a job perk.”

“Can I take off and go fishing?” Will asked Domo.

“You can try, but the goblins will follow you.”

“That figures,” Will said in disgust. “London, I appreciate your offer, and I may have to take you up on it later. For right now I’m just heading out for something to eat.”

London smiled. “Domo’s showing you where to get real food, huh? We can do the honor guard thing, too. You know, make sure nobody gets too close and rough them up if they do.”

“You have issues with violence, don’t you?” Will asked.

Brooklyn smiled. “Everyone needs a hobby.”

* * * * *

Night was fast approaching when they reached their destination. It turned out that an hour’s walk south of the goblin capital was the border with the nearest human kingdom, and not far beyond that was a small town. Unlike the Kingdom of the Goblins, this land was nearly idyllic, with quaint peasant houses, ox carts loaded with produce and plow horses working in the fields. There were vast fields of wheat, peas and turnips tended by farmers. Windmills seemed to be the most advanced form of technology these people had. The locals wore simple cotton clothes and leather shoes, and they looked healthy and well fed. More ominously, they ran away when they saw Will and his followers walk down the road.

Worried, Will asked, "We're not too popular, are we?"

"People of all races view goblins the same way they view roaches—not dangerous, but definitely something you'd rather not have around," Domo told Will. "I don't think we'll attract a torch-wielding mob in the short time we're here."

"That happens often?"

Mr. Niff nodded. "All the time. It's fun and a great form of exercise. We sell books on how to deal with mobs."

When they reached the town, they found it clean and quiet. There were just over a hundred houses clustered around a blacksmith's shop, a stable, three stores and an inn. The buildings were made of wood, well built and in good repair. Most of the people were either still coming in from their fields or already inside their homes, leaving Will and his followers alone on the streets.

Domo pointed his walking stick at the large inn near the center of the town. "This is the closest place where you can get a bite to eat. Oh, and in case you're thinking about going out the back and running off, I think you'll find all the roads you take lead back to your kingdom."

"Another part of my contract?" Will asked bitterly.

"Article ten, subsection four, paragraph two, line eighteen. Right after the part where you can't escape by giving away your job as a raffle prize."

Will looked dubiously at the inn. His first inclination was to find someplace Domo *didn't* recommend, but he was hungry and he couldn't stay long if the goblins were going to attract trouble. Before he went inside he told the others, "Don't do anything stupid while I'm eating."

"That rules out everything except breathing!" Mr. Niff protested.

Inside, the inn was noisy and smelled of roast chicken and salted meats. There were a dozen other patrons and an innkeeper who looked big enough to double as a bouncer. The inn was warm and well lit, but not very friendly. The other patrons kept their distance from Will. They glared at him as he entered, and most of them grumbled.

Will found a seat at a sturdy table and smiled when the innkeeper marched up to him. "Hello, my name's Will, and I'm—"

"—the new King of the Goblins," the large man interrupted. He wore scuffed up clothes and a leather apron. "I figured that out from the outfit. I thought when their last king got away there wouldn't be any more, but they found another fool."

"In my defense I was tricked," Will said. "Tricked by lawyers."

The innkeeper shrugged. "That figures. Lawyers, can't live with them, can't get rid of them. I'm guessing you're here about a meal."

"Yeah, and I hope I'm not putting you out too much."

"No, I can manage. I got an understanding with the goblins that I keep their kings fed and they don't do anything to my inn," the innkeeper said.

Curious, Will asked, "Do something like what?"

The innkeeper's response was surprisingly casual. "TP it, egg it, fill it floor to ceiling with road gravel. They're small, but they're dirty fighters. One man kicked a goblin once, and the next day his kid found an application to law school in his room."

Will shivered. "That's low. I'll see what I can do to keep them out of your way."

"I'd appreciate it."

The food was extremely good, with roasted chicken, pan fried potatoes and a bowl of corn chowder. Free food was a definite bonus, maybe even a necessity since Will hadn't found anything in his contract about a salary.

Will took some leftover food and left quickly. He found his followers outside, the trolls playing poker while Domo napped and Mr. Niff tied a rake to a horse's tail. "Come on, let's get you out of here before the neighbors complain. I want these people to like me if I have to come here a couple times a day."

With the sun setting behind heavily forested hills, Will led his motley band back to goblin territory. He'd only gotten a hundred yards toward home when he heard a distant rumbling noise. He didn't see any clouds, so that ruled out thunder. Will was about to question his followers when he saw Mr. Niff pull a paperback book out of a pocket and start paging through it. The book was titled *How to Attract, Antagonize and Escape Angry Mobs for Fun and Profit.*

"Here we go," Mr. Niff said happily. "Chapter two, stoking the flames of an angry mob. There are some real good insults in here I haven't used in months."

Panicking, Will asked, "We've only been here a half hour and they're going to attack us?"

"They're getting more organized," Domo replied. He didn't seem much bothered by the approaching mob. "It used to take them days to get mad enough at us to get a group like this together."

It was a mob, all right, over a hundred strong. They were shouting, shaking their fists, and waving pitchforks and lit torches as they closed in on Will. To his surprise, Will saw women and children in the crowd. Evidently mob action was an equal opportunity employer. Once they were close enough, Will could make out what they were shouting.

"Get them out of here! We don't want them!"

London and Brooklyn grinned and balled up their fists for a fight. Mr. Niff found a good page in his book and opened his mouth, obviously to no good intent. Domo leaned back against a barrel to watch the chaos unfold. The people in the crowd kept surging forward. Will wasn't sure he could outrun them, and his followers didn't look like they wanted to. He had to make this stop quickly.

That's when the best advice his father ever gave him came back: when in doubt, pretend you know what you're doing.

"People, people, please, one at a time!" Will said as he walked in front of the trolls. "Come on now, no need for pushing. We are a civilized people."

That was, without a doubt, the last thing anyone expected to hear from him. The mob stopped with dumbfounded expressions on their faces. The trolls looked disappointed that the fight was being delayed. The two goblins stared at Will in utter disbelief.

"Now then, is the mayor or sheriff of this fine town somewhere in the mob?" Will asked. "Come on, don't be shy."

Someone near the middle of the mob raised his hand. Will smiled and nodded to the man. "My name is Will Bradshaw, and I have been tricked into being the latest King of the Goblins. It's nice to meet you. I, uh, see some people here are upset. I assure you I am new here, very new, and I don't know much about the problems you've had with these little guys."

"You don't know?" a man asked dubiously.

Will smiled and prayed this would work. "No. You see, I'm from very far away, and I was hired by a lawyer who—"

"Oh, a lawyer," the man said. The people in the mob nodded. One man offered Will a pat on the shoulder and some comforting words. The man who was speaking for the mob said, "That figures."

Will held back a sigh of relief and said, "Right, glad to see you're so understanding. Anyway, it looks like you've got some issues with these little guys, so what are they?" The mob wasn't shy in answering.

"They scare children!"

"They lower property values!"

"They pee on dogs!"

Will looked at Domo and Mr. Niff. "You do all that?"

Domo smiled. "Wow, our public relations department must be working overtime."

Mr. Niff didn't answer. He'd wandered away and was playing with two small girls. They were playing jacks and Mr. Niff was losing.

A member of the mob shouted and got Will's attention back. "They're a threat to the well-being of our town, and we want them out!"

The mob roared in agreement and got back to shaking their fists and waving their torches. Some of those torches had gone out, and the unlucky owners ran off to get fresh ones.

The two trolls watched Will curiously now that he had the mob almost under control. Domo yawned and picked dirt from between his toes, neither scared nor impressed. Will glanced over at Mr. Niff and saw he was still playing with the two girls. The three of them were throwing knives at a tree stump. Will had to admit Niff had very good aim.

Will got the mob to quiet down with difficulty. "So you want them to go?"

As one they screamed, "Yeah!"

"Would you *pay* to get rid of them?" Will asked. Domo and both the trolls perked up when they heard this.

The offer took the mob by surprise. The people muttered to one another in hushed tones as they debated the merits of Will's question. After a few moments they reached a consensus and a man at the front of the mob hesitantly said, "I guess so."

Will clapped his hands together and smiled. "Good to hear it! Okay, seeing as I am the King of the Goblins, I believe I can handle this problem for you. I'll pass my hat around, you toss in a few coins and in return I promise to take these two troublemakers out of here this instant."

The people talked to one another and accepted the offer. Will handed his hat to the mob and it came back with a handful of copper coins and half a silver piece. A few members of the mob shook Will's hand and thanked him for removing the threat to their community. Will grabbed Domo by the hand and pulled him away while the trolls followed him and tried to keep from snickering.

"Niff, we're leaving," Will said. Mr. Niff was playing jump rope with the girls, and Will's shout broke his concentration. In seconds he fell tangled in the rope, to the amusement of the giggling girls. They untangled him and he ran to catch up to Will. The mob gradually dispersed as Will walked away from the town. Some of the people waved goodbye.

"They're not too bright, are they?" Will asked.

Domo smiled. "We like them that way."

Chapter Four

The next morning, Will woke up slowly and pushed aside the piles of rubbish he'd been sleeping on. Goblins didn't quite understand the concept of 'bed', and made do with sleeping on piles of rags, grass and the odd scrap of paper. He'd accidentally incinerated his last 'bed' with his fire scepter, and the goblins had thoughtfully replaced it with another pile of rags. As their king, Will was afforded their finest, since he slept on rags that weren't moldering or covered in mildew. Rank had its privileges.

"I have got to get some furniture in here," he muttered.

"The boss is up!" a goblin shouted. Will's bedroom wasn't any more private than his throne room. At any given time a couple of goblins could wander in, or he could get dozens of the little pests hanging around for hours on end. The bedroom consisted of the aforementioned rag pile, a wooden bucket that served as a chamber pot, his ill tempered magic mirror and a doggie bag he'd gotten from the inn last night.

Goblins scurried around him, eager to get his attention. "What're you going to do today, boss?"

"What weighs more, a pound of lead or a pound of feathers?"

"How much wood could a woodchuck chuck if a woodchuck could chuck wood?"

Will pushed aside the nearest goblins and grabbed his doggie bag. Still groggy from a rough night's sleep, he mumbled, "Uncle Will is going to spend the day ducking his responsibilities and trying to find a way out of this madhouse."

"Ambitious!" a goblin with mottled skin cried. "No one has gotten out of a king contract in less than three months, and he thinks he'll get out in a couple days."

"Maybe he knows what he's doing?" a clearly horrified goblin suggested. The other goblins looked at the speaker, then at Will, and broke out laughing.

Will finished eating and looked around. "Where did Domo go off to?"

"Here, Oh King," Domo said as he hurried into the bedroom. "Your moderately faithful servant is at hand for another day of chaos and mayhem."

Will dug through the mess in his room until he found his contract. He stumbled to the mirror and tapped the glass. "Gladys, I need to talk to you for a second."

The mirror's surface clouded up until Gladys' pouting form appeared. "What are you doing waking me up so early? I need my beauty sleep."

"So you'll be out for a few centuries?" Domo asked. The mirror kicked him in the shin. That sent him back, yelping and hopping on one foot.

"Watch it, freak!" Gladys shouted.

Will tapped the mirror again. "Focus, Gladys. I need you to do some work for me."

Gladys pointed an accusing finger at Domo. "How come you don't support me when these vermin go and insult me? What kind of a leader are you?"

Will asked, "Do you really think they'd listen if I told them to be nice to you?"

Sulking, Gladys replied, "It'd still be nice to hear it."

"Gladys, is there anyplace in the kingdom where there aren't any goblins?"

Gladys frowned. "Don't know, let me check." The mirror fogged up and then began displaying scenes of the goblin lands. Will saw caves and tunnels, ruins and roads, scrub forests and wastelands, gullies and swamps. The only place where there weren't many goblins were the edge of the wastelands, a barren and rocky place so dismal even he didn't want to go there. Watching the scenes flow by showed Will just how big the kingdom was and how little of it he'd seen.

"Nope, the creeps are everywhere," Gladys reported.

"Can you find me a quiet place, then, somewhere I can work on my contract?" Will asked.

Gladys pouted and grumbled, then relented. "Fine, if it means I can go back to sleep."

More images flowed over the mirror's surface. It occurred to Will that Gladys was hampered in her search by the need for those scarecrows. If she could only view locations where a scarecrow had been set up, then she only saw those parts of the kingdom where the goblins had bothered to place them. That was something else to work on.

Gladys reappeared on the mirror's surface. "The mushroom caves are pretty quiet, but the creeps are going to follow you if they see you go in there."

"Thank you, Gladys," he said. Will looked at the goblins, at least some of whom were going to stay around and tease the mirror. "Domo, I need you to show me where those caves are. As for the rest of you, come on, let's head out."

Will left and a mob of goblins followed him. With Domo in the lead, the group wandered deep into the tunnels and caves below the city. Several more goblins saw Will and joined him, much to his annoyance. With an ever-growing mob of goblins in tow, Will went deeper into the tunnels.

"Here we are," Domo said triumphantly. He stood at the mouth of a large natural cave as big as a shopping mall. Unlike the other caves, there was no trash here, and the stalactites and stalagmites were intact. The huge cave was filled with giant mushrooms, the largest of them forty feet tall with trunks two feet thick and caps fifty feet across. The mushrooms were a variety of colors, mostly browns and whites, but there were also yellows, reds, blacks, and one that was bright blue.

"Wow," Will said, momentarily too awed to speak much. "This is...it's impressive. Do you guys eat these things?"

"Heavens no," Domo said. "If we did that there'd be no new goblins."

Puzzled, Will admitted, "I don't follow you."

Domo frowned. "Didn't your parents tell you where babies come from?"

"Yes, and mushrooms weren't involved."

"In our case they are," Domo said. "In hidden caves and forgotten places like this, special breeds of mushrooms grow to incredible size. It takes them years to get this big. Once they reach maturity they open their caps and send out clouds of spores to grow more mushrooms, but they also drop young goblins out. That's how we reproduce. Come on, Will, you must have noticed there were no women goblins in the city."

Will scratched his head. "That was one of many questions I really didn't want an answer to."

"Ah, we're in luck," Domo said. He pointed his walking stick at a smaller mushroom, only thirty feet tall. The towering brown mushroom shivered and gave off tiny wisps of spores. "That one's going to open any second."

The mushroom creaked and shuddered, the tightly closed cap trembling as it prepared to open. "Once the goblin falls out, members of a goblin guild will arrive and recruit him into their mob. Nearly all goblins are part of a guild," Domo added proudly, "except for strong-willed goblins like myself."

The mushroom bulged and creaked before the cap popped open and stretched out to its full width. A billowing white cloud of spores erupted from the mushroom. Along with the spore cloud, a small goblin with pointed ears and red skin fell out and hit the ground. He bounced on the soft mold that covered the ground. Dripping wet, the little goblin opened his eyes, stood up and looked around with an expression of wonder.

There was a rumbling as a mob of ten goblins ran across the cave floor. This bunch was dressed in German World War I infantry uniforms, complete with spiked helmets. In place of guns they were armed with rubber chickens, rolling pins and large fish they used as clubs. The mob surrounded the new goblin and tackled him. A flurry of activity followed and the mob ran off, leaving the newborn goblin behind.

The little goblin was back on the ground again after the mob knocked him over. He got up and looked at himself. He was now dressed in the same kind of uniform as the others and was armed with a bowling pin. For a second he looked confused, then screamed a battle cry and ran after the mob.

"And thus is born another productive member of society," Domo said. "He'll spend his first month with the gang that recruited him, learning by example and osmosis. Once he's absorbed what little they can teach him he'll be a fully trained warrior."

"What if a really competent goblin recruited a newborn?" Will asked. "He could pass on important skills and get the next generation off to a good start."

Domo pointed his walking stick at Will and announced, "Now that is some clever thinking! There are just two tiny problems with it. One is that there are no really competent goblins, or even mildly competent goblins. Seriously, it's a minor miracle that the guys can even remember to wear pants. Two is that newborns don't absorb all the skills of the goblins that recruited them. More than half the skills and knowledge gets lost somehow during transmission and have to be learned the hard way."

Will looked around the cave and counted the towering mushrooms. "There aren't enough mushrooms here to make all of you guys if they only make one and then die."

"Quite observant of you. This cave can only make ten goblins a month. There are more caves and hidden places like this scattered throughout Other Place, each one producing more goblins."

"So why do they all come here?" Will asked.

Domo sat down on a mushroom the size of a footstool. "About a hundred years ago, everyone in the other kingdoms got quite annoyed with us. We were scattered around and could be found in every city, forest, mine, port and prairie. The men and dwarves and elves couldn't stand dealing with us day after day."

"I can sympathize with that," Will said.

"A cabal of wizards and a firm of lawyers got together and hatched a plot to get rid of us. They convinced four kings to give up parts of their kingdoms, mostly worthless land they couldn't collect taxes from. The wizards and lawyers took this land and performed a mighty ritual to make it the Kingdom of the Goblins. The spells and contracts they wrought drew in goblins from across Other Place."

Domo chuckled and rocked back and forth on his makeshift chair. “But goblins being goblins, it didn’t work out as they planned. We’re stupid and a bit crazy, so the spells and contracts were only able to lure in about a third of all goblins. Worse, the ritual that made our kingdom demanded that there be a king, and no goblin was qualified to rule.”

“Obviously,” Will said.

“So they had to trick other people into becoming the King of the Goblins. Whenever there is no sitting king the spells and contracts weaken and goblins start wandering off. And of course nobody wants to be King of the Goblins, it being a thankless and maddening job. In ninety years there have been 47 kings, and as of yesterday that number grew to 48.”

Domo looked up at Will and smiled. “I figure we’ll be rid of you in a month or two. Cickam, Wender and Downe is good as law firms go, and their contract will be hard to escape. But you seem moderately bright, and being surrounded by goblins is an excellent incentive for you to be creative. Add in the fact that the longer you stay the more goblins will show up, and I think that you’ll find some way out of this mess.”

“Wait a minute,” Will said excitedly. “You want me out of here?”

“Of course,” Domo said. “If you stay this place will be flooded with goblins, and I find my kind almost as annoying as you do.”

“Then help me escape!”

Domo laughed. “I said I wanted you to leave. I didn’t say anything about wanting it to be easy for you.”

Will stared at Domo, all his loathing and anger showing through. Domo just smiled and laughed. “Keep looking for a way out, Oh King. I’d be quick about it if I were you. More of your followers are on the way.”

Sure enough, another crowd of goblins was heading toward them. Will muttered angry words under his breath and marched off. He didn't care where he was going as long as it was away from Domo.

* * * * *

Article 19, subsection 1, paragraph 8, line 15: The King cannot sell or trade his kingdom to another party, even if it is in exchange for a mint condition issue of Spider Man #1. That was another line of escape closed, not that Will thought he could find anyone who'd buy the place.

His contract was insane. The print was so small and close together that Will's eyes hurt just trying to read. There were hundreds of sections and subsections covering countless potential escape routes. He'd come up with three ways of escaping his contract and found all three blocked. In fact, he discovered two dozen very inventive ways to escape that he hadn't considered already disallowed in the contract. Whatever his faults, Twain was extremely thorough.

Will wandered through the tunnels until he came out onto the surface. He walked to the south where men lived so he could get some lunch. As he walked, he read his contract and shooed away the inquisitive band of goblins following him.

Scattered across the lush landscape were small homes the goblins had built. There were mud huts with thatch roofs, crude cottages made from piled up stones, and simpler homes such as hollowed-out tree trunks. There were goblins living underground as well, either in tunnels dug straight into the dirt or secret chambers cunningly hidden in the sides of hills. These last ones were often undetectable until concealed doors popped open and a goblin scurried out to follow Will around.

"Ooh, hey look at that," a goblin with pointed ears said.

Will looked up from his contract, dreading what he would see. He was surprised to realize just how far he'd gone without paying any attention to his surroundings. He found himself at the mouth of a small canyon with limestone cliffs going up twenty feet on either side. The land was lightly forested and a small stream gurgled out of the canyon.

"Kind of pretty," Will said as he stepped over the stream.

"Not the water," the goblin said. "Look at those guys working over there. I wonder what they're doing?"

Farther up, the canyon widened to a sizeable clearing. A team of twenty or so goblins were digging into the limestone and hauling away broken rocks. They all seemed very cheerful, which made Will suspicious.

"Let's find out," he told the mob following him, and marched up the canyon.

As he approached, he saw that the goblins had steel picks and shovels. The tools were so small that Will figured they were made rather than stolen. That was another surprise, since he hadn't thought any of his followers were capable of making anything more complex than a club.

"Wait a minute, I recognize these guys," Will said. "They're the ones I told to dig a bottomless pit yesterday."

"You gave an important job like that to them and not us?" a goblin with webbed fingers asked. "Sire, I'm deeply hurt."

"You weren't even there at the time," Will replied.

"What's that got to do with it?"

Will ignored the goblin (something that was getting easier to do by the hour) and walked over to the pit. The second group of goblins was already two feet down and working hard to make the pit even deeper. Perhaps he could get a few of the goblins following him to join this bunch. Will turned around to see if he could persuade them, only to find Domo standing in the front of the mob.

Angry, he told Domo, “If you’re not helping, then bug off.”

“I do my best to help. I just do it when it’s fun.”

Will muttered to himself and looked back at the working goblins. They certainly were industrious. Will couldn’t figure out why the kingdom was in such a sorry state if goblins could work so hard. Maybe they only worked hard for a leader. Based on what Vial and London had said yesterday, their last king wasn’t the sort to inspire loyalty.

“How exactly does this work?” Will asked. “Digging a bottomless pit, I mean.”

“Goblin magic,” Domo explained patiently. “All races have certain magic they’re best at. Humans use elemental magic, elves use nature magic and dwarves can make items with magic power. We goblins have magic based on stupidity.”

“I know I’m going to regret asking, but what does that mean?”

“As I said earlier, goblins are stupid and a little crazy,” Domo replied. “When there are enough goblins in the same place, you reach a critical mass of stupidity and craziness.”

“Like Congress,” Will said.

Domo nodded. “Or Parliament. Once that happens, their collective stupidity and craziness starts to warp space. Bottomless pits are one example of that magic. If these goblins dig down deep enough, at some point the pit will simply become bottomless. Once they’re made, we use bottomless pits to get rid of hazardous waste and incriminating evidence.”

"Oh," Will said. He had to think about that for a moment before a problem appeared. "Uh, Domo, what happens to the goblins digging the pit when it suddenly becomes bottomless?"

As if someone flipped a switch, all work stopped. The goblins digging the pit dropped their tools and looked up in shock. Obviously the question hadn't occurred to them. Their eyes focused on Domo, who was smiling.

"We will miss them terribly."

His answer caused instant panic. Goblins screamed and threw down their tools, scrambling out of the pit as fast as they could. The goblins that followed Will into the canyon also panicked, adding to the confusion. Within seconds there was a riot as the goblins went out of control.

"Stop it!" Will shouted. "Everyone stop doing anything! Come on, calm down! You, stop chewing on that guy's foot! Everybody just stop!"

Calm gradually returned to the canyon. The goblins stopped running around and looked at their king. Judging by their fearful expressions they were hesitant to get near the pit again. Will got his breath back after shouting so much and stepped in front of the unruly mob.

"Okay, uh, everybody, I don't want anybody to fall in when this is done," Will said. He also didn't want them to stop working, because if they did they'd start following him around again. If that happened he'd never get a spare second to study his contract. He had to find a way around this problem.

"So, uh, okay, I have an idea. Before you dig any deeper, you guys can drive stakes into the ground around the pit, okay. And, uh, you'll tie ropes around your waists and to the stakes. That way, when the pit becomes bottomless, no one will fall to their deaths."

The goblins looked at one another and murmured. After a few seconds they nodded in agreement with Will's plan. They were nearly calmed down and ready to get back to work when Domo smiled.

"Inevitable deaths," Domo said. The riot started all over again.

"Stop it, stop panicking!" Will shouted. He turned to Domo and yelled, "You're not helping!"

"Sorry," Domo said. He sounded anything but sincere.

* * * * *

"I am very disappointed in you," Will said angrily as he marched through the woods. Domo hurried to follow him. Besides him, Will was alone. After an hour Will had managed to get the original crew back to work and talked the goblins following him into joining the project. Once he'd convinced them they weren't in any danger they were quite happy to help.

"Oh come now, what were you expecting?" Domo replied. "I am a goblin, after all. If you want slavish obedience, try switching jobs with a human king."

"Can I do that?"

"No, but you could try," Domo replied.

Will whirled around and folded his arms across his chest. "Domo, if you're going to follow me around then you have got to at least try to be helpful. If you sabotage me like that again, I'll get even with you. I mean, come on! You said you don't want goblins around anyway, so why screw things up so they'll come back to the city?"

"Screwing things up is what goblins do best," Domo said with a smirk.

Will turned around and marched on. "Some of you seem better at it than others."

Domo puffed out his chest in pride. “Praise from Caesar.”

The tavern had an excellent beef stew cooking, and Will took enough home in a pail that he wouldn’t have to come back for dinner. The locals were beginning to accept his presence. They didn’t like his followers (for which Will could hardly blame them), but they were sympathetic to his plight. Will left the inn and was just outside of town when he heard a voice cry out.

“It’s him!”

Fearing what he’d find, Will spun around and saw who was speaking. Tramping out of the woods was a mob of fifty goblins headed straight for him. They ran up and gathered around him, cheering and waving.

“It’s true! We have a new king!” a goblin shouted.

“Happy days!” cried another wearing a pot on his head.

“For some of us,” Will said. “Domo, is this what you were talking about when you said more goblins were coming?”

Domo had to shout to be heard over the mob. “This is just the beginning! They’ll come by the hundreds every week. If you think it’s crowded now, just wait a year.”

A goblin with a huge nose grabbed Will’s hand and shook it vigorously. “Sire, this is such a pleasure! Me and the boys were just wandering around, living in abandoned barns and tying cats to anvils, when a goblin runs up to us and says we’ve got a new king. And he’s a man with plans, too! Which is kind of surprising considering the talent we usually attract, but it’s nice.”

“Wait, what do you mean a man with plans?” Will asked.

The goblin smiled and jumped in excitement. “The guy said you were fixing up the old maze and digging a bottomless pit! And he said you were touring the kingdom. The last guy in charge didn't do half that much in a whole year!"

Will looked down at Domo in cold fury. Domo waved his hands. "Hey, this isn't my fault. I didn't send out any messengers. The guys do this on their own."

The goblins crowded around him, grabbing at his clothes. "What are you going to do next?"

"Why is grass green?"

"Does pig iron have pigs in it?"

Will pushed away the more aggressive goblins and managed to smile nervously. Hundreds more goblins would come each week and all of them bored and stupid? His job just proved it could get worse. Now he had even more of them to get rid of.

Calm down, he told himself. *Relax, don't show fear, and look for a temporary fix.*

"Okay, it's good to see so many new faces today," Will said with false cheer. That got them to shut up, if only because they were stunned to hear it. "I am so glad to see so many goblins coming to help out. Yes indeed, there's so much work to be done, and what happens but more guys show up to help."

"Work?" a goblin asked suspiciously.

"Help?" This one sounded vaguely hopeful.

"Oh yes," Will said. "Have you guys been in the maze recently?"

The goblins looked at one another and muttered back and forth before one said, "Not really recently."

Will smiled and nodded. "Well, the place is a bit of a mess. It's not your fault, of course. These things happen. A couple of goblins are patching it up, but for a project this important it would mean so much to me if you could help them out."

"Really?" a goblin asked eagerly.

Another goblin pushed his way to the front of the mob. "Fix the maze?"

"Yep, fix the maze," Will said. "The other guys are good enough, I guess, but I bet you'd be even better at the job."

"Wow, we just got here and he's trusted us with working on the maze!" a goblin exclaimed.

Will patted the goblin on the shoulder. If he could just keep them busy they wouldn't have time to cause him any trouble. Now he just had to make sure they didn't wander off or get sidetracked. "Come on, guys. I'll go with you."

Leading the crowd of eager goblins, Will walked through the woods with Domo following close behind. His followers were loud and obnoxious, but manageable for short periods of time. The trick seemed to be finding them something they already wanted to do.

"This won't hold them for long," Domo said.

"Another word out of you and I'll have London rough you up," Will threatened. "And no trying to make them panic."

Domo rolled his eyes. "Killjoy."

As they approached the city, Will saw a large crowd of goblins in front of the maze. He recognized Vial and his lab rats, but the rest were new to him. Vial stood next to an open pit mixing cement with a long pole while his followers added water. There were over a hundred other goblins milling around. It looked like they were celebrating.

"It's the King!" A floppy-eared goblin shouted. In seconds the larger crowd merged with the mob he was leading. They cheered and hooted. "We did it, boss!"

"Did it? Did what?" Will demanded. "Please tell me you didn't do anything to the inn."

"Oh no, we did just like you said," the smiling goblin said. "We patched up all the holes in the maze and cleared out the junk. Just a few more finishing touches and it will be good as new."

Puzzled, Will said, "But I only told you guys to do that yesterday."

The floppy-eared goblin nodded. "It was easy. Most of the bricks we needed were still in the maze, just sitting on the floor. Vial came out and made us some cement, we plastered everything in place and now it's drying."

"Oh no," Will whispered. This was terrible! He had hundreds of goblins (some of whom made explosives), and they were going to follow him around and pester him. He looked inside the maze to see what they'd done, and sure enough all the major holes were patched. "How did you finish so fast?"

"Lots of guys came to help," the group's ringleader said. "Once the word got out you wanted it done, the builders insisted they had to come and help. And with Vial's cement, whatever we put in stayed in."

"A very useful recipe, I must say," Vial said. Behind him, a lab rat goblin hopped across the ground, his feet stuck in a block of cement. "And most definitely a learning experience, in that we learned not to mix cement by stepping on it."

"I can't remember the last time it looked this good!" another goblin shouted. More voices rose up in agreement. Even Domo seemed pleased with the result.

Will fought back a growing sense of panic and managed a weak smile. "Well done."

The assembled goblins froze and stared at him. Their mouths fell open and they dropped whatever they were holding. One of the goblins managed to find his voice while the rest stood dumbstruck.

"He praised us," the goblin whispered. The crowd broke out of their shock and screamed in delight. They ran around, whooping and hollering, throwing stuff in the air (most of which hit other goblins when it came down). It was a blend of a riot and a party.

"Think of something," Will whispered nervously to himself. "Think of something or they'll never leave you alone."

Will took a deep breath, let it out, and forced himself to smile. "Yes, very well done. And you know what, seeing the maze look so good has given me an idea!"

The goblins gathered round him, their eager eyes fixed on Will as he spoke. "This is a very nice maze, but what I was thinking was it could use a second floor."

"A second floor?" a goblin asked.

Will nodded. "Yes, a second floor would make this an even better maze. People would never be able to get through it that way, not unless they had one of you to guide them. And you could add traps. Traps that would, uh, drop them back to the first floor with chutes."

"Amazing," a goblin replied.

"Astounding," said another.

A third goblin took off a chewed-up hat and said, "The man is a genius."

The goblins cheered again and shook Will's hands. Domo, however, looked skeptical, and opened his mouth to no doubt spoil the mood. Not willing to let him dampen the crowd's enthusiasm, Will clapped his hand over Domo's mouth.

"I brought a group of goblins with me who'd like nothing more than to help with this monumental project," Will announced. Hopefully it would be monumental in terms of time needed to finish it, keeping some of the little pests busy for at least a few weeks. "And Domo will help you design the traps."

Domo pulled Will's hand away from his mouth. "I'm doing what now?"

"It's called payback, Domo," Will said. Then he gave Domo a push and sent him into the cheering crowd. "Make me proud, guys!"

Will edged away from the cheering goblins and headed toward the city. He felt reasonably sure he could find his way back to the throne room or some other isolated place to work on his contract undisturbed. If another group of goblins found him, he could send them to join the ones working on the maze.

"Hey there, boss." It was the trolls, London and Brooklyn. The brothers ambled out of the city and came up to Will. "We were wondering where you wandered off to," London said. "We looked for you this morning and couldn't find you anywhere."

"You shouldn't go places without your bodyguards," Brooklyn said. "You could have gotten in a fight without us, and we don't like missing fights."

The sound of cheering goblins interrupted them, and the trolls saw the celebrating goblins heading for the maze. London asked, "What did they blow up this time?"

"Nothing, but as long as you're here I need you to break one of the goblins out of a cement block he got stuck in," Will said. He pointed at the unfortunate lab rat, who was hopping toward the maze to join the others working on it.

Brooklyn laughed. “That’s a new one! Just when I think I’ve seen them do it all, they find a new way to get into trouble.”

With so many goblins busy, Will would have time to work on finding a way out of his difficult-to-read contract. But there might be help at hand for the problem. “While you’re at it, ask Vial if he has a magnifying glass I can borrow. And when I say ask, I don’t mean mug him, I mean ask.”

“Can I make the asking sound intimidating?” London pleaded.

Will raised an eyebrow in surprise. “You want to try to intimidate someone who makes explosives for a living?”

London smiled and gave Will a thumb’s up.

A fierce wind rolled over them, distracting Will from his attempts to convince London that a professional bomb-maker was a poor choice for a victim. Will grabbed his hat to keep it from blowing away. The sudden windstorm was strange, more so because Will noticed that the wind was surprisingly localized, with trees a half-mile away undisturbed.

“What’s the deal with this wind?” he asked.

Brooklyn didn’t seem bothered by the windstorm. “Oh, that’s just Barbie.”

The source of the wind landed in the grassy field in front of the Goblin City. It was a dragon, a fifty-foot long monster with crimson red scales and the wingspan of a Boeing 737 jet aircraft. The dragon had yellow eyes, curving horns on its head, claws longer than Will’s arm, and a long serpentine tail that ended in a sharp bone spike. Will guessed that the dragon weighed somewhere in the range of ten tons, all of it muscle and bone. He could see muscles ripple and bulge beneath its thick scales as it moved. The dragon folded its wings against its back and lifted its head high into the air to survey the gathered goblins with obvious disdain. As it opened its mouth, wisps of fire slipped out and rose into the air.

In a booming and oddly high-pitched voice, the dragon demanded, "Okay, where's your king?"

Chapter Five

The goblins looked at the dragon with curiosity rather than fear, neither running from it nor attacking it. London and Brooklyn seemed equally unimpressed. Based on their reactions, or lack thereof, Will was reasonably certain it wasn't going to attack. Then again, a goblin had just sealed his feet in a block of cement, so Will wasn't sure he should trust their judgment on anything.

"Come on," the dragon said in a high-pitched voice. "The word got out there's a new king. If he's not here, find him and bring him out."

Doing his best to fake bravado, Will walked up to the dragon. He had his scepter, but he was pretty sure fire wouldn't hurt a fire-breathing dragon. That being the case, he figured the best weapon available to him was bluffing. "Hello there, William Bradshaw, King of the Goblins at your service."

Brooklyn followed Will and waved to the dragon. "Hi, Barbie!"

"That's Barbecue!" the dragon bellowed. The roar almost knocked Will over, and did send several goblins flying through the air.

"Don't do that again," Will told Brooklyn. He smiled at the dragon and said, "Sorry about that, no insult intended. This being my second day on the job, and what with there being no training beforehand, I'm sorry to say I haven't had the pleasure of making your acquaintance."

The dragon seemed satisfied. "It seems the lawyers found someone with manners to rule these cretins."

Will smiled. "No, but I do a very good job of pretending I have manners. So tell me, is this a social visit or is there going to be property damage involved?"

"Neither," the dragon said. "Walk with me. There's something I need to talk with you about."

The two of them walked into the light forest alone as the goblins got back to work and London went to find Vial. The dragon walked slowly so Will could keep up with her. Once they were half a mile from the city, she began to speak.

"My name is Barbecue. I live a hundred miles to the east of here with my husband and four kids." The dragon was female, Will thought. That explained the pitch of her voice. She continued talking as they walked. "Just so you know, I don't burn down cities. I don't eat people, either. I don't know how stories like that get started. You people taste worse than wolves."

"That's a load off my mind, but I should warn you that burning down this city might be considered a public service," Will said.

Barbecue shrugged her huge shoulders. "Ehh, everybody's got to live somewhere, and better they're here than close to me. Besides, goblins might annoy other people, but not me."

"Yes, well, what with you being a dragon, I imagine even these guys have the brains not to bother you."

Barbecue snickered. "You'd be surprised how many problems go away when you can breathe fire. Anyway, my family and I live in a cave just outside your kingdom, and we've had good relations with the kings before you. That's why I dropped by."

"To say hello?" Will asked hopefully.

"To get some help," she corrected him. "You were brought here with a lawyer's contract, right?"

Will took out the offending document and held it up. "Yes, and if you know a way out of it, I'd really appreciate it."

Barbecue shook her head. "Sorry, kid, not one of my strong points. I have a problem with lawyers myself. The human king south of here has just come to the throne. His name is Kervol Ket and he's been in office less than a month. He inherited the job from his dad and he's worried he won't keep it if he looks weak. Anyway, the fool went and hired a lawyer to help him get a firm grip on the kingdom."

Will scratched his head. "Sounds like asking a shark for a life preserver."

"Ha! Yeah, brains aren't a requirement for being king. Anyway, the lawyer got him a princess to marry with a happily-ever-after clause in her marriage contract. But for the king to look heroic to his people, he has to rescue her."

Will swung his scepter like a golf club. "Ah, a picture begins to form. Brave king rescues beautiful princess from savage man-eating dragon. The dragon surrenders, the king gets the girl and a big celebration follows."

The dragon laughed. "You're good at this."

"I learn fast."

Barbecue nodded. "Yeah, I look kind of bad, but there's a fee involved. As a bonus, stunts like these keep tourists away. The contract calls for the king to face minor perils before he meets and defeats me. That's where you come in."

"Minor perils?" Will asked. "Okay, am I understanding this right? You *want* some of my goblins?"

"Only for a little while," Barbecue said hastily. "You'll get them back. I just need them to shout at him a bit, maybe throw some rocks. He'll chase them off and then come after me. The whole project shouldn't take more than a day."

"Is there any way I could talk you into keeping them a little longer?"

Barbecue shook her head. "Bad idea. My kids don't play well with others. Plus your goblins might wake up my husband if they stay too long. He's asleep in the den, has been for months."

"Big help with the kids, is he?"

Barbecue snorted fire. "Oh don't get me started or I'll go on all day! So, can you spare me some goblins?"

Will looked back at the goblin work crew. He really didn't want to disturb them when they were having fun. Then again, there were a lot of other goblins that weren't working on the maze. Earlier Domo had said there were warrior goblins. Maybe he could round up a few of them.

"I can spare some," Will said. "How many do you need?"

The dragon thought for a second and mumbled some numbers. "Eight should do."

"Stay away from our king!" It was Mr. Niff, running to the rescue. Mr. Niff pulled a knife from his belt and got between Will and the dragon. "You can't get away with threatening our king just because you're a living engine of destruction."

Barbecue offered an indulgent smile. "Hi, Niff."

Will grabbed Mr. Niff and pulled him aside. "Hold on, nobody's threatening me. Say, Niff, how would you like to help me out in a very important job?"

"Me? No fooling?" Mr. Niff asked.

"No fooling. I need eight warrior goblins with you leading them. You guys need to pretend you're guarding Barbecue's lair. Sounds exciting, huh?"

Mr. Niff's face lit up with a smile from ear to ear. "Oh boy, it's a happily-ever-after contract, isn't it?"

Will patted the goblin on the back. "Got it on the first try. You just need to pretend to fight, then run off."

"I can do that! Nobody's better at throwing fights than goblins."

London came up behind Will and tapped him on the back. Will turned around and saw that the troll was smoldering and covered in soot. London proudly held up a magnifying glass with a copper handle and said, "Mission accomplished, boss. The little guy put up quite a fight, but I got it for you."

Will took the gift and glanced over at Barbecue. "Would you like to borrow a troll while you're here?"

"Sure!"

* * * * *

An hour later Barbecue took off, carrying London, Mr. Niff and seven other goblins. She promised to have them back by sunset. Will had no intention of holding her to that. Now that he thought about it, this could be good for him. After all, being on the good side of a fire-breathing dragon seemed very forward thinking. And if this worked out, he might be able to loan her some more goblins later on.

Will retreated into the Goblin City and found a quiet place in an alley to sit down and study his contract. With Vial's magnifying glass he could make out all the fine print. Seeing it clearly actually made things worse. There were hundreds of lines of extra text on the front of the contract and thousands more lines on the back!

Article 29, subsection 11, paragraph 12, line 41: The King cannot escape his job by running off to join the circus. He also cannot run off to join the British Navy, the Salvation Army or the Arbor Day Foundation.

"Well thank you very much!" a squeaky voice shouted.

"Hello, Domo," Will said with a total lack of interest. "How's the maze coming along?"

The little goblin stomped up to him and held up his mud caked hands. "Do you see this?"

Will glanced over. "Good work, Domo, you've discovered mud."

"They had me digging pits for Vial to mix cement in! I escaped after they got into a discussion over whether or not zero is a number."

"I thought you were going to design chute traps for them," Will said. He went back to studying his contract.

"Yes, and when that was done they had me carrying bricks, tell the cooks to bring lunch out and dig those pits. I worked very hard not to become a builder, and I didn't do that so I could be forced back into it."

Domo grabbed a bucket from someone's house and set it upside down in front of Will. Muttering angrily, he climbed on top of it so he could almost look Will in the eyes. "Do you have any idea what it's like being stuck in the builders' guild? They recruited me after I was born and it took me three years to get away. All the dirt and dust and accidents, most of which were not in the least bit accidental!"

Will leaned down until his face was an inch from Domo's. "Gee, being dragged into a bad situation against my will, how would I know what that feels like? Hmm, oh wait! *Maybe* because *I* got hijacked for *this* job."

Domo held his ground for a few seconds before he looked down. "Yeah, sorry. I guess it's not much different for you. But I'm not the one who recruited you, so don't blame me for it. And once you find a loophole in your contract you can leave like the other kings did. Me, I'm stuck here."

"You can't leave?" Will asked.

Domo sat down on the bucket and sighed. "I can leave, but there's no place to go. Most people consider goblins vermin. They say we're worse than rats. There's some truth to that, but I've seen how the other races act. Some of the things they do would put you off red meat for life. A kingdom east of here has 'Your suffering amuses us' as their national motto, and they've been known to balance their books by selling their own people to slave markets."

"I'm sorry," Will said. He put his contract away and sat down next to Domo. "I spent a long time with people looking down on me, too. It's no fun."

He patted Domo on the back. "Hey, is there anybody here good at making those scarecrows?"

Domo looked at him, clearly puzzled. "I don't know. Why?"

"Gladys needs those to see the kingdom. I only saw a few of them when I was outside the city. If we can get some more up she'll be able to see more and I can do a better job of keeping an eye on things."

"Makes sense," Domo said. "There are always extra uniforms around, and scarecrows are easy enough to put up."

* * * * *

An hour later, Will was standing in a field of sweet smelling white and purple wildflowers buzzing with bees. He looked up from his contract and said, "Guys, no, the scarecrows don't do any good if they're facing trees."

The five goblins looked away from the scarecrows they'd just set up at Will's instruction. One smiled and said, "Yeah, but it really steams Gladys off. One time we turned them all backwards and she couldn't see anything."

"If she can't see anything then she can't help me," he replied. "Turn it around."

Grumbling, the goblins turned a scarecrow around so its back was to the tree. Domo had rounded up five warrior goblins for this project, and he was helping Will to keep an eye on them so they didn't goof up too badly. Will was beginning to think goblins didn't so much screw things up as they intentionally sabotaged them as a joke.

So far the work was going well. Will had found a place with few scarecrows and the goblins put in new ones at his direction. The scarecrows were copies of his uniform tacked onto a post and crossbeam. The goblins already had three new scarecrows up and the uniforms and posts to put up five more. Once that was done, Will could ask about getting more made. Until then, a few bored goblins were kept busy and he had some quiet time to work on his contract.

"How many scarecrows do we have?" Will asked Domo.

"Not sure. Nobody's been putting them up since the last king left, and they can get blown over in storms or burned down by angry gnomes."

"Why would they do that?" Will asked.

"It has to do with a poorly timed joke made many years ago. Who could have guessed they were so sensitive about lawn ornaments?" Domo replied. "Anyway, we don't use the mirror so we don't spend much time putting up scarecrows. Now that you're here we'll need more just so you can make timely escapes."

"I can escape with these?" Will asked hopefully.

"Your contract, no, but if you're in a pickle you can jump from where you are to a scarecrow."

Will perked up. "How does that work?"

Domo pointed at the newest scarecrow. "It's goblin warp magic. If you can see a scarecrow, you can fall backwards into your cape and warp over to it.

You trade places with the scarecrow. King Daniel the Easily Startled used that trick many times."

"Really?" Will asked. "The contract didn't say anything about this."

"It wasn't written to be helpful."

"Yeah, tell me about it," Will replied bitterly. *Article 31, subsection 1, paragraph 28, line 4: The King cannot escape his duties by pretending to be a blithering idiot. If he is a blithering idiot, he risks reelection or promotion.*

Will put the contract away and studied the nearest scarecrow. "So if I just fall backwards like so, I'll—"

Whoosh!

Will found himself standing in front of the five goblins with his back to a poplar tree and the scarecrow's post. He was now wearing the uniform that had been part of the scarecrow, while the one he'd been wearing fell to the ground next to Domo. The assembled goblins clapped and cheered.

"Well, that's helpful," Will said. He checked his belt and found his fire scepter had been transported along with him. That was a bonus; he didn't want to be disarmed when he used this trick. "You say this is part of the warping magic you do?"

"Yeah," Domo replied. "We discovered it fifteen years ago when somebody nailed King Richard the Yeller's clothes to a tree. He was running after us, shouting as usual, when he tripped and warped over to the tree."

"Cool," Will said. "Is there any limit to range?"

Domo shrugged. "Not that I know of. The farthest I've ever seen a king warp himself is fifty feet to get away from a rabid insurance salesman."

"Not just the warping," Will replied. "I mean is there a limit to how far away a scarecrow can be and Gladys can still see through it?"

Domo smiled. “Ah, you’re planning on doing some spying!”

“Uh, no, but I—” Will began nervously.

“No, he’s going to set them up to look at pretty girls,” a goblin suggested. That made Will’s face turn as red as a beet.

A warrior goblin jumped up and down. “Or to watch rich people and see the naughty stuff they do. Ooh, I smell blackmail!”

“No blackmail!” Will shouted. “I just want to know if we can put some on the edge of the kingdom and see threats coming. You know, like fire-breathing dragons dropping by for a visit.”

“Clever thinking,” Domo said. “There’s always somebody on our borders causing trouble.”

Worried, Will asked, “Really?”

Domo smiled. “Oh yeah, the humans to the south hate us, the dwarves to the west hate us, the elves hate us.”

“Be fair, the elves hate everyone,” a bug-eyed warrior goblin said.

Another goblin nodded in agreement. “It’s true. They don’t even like other elves. They’re always fighting duels with one another.”

“Their word for an elf neighbor translates to ‘disgusting creature I do not yet have a reason to destroy’,” Domo added.

Exasperated, Will asked, “Does everybody hate you guys?”

“No,” Domo said. “The trolls ignore us. I would like to point out that while the other races loath us, they don’t especially like one another, either. The different human kingdoms hate each other, dwarfs don’t like anybody who isn’t a dwarf, and trolls ignore everybody. Elves look down on other races and really hate other elves.”

Will shrugged. "I guess some things don't change no matter where you go."

Domo slapped his hand against the side of his head. "I forgot! There is a group that likes us. The Purple Puppet People get along really well with goblins. Always have."

Will rubbed his hands together. This was information he could use! "Where do they live?"

Domo pointed to a tall dead tree in the distance. "You see that tree?"

"Yes."

"Okay, you head over there and take a left until you reach a gully, go up the gully until you reach a pond. After that you walk a hundred paces to the hut of Esmeralda the witch (she's crazy), and go north until you see the Perilous Peaks gift shop. Walk seven hundred miles due east and you're there."

"Seven hundred miles?" Will asked. Domo nodded. "I take it I won't be seeing much of them."

"Not necessarily," Domo said. "From time to time one of them comes by to borrow a cup of sugar."

"Hey, boss, we're out of scarecrows," a warrior goblin said. Sure enough, all the scarecrows were in place, each one pointed in a different direction so Gladys had a perfect view of the area.

"We'll head back to the city and see about getting more uniforms," Will said, and led the goblins away. Out of curiosity, he asked, "This new human king, Kervol, what can you tell me about him?"

"Not too much," Domo admitted. "He got the job three months ago after the last king slipped on a banana peel, fell down an open sewer grate and had a cow fall on him. That's the third time that's happened to a king this year.

Nobody knew anything about this Kervol guy until he inherited his dad's job. Since he took power he's raised taxes to pay for his coronation and upcoming wedding."

Will scratched his head. "Uh, how do you know all this if humans don't like you? I mean, I can't see them telling you these things."

Domo smiled. "Like it or not, goblins are everywhere. If somebody says something juicy, chances are a goblin is close enough to hear it."

"Is there any chance I'll get along with Kervol?" Will asked.

Domo looked doubtful. "It's possible, but if I had any money I wouldn't bet on it. Besides raising taxes, the guy likes making long speeches. So far he's promised to make new anti-goblin laws, stuff like 'no goblins in a town after dark', 'no goblins in a tavern at any time', and the ever popular 'no peeing on dogs'."

Will frowned. "You guys don't actually do that, do you?"

"I don't, but I can't speak for the rest of them," Domo replied. "I wouldn't expect any trouble from Kervol. One of the warrior goblins brought back a flyer that listed job openings in his castle. He's looking to hire musicians, a pastry chef, an interior decorator and a hair stylist. The only thing he'll threaten is the royal treasury and possibly the laws of good taste."

"And there's no chance he'll attack us if he runs low on money, because we don't have anything," Will suggested.

"We have plenty of stuff," Domo corrected him. "We just don't have anything that can be sold for petty cash."

* * * * *

Back at the Goblin City it was pure chaos. Goblins scurried around bearing tools, building materials, food and, for some reason, live frogs. The crowd of workers outside the maze had doubled since Will last saw it. As he watched, a goblin ran into the maze leading a group of volunteers. It was starting to get dark, but the work wasn't stopping.

"There must be a thousand of them," Will said.

Domo snorted. "Yeah, everyone wants to get in on a big project like this, if only to say they were there. I'm guessing only about a third of them are actually doing anything useful."

"But the extra goblins won't try to mess things up, will they?" Will asked.

Domo clapped a hand over his heart. "Never! This is a national landmark and a source of pride for goblins everywhere. It also lowers property values in a fifty mile radius and causes incontinence in farm animals."

Will opened his mouth, a protest or maybe a demand for sanity on his lips, but he shrugged and gave up. He started to walk into the city and stopped halfway there.

"Domo, why is the air shimmering like that?" he asked. The air above the maze rippled the same way it did over a highway on a hot summer day. There was a funny smell to the air, sort of musty, and Will's skin tingled.

Domo looked up and chuckled. "Oh, this is going to be good."

"What is?" Will's question was answered when a small green frog fell out of the sky and landed on his hat. Hundreds more followed, and were soon joined by small fish. After that came combs, key chains, loose change and other things that end up lost under couch cushions. Lastly came socks, hundreds of them, and no two alike. The rippling in the air disappeared as the last sock landed. None of the goblins seemed to take notice of this except to eat the fish and collect the frogs as pets. Will watched the bizarre scene and said, "I keep thinking things can't get any weirder. I haven't been this confused since I tried to do my taxes last year."

Domo ate a fish off the ground and said, "This is goblin magic. There are too many goblins in the same place at the same time. Their innate stupidity and craziness is warping space. All this stuff is being taken from random places across the universe. If your coronation had lasted any longer it would have happened then, too. "

"And this is going to happen often?"

"You bet," Domo told him. "This many goblins together will warp space at least three times a day. You may want to stay clear until they're finished working, or at least find a good place to hide if it starts raining anvils."

Will took a deep breath. "Okay, I need to keep the goblins busy or they'll hound me until I go crazy. I need to keep them in small groups or heavy objects could suddenly fall on me. My followers either can't or won't do anything right unless they feel like it. All the neighboring kingdoms either hate me or completely ignore me. Am I missing anything?"

"There's more, but that's all the big stuff." Domo looked off into the distance, squinting at a tiny shape in the sky. "There is the dragon."

"Her I can deal with."

The approaching dot grew larger and belched out a plume of fire. Domo backed away and said, "I hope so. She looks pretty steamed."

Will saw the dragon fly toward the city and pick him out of the crowd with laser-like precision. Barbecue roared as she flew in. She was clutching London and the goblins with her front feet, and she also held someone dressed in white. Screaming goblins dropped what they were doing and scattered as the angry dragon soared through the air. Will threw himself to the ground, accidentally warping to a nearby scarecrow. *Whoosh!* It didn't help. Barbecue saw him, and with a quick turn landed right in front of him, tearing up the grass and crushing a bush under her clawed feet. She was breathing hard and her teeth showed as she growled. The dragon smelled of burnt sulfur and ash.

"I'm a fool!" Barbecue roared. "Of all the brainless things I could have done, I trusted goblins to do something right!"

"What's the matter?" Will asked as he struggled to his feet. "What happened?"

Barbecue brought her head within inches of Will and stared hatefully at him. He backed away and covered his face, certain that the dragon was going to bite him in half. But instead of attacking, the dragon spoke in a low, dangerous voice. "You want to know what happened? Your goblins, your rancid smelling, half-witted goblins screwed up everything! I should have seen it coming a mile away. You know what? Your guys messed this up, so you can fix it!"

Barbecue tossed London and the goblins to the ground. As best Will could tell they were miserable but unhurt. Then the dragon tossed down a young woman with golden blond hair and a stunning figure. She wore a dazzling white dress and had a silk purse and a tall cone-shaped hat. Once the woman was on the ground, Barbecue flapped her huge wings, rose into the air, and flew away while muttering insults about goblins.

Will walked over to Mr. Niff and helped him up. He pointed at the woman and asked, "I'm afraid to ask, but who is this?"

Mr. Niff cleared his throat and said, "Uh, boss, meet Princess Marisa Brandywine, fiancée to King Kervol Ket."

The princess looked at Will, sneered, and said one word in a high-pitched, squeaky voice. "Creep."

Chapter Six

"How?" Will demanded. He and the others stood in the grassy field in front of the Goblin City. Curious goblins began to gather around them now that Barbecue was gone. "How on Earth did this happen?"

"Uh, technically we're not on Earth, we're on Other Place," Mr. Niff said nervously.

"Answer the question!" Will shouted. The goblins looked away and London studied his toes. Will threw his hands in the air and said, "All you had to do was make some noise and run away. How did you screw that up? London, did you tackle the guy?"

"Oh no sir! I didn't lay a finger on him, honest. I might have roughed up a couple of other people, but that's it!"

"A couple of other people?" Will asked. London nodded. "You chased off the king and a couple other people, too? You were supposed to lose!"

"We tried!" Mr. Niff cried. "We couldn't!"

London nodded. "He's right, boss. It was a setup, I'm sure of it. Their King came with this thin little sword, like something you'd roast marshmallows with over a fire. I thought it was a bit of wire, but he kept calling it a sword."

"A foil?" Will asked. "He went to fight a dragon with a foil? That's a fencing sword!"

"He didn't have armor on, either, not one piece" London said. "Real fancy clothes, but no armor."

Mr. Niff fell at Will's feet and groveled. "It's all true, boss, every word! The guys and I ran out and threw rocks at him and shouted a bit. Then this big group of people came, maybe twenty of them bunched together."

Exasperated, Will asked, "You chased off twenty people?"

"It's not like that," Mr. Niff pleaded. "None of them had armor or weapons. There was a hairdresser, a nail technician, a publicist, a script writer, a makeup artist, two guys for his clothes, a minstrel and a bunch more."

"The minstrel was the worst," London said.

Mr. Niff grabbed Will's hand and looked up into his eyes. "No matter how bad their King screwed up, the minstrel kept playing a lute and singing about how the guy was winning and being brave. Even when Kervol tripped on a tree root, sprained his ankle and fell face first into a mud puddle, the minstrel said he leapt into battle and divided the enemy. The minstrel wouldn't stop it until London broke his lute, kicked him in the shin and made him eat a bug."

"We tried to lose, boss," Mr. Niff implored. "We really did! One of the guys tripped over his own feet, we missed with all the rocks we threw and London accidentally kicked me in the back of the head." Mr. Niff paused and looked at London. "That was a mistake, right? I mean, you didn't mean to do that."

"Then what happened?" Will asked. "How did you drive him off?"

"He swung his sword at London and hit a rock instead," Mr. Niff explained. "It bent and he went home with the other people, vowing vengeance against us all. Uh, London, I mean, you weren't aiming for me or anything, were you?"

London twiddled his thumbs. "Uh—"

"Enough!" Will shouted. His followers shut up and looked at him. They were upset about this, he could tell. Whatever their failings—and they had a lot of them—he didn't think they were lying about what happened.

"Okay," he began, "this is a problem we're going to have to work around. I guess it's not too surprising this king is a moron. After all, most of the people I've met here have an IQ south of a hundred. We're going to give Kervol his princess and we're going to apologize for making him look stupid. Hopefully that will make everything okay."

Will turned to the princess and smiled. The woman was a beauty! She was young, pretty, slender, and had perfectly styled blond hair that reached down to her waist. Dressed in a stunning white gown and wearing dainty white slippers, she practically glowed in the sunlight. The only thing ruining an otherwise perfect appearance was her ridiculously tall white cone hat. Even with her silly hat, she had a kind of spellbinding beauty that made it hard for Will to look away from her, and he couldn't seem to think straight.

Trying to sound both polite and apologetic, Will said, "Princess, I am very sorry about all this. There's been a terrible mistake, and my, err, friends, and I will do everything in our power to get rid of you. No, wait, I mean get you home!"

"You'd better!" the princess screeched. Good Lord! Whatever influence she had over Will vanished when she spoke. The woman had a voice that sounded like nails scratching a chalkboard. "Do you know who I am?"

"Princess Marisa Brandywine." Puzzled, Will said, "Niff already introduced us. Did he get it wrong?'

She stamped her foot, which was enough to send her ridiculously tall cone hat flying to the ground. "It's supposed to be Queen Marisa Ket, you moron! I'm supposed to be at the altar getting married, and because of you I'm not."

Marisa grabbed her hat and put it back on. Will backed up a bit and said, "I am very sorry about that, and I'll do whatever—"

"Queen!" she shouted. "K-W-E-N queen! No more beauty pageants trying to get noticed by rich guys, no more pretending I'm sweet, no more putting up with creeps! I'm supposed to be rich and powerful and able to step on people like you. I could have you locked up and throw away the key. And then throw away the cell," she added with a vicious glare. A stray breeze blew her hat off again and she snatched it off the ground. "I'm throwing away this stupid hat first."

Will frowned and asked Domo, "How quickly can we get Kervol here?"

"Not fast enough."

Brandywine reached into her silk purse and pulled out a sheet of paper. She stomped over to Will and held it up an inch from his face. "My happily-ever-after contract says I'm supposed to be married today. I'm supposed to have a castle and servants and horses and flowers. And if you messed it up you're in deep trouble, pal!"

"May I see that," he asked innocently.

Brandywine sneered and pressed her contract into Will's hands. "Read it and weep, chump. I'm going to be rich and powerful."

Mr. Niff waved his hand. "Maybe we can make this up to her. She's got a wedding coming up. We could buy gifts, like silverware."

"Too expensive," Domo said.

Marisa noticed that no one was paying her attention, an intolerable situation. "Hey, I had to hire a genealogist to find a royal ancestor so I could call myself a princess. The geezer went back ten generations in my family and made up some stuff so I could get this marriage. Do you have any idea how much that cost?"

"Hmm," Will said. He took out Vial's magnifying glass and studied the fine print in Marisa's contract.

"We could get her flowers. Those are cheap," Mr. Niff suggested.

Domo shook his head. “They’ll already have flowers.”

Marisa stamped her foot. “I’m talking, so shut up! I’m going to be rich and you’re slowing me down. I’m going to have gold and silk and jewels and perfume, the good kind, too!”

“And seven sons,” Will added.

Marisa’s face went from snarling to completely blank in a second. “What?”

Will pointed to a line in her contract. “You’re going to have seven sons and a sufficient number of daughters to be used in politically arranged marriages. It says so right here.”

Mr. Niff clapped his hands together. “Maternity clothes!”

“Perfect!” Domo cried.

Marisa ran over and snatched the contract from Will’s hands. She read it quickly, mumbling as she did, until she reached a spot camouflaged by legal jargon. All the color drained from her face. “Oh…my…God!”

Will patted her on the back. “Yeah, the fine print will get you every time. Trust me, I know. Well, Miss Brandywine, I don’t think I can get you to the altar on time, but I’ll get you there eventually. Niff, if you and London can look after her then I’ll go with Domo and Brooklyn to sort thinks out first thing in the morning.”

* * * * *

The next morning was beautiful, warm and sunny, and the air was heavy with the sweet smell of wildflowers. This almost made up for having Princess Brandywine complain the entire night and scream at everyone. Will figured that was the same reaction most people would have to spending a night surrounded by goblins. Then again, Brandywine made it clear anyone was a worthy victim of her sharp tongue.

"Don't worry, I'll have this settled by tonight," Will told her. He, Brooklyn, and Domo were at the gatehouse, prepared to go off and arrange for the king to collect his bride. Will brought his fire scepter, some food, a few coins and a spare scarecrow folded up for the trip. Domo had his walking stick and Brooklyn carried a branch he'd broken off an oak tree to use as a club.

Brandywine sneered. "You'd better! I want this done properly, with a white stallion and a gilded carriage and roses and attendants."

"I'm not sure about all of that stuff, but Kervol seems to have the attendants ready." Will patted London on the shoulder. "Sorry about this. Try to keep her from killing anyone. And don't kill her, no matter how tempting."

London leaned in close and whispered, "Boss, that bottomless pit you ordered will be done in a few days."

Will's eyebrows went up. "That fast?"

London nodded. "Goblins work quick when they're making mischief. If you want there to be an accident while you're gone, it can be arranged."

"No," he said reluctantly.

"There won't be any evidence," London added hastily. "And with you out of the kingdom there's plausible deniability."

In the distance, Will heard Marisa scream at the goblins. "You call this steak?"

"That's what the cook at the inn called it," Mr. Niff said.

Marisa took a bite and spit it out. "It tastes like a badly cooked boot. I'm not eating this!"

Will took a coin from his pocket and flipped it. "Tails. Sorry, London."

Will headed south, leaving Princess Brandywine to the mercy of the goblins, or maybe the other way around. He figured she couldn't do too much damage in the time he'd be gone, and he had to get rid of her. Despite London's offer this had to be done right or he'd have a king angry with him. Of course the king might be angry with him once he got to know the princess, but that was a problem for another day.

"How are we going to handle this?" Domo asked.

"First thing we have to do is make contact with Kervol so he knows we have his princess," Will replied. "After that, we arrange for him to come over and take her off our hands. We'll put on a nice show for everyone to watch, he'll get the girl—God help him—and I can get back to looking for loopholes in my contract."

Brooklyn swung his club and knocked a tiny, white-skinned pixie out of the air, then stomped on it. Will looked at the tiny flattened creature and asked, "What did you do that for?"

"It's our civic duty to squash them," Brooklyn said matter-of-factly.

"It's a pixie," Domo explained. "Sure, one's pretty harmless, but once they get to breeding there can be clouds of them. Have you ever seen a plague of pixies? They're vicious little monsters. They can strip all the meat off a cow in six minutes."

"No more milk and cheese," Brooklyn said. "Kind of hard on the cow, too."

"Lovely," Will said. "Back to the topic at hand, we'll pass our message along at the nearby town and wait for him to show up. I figure he'll be here by tonight."

The trio walked to the same town Will went to for his food. They found the town peaceful and the people hard at work. The locals were harvesting winter wheat, milking cows, chasing chickens and carrying out all the other daily farm duties that take up so much of the day. A few people recognized him from his previous visits and waved.

"Excuse me, I'm looking for the mayor," Will asked.

One of the farmers pointed at a barn. "He's milking cows in there."

Surprised, Will asked, "The mayor milks cows?"

The farmer shrugged. "Not much point feeding them if you don't milk them."

Will frowned. "That's not what I meant. Never mind. I'll go talk to him."

The barn was large and painted with whitewash. Inside were assorted farm animals in stalls, all of them healthy and well cared for. A large man with a full beard and dressed in coveralls was busy milking a cow.

"Hi, I'm Will Bradshaw. Are you the mayor?"

The man didn't look up or stop milking. "That's me."

"I'm kind of surprised to see a mayor working in a barn," Will said. He wanted to make sure he had the right person before he asked for help. The man certainly didn't look like a mayor.

The man didn't stop working. "Surprised to see a king in a barn."

"Yes, well, I'm not much of a king. I have a problem, and I think you can help me."

The mayor chuckled. "Don't see how."

Will smiled and said, "You see, I am currently in possession of a princess, which sounds a lot nicer than it really is. This princess should be marrying your king and I'm trying to return her."

The mayor pointed at several more cows awaiting his attention. "Kind of busy to deliver her for you."

"That's perfectly understandable. I was kind of hoping you could send a message to him saying where she is and asking him to come get her."

The mayor stopped milking. He jumped up, his face twisted in fear. "I can't do that! Anything but that!"

"What's the problem? I just need you to send him a message."

People ran into the barn to see what the shouting was about. A crowd of fifty people formed in seconds, surrounding Will, Brooklyn and Domo. The mayor pointed an accusing finger at Will and said, "He wants us to send a message to the king."

"Mercy no!" a woman cried. The rest of the townspeople chimed in.

"Horror!"

"We're doomed!"

"Okay, hold on just one minute!" Will yelled. More people poured in and they were all panicking. Will had to shout to be heard. "What's wrong with you people? This guy isn't just harmless, from everything I've heard he's an idiot! Why are you so scared of him?"

"It's not like we expect him to hurt us or anything," a farmer said, "but we can't ever talk to him."

"Why not?" Will asked.

The mayor smiled weakly and said, "You see, ten years ago we bribed the royal cartographer, err, that's the mapmaker, to leave our town off the royal maps."

Will scratched his head. "And you did this because…come on, help me out here, people."

The mayor looked embarrassed. "Uh, you see, none of the royalty ever came this way before, seeing as there's nothing but farmland. So if a town isn't on the royal maps, and the king doesn't actually see us or hear from us, then he doesn't know we exist. And if he doesn't know we exist, he doesn't send a tax collector."

"You haven't paid taxes in ten years?" Will asked.

The mayor nodded. "We'd like to keep it that way."

Will's eyes opened wide. "Wow. That's a sweet deal. Domo, I'm a king, do I get paid taxes?"

Domo snorted. "You wouldn't want anything the goblins might bring you."

Will threw up his hands. "Figures. Okay, you've got a good thing going, and I don't want to ruin it for you." This was met with sighs of relief and scattered applause from the crowd. "But I still need to talk to your king. Is there a town around here that does show up on the maps where I can send a message?"

The mayor scratched his head. "There *might* be. The mapmaker retired ten years ago after he finished the royal maps. He bought himself a mansion, and we didn't give him that much money."

Will was getting a headache. Worse, he could see where this was going. He rubbed his forehead and asked, "By any chance, was it the mapmaker who suggested this little scheme?"

The mayor nodded. "Now that you mention it, yes."

"So there's a very good chance he made the same offer to other communities, and there are exactly no towns or villages in these parts that want to come to the king's attention."

The mayor smiled. "In a strictly legal sense, there aren't any towns here at all."

Grumbling, Will said, "This has 'long day' written all over it."

* * * * *

It was well past dark when Will came back to the Goblin City with Brooklyn and Domo. The little goblin was so tired that Brooklyn carried him the last hour of the trip. They returned to find that the goblins were finished adding onto the maze. They'd put in a good day's work, and the maze was noticeably larger. Most of Will's subjects were asleep, but a few came out to greet him.

"Boss!" Mr. Niff ran up and shook his hand. "Good to see you. You had us worried not coming back for so long."

Tired and disgruntled, Will replied, "Yes, well, we were busy visiting five towns that don't exist. Apparently there aren't any towns within fifteen miles of the border, and all the people who live in them want to keep it that way. I had to settle for asking a traveling salesman to tell King Kervol that we have his fiancée and we want to give her back. There's no telling how long it will take the message to get to him."

Will looked around and listened. "I don't hear any screams or insults. What did you guys do to the princess?"

"Nothing, honest!" Mr. Niff replied. "She got all tired out from screaming at us and went to lie down."

"Thank God for small mercies," Domo said. Brooklyn put him down and the goblin wandered into the city. "I'm going to bed. Don't wake me unless the city is burning down, and only then if the fire is getting close."

Will wanted to join him, but he heard noises outside the city walls. There were things scrambling around in the darkness outside the city. Will could barely make them out in the moonlight. He held up his fire scepter. "Small fire, okay? Like a flashlight, or a torch. I just need a very small—"

FOOM! The scepter spit out a wall of fire that lit up the sky, and for a few seconds Will could see perfectly. There were dozens of goblins scampering around. Among them were other things, three-foot tall creatures dressed in rags, creatures with wings too small to fly with, short horns or long shaggy hair. Most of them were pushing carts or carrying large leather sacks. They winced from the intense light, and as it faded they continued their scurrying.

Puzzled, Will asked, "Who are they? Or what are they?"

Domo looked back at the creatures. "They're goblins. I know, I know, they look even weirder than the rest of us do, but they're goblins. About a third of all goblins come out at night to forage or fool around. Some of them will keep up work on the maze during the night and others will bring in food. By the looks of it, this lot is back from foraging in the human kingdom."

"They don't get in trouble for that?" Will asked Domo.

"Oh please. You've seen what we consider food. You did notice that there were no garbage dumps in the towns we visited, right?"

"You mean did I not see something in all those towns that don't exist?" Will frowned and said, "Now that you mention it, there weren't any dumps."

Domo yawned. "Nobody likes having us around, but we're useful to them. The other races will drive us out of town, or at least the nice parts where rich people live, but they're careful not to hurt us. They need us to clean up after them."

"They need you and they treat you like dirt?" Will asked.

Domo shrugged and walked into a tunnel entrance. "We're used to it."

* * * * *

Will had two days of relative quiet after that. The goblins worked hard on expanding the maze. Having so many of them together warped space three times a day, producing rains of frogs, clouds of presidential campaign literature from the 1970s and a 300-pound bronze statue of a wombat that fell from the sky. This last item was carried away with much fanfare and hidden deep underground.

Princess Marisa Brandywine did her level best to make life miserable for everyone she could see, which proved to be mostly Will's problem. Brandywine figured out early on that the goblins didn't care one bit about her or her ambitions, and most of them could give insults as well as they took them. She didn't try irritating the troll brothers, since even she could see how badly that would end. Searching for a more receptive audience for her abuse, she settled on Will. This ruined an otherwise perfect chance to find a way out of his contract. *Article 38, subsection 5, paragraph 19, line 2: Don't even think about trying to burn the place down and blaming it on an electrical fire.*

"How can you stand it?" Brandywine screeched. "This place is so filthy calling it a pigsty would be an insult to pigsties everywhere. Don't you have any pride?"

"I gave up on that a *long* time ago," Will said. It was midmorning and Brandywine had been on his case since dawn. Currently she had him cornered in an alley in the Goblin City. Will had figured there was enough trash in the alley that the princess wouldn't follow him in, but she proved him wrong. She didn't look like she was getting bored with pestering him, either. "Lady, I'm trying to find a way out of my contract. I suggest you look for a way around the clause in yours. You know the one I'm talking about."

"The name's Princess Marisa Brandywine, pal, and don't you forget it! And as for the contract, I'll be rich soon so I can hire a lawyer to handle that."

Will laughed. "A lawyer got you into this mess."

"And another one will get me out of it," she retorted. "Even if they can't, I'll be a queen and you'll still be here in this mess."

Will decided he'd put up with this abuse long enough. He tucked his contract into his belt and stood up, his arms folded across his chest. "Why are you still here? You're in good health and your future husband isn't too far south of us. Exactly why haven't you gotten off your butt and walked out of here? Nobody's making you stay."

She sneered. "You must think I'm stupid."

"No, I think you're an arrogant gold digger getting by solely on your looks."

"You got that right, pal!" She paused for a second and looked confused. "Wait, was that an insult? It doesn't matter. I'm looking out for myself, and if this stupid fairytale wedding and happily-ever-after clause in my contract says I have to be rescued, then you'd better believe I'm going to get rescued! It took a lot of begging, backstabbing and bribes to get me this far. I'm not going to risk losing it when I'm so close."

Will walked away from her, not much concerned with where he was headed. "No man deserves such a punishment."

The princess kept shouting at him for a while, but he tuned her out. He eventually stopped next to the maze. Over a thousand goblins were working on it, and making enough noise that if Brandywine did follow him he couldn't hear her.

London ambled over to Will. "I know you said no before, but the pit's almost done if you want to throw her in."

"It might come to that," Will muttered. He sat down behind a stack of bricks and got back to his contract. Blast it, another day with that woman would drive him mad! She was worse than the goblins. They might sabotage his efforts or annoy him, but they didn't think they were better than he was. Will experienced that too much back home to put up with it here. He rested under the shade of a scarecrow and prayed King Kervol would come soon.

"The King of the Humans is coming!" a goblin cried out. The shout broke through the air like blessed relief. Work on the maze stopped and the goblins ran over to see the guy. Will dusted himself off and went out to greet him. He saw the king and future victim of Brandywine's abuse approaching the Goblin City with a group of people following close behind. Will raced toward him and met Kervol a hundred yards south of the gatehouse. Time to get rid of the princess!

There he was, King Kervol Ket. The man managed to look majestic and stupid at the same time. He was tall, dark, handsome, and had a stupid smirk on his face like he had an IQ somewhere between that of a turnip and a soap bubble. His clothes were made of fine silk dyed blue and red, which looked great and was totally unsuitable for a trip outdoors. His boots were scratched up, and he already had a tear in his pants leg. Kervol held a wire-thin fencing sword called a foil in one hand and a bouquet of roses in the other.

Behind him was his entourage, all twenty of them. They were dressed fashionably, but not so well they looked better than their king. They came burdened with makeup, more fashionable and totally inappropriate clothes, rich food, wine, musical instruments, flowers, sweets and bottles of perfume. In short, they had everything you didn't need for the trip through the wilderness to get here, or for an epic fight to rescue a princess. One of the men carried a flag with Kervol's emblem, a blue peacock on a white background.

"*Knave!*" Kervol shouted theatrically. "*Villain! Scoundrel!* Uh, uh…line!"

One of his female followers paged through a stack of papers and prompted him. "Base and ignominious fiend."

"*Base and ignominious fiend!*" the king bellowed. "*I have come for my betrothed and will face any peril to reclaim her.*"

"She's right over there," Will said. "Listen, I am real sorry about all this and—"

Kervol went on shouting. "*I have faced blackguards and rogues of all manner to reach this foul and degenerate bastion of evil, and I have swept them aside. I have prevailed over untold hardships.*"

"Ran out of wine, did you?" Domo asked snidely.

"Halfway through the trip, yes, but we found a store," Kervol replied. "Oh blast it, you made me lose my concentration. Line!"

The same woman looked over her pages again. "And now I face you, foul worm, beast of fire and death."

"*And now I face you, foul worm, beast of fire and death.* Wait, that was for the dragon. Do we have a line for him?"

Will shook his head. He said to Domo, "He's not listening to me. Do I even need to be here?"

"I think it's expected you stay," Domo explained.

Will managed a phony smile and walked up to King Kervol. "Hi there, William Bradshaw, King of the Goblins at your service. This whole thing with your lady was a big mistake on my part. It's my fault, and I should have come along to supervise your fight with my guys. I'm new at this and I didn't realize just how badly things could go wrong. So I'd like to apologize and wish you and the young lady a long and happy marriage."

"He said that last bit without laughing," Mr. Niff said proudly.

Domo nodded. "A fine actor."

Kervol looked at Will as if he'd grown a second head. "What are you doing?"

"Apologizing."

"No, no, no," Kervol said. "My speechwriter prepared lines for you. Greta, hand him his lines."

The speechwriter handed Will a wad of dog-eared and coffee-stained papers. He took it and said, "You could have given this to me to start with."

Kervol looked confused for a second, and then slapped himself on the forehead. "Blast it, these last-minute changes always screw things up. Greta, where does he come in?"

"On page 19, with the words *weakling king, I will crush you like the bug you are*."

Will quickly read through the script. "Uh, are my lines the ones in red?"

"Yes, yes, get on with it," Kervol snapped.

"But is says I eat puppies."

"You don't?" Mr. Niff asked Will.

"Surprisingly, no. And this bit about capturing maidens, well, maybe in a dream or something. Hold on, it says I steal gold and burn villages, and…is this last one anatomically possible?"

"It doesn't matter!" Kervol yelled. "Listen here, bucko, your followers are right noxious monsters and you're no better. Everyone knows it. Worse, you've upset a very delicate timetable. The wedding cake went flat, the flowers wilted and I had to pay the wedding guests to keep them from leaving! It's going to cost a lot of money fixing this mess, and you and your filth-ridden followers are to blame!"

"I already apologized," Will said. "Okay, this is my fault, I admit it, but you're not doing this right, either."

In Kervol's entourage, a minstrel began playing his lute and singing. "*The vile and horrid King of Goblins dared to oppose our noble king with words and deeds most foul.*"

"Shut up!" Will shouted. "Kervol, you don't have any armor and you're using a stupid little sword. Come on, what kind of dramatic rescue is this?"

Kervol handed off the roses to an attendant and marched up to Will. "Look here, you sniveling rat-faced twerp, this outfit is the proper attire for a king. All the monarchs are wearing it this year. And this sword is the weapon of a gentleman."

"Are you listening to anything I said?" Will asked. Quickly losing his temper, he shouted, "You have no armor! If even one of my goblins started throwing rocks at you you'd be on the ground in seconds. You don't go into a fight dressed like that! My kingdom came with a magic scepter. It's too enthusiastic, but it's mine." The scepter hummed in appreciation. "If a dirt poor kingdom like this came with a magic weapon, don't tell me yours didn't."

The minstrel kept playing: "*The King of Goblins, with a sneer and scowl, did stand against our king.*"

Grudgingly, Kervol said, "There is a magic sword, but it's stuck in a rock. Even if I could get it out, it's not fashionable. It's an old design and the handle looks funny. None of this matters! Listen, just read the stupid lines and get a few goblins for me to run through. The minstrel and official record keeper will record the whole thing and I can go home."

The minstrel went on playing, oblivious to the dark looks he was getting from Will: "*Bravely did our king issue forth his challenge to the foul and fetid horde.*"

Will gave the minstrel a withering glare. "London, if you could take care of that for me?"

"I thought you'd never ask," the troll said. He smiled evilly and lumbered toward the minstrel.

Will opened his mouth to continue the argument, then froze. Something Kervol said earlier didn't sound right. "Back up a bit. You mentioned running through a couple goblins, didn't you? As in stab?"

Kervol rolled his eyes. "Yes, yes, there's supposed to be bodies after an epic battle between good and evil. Everyone knows that. Pick out someone expendable."

Princess Brandywine heard the commotion and came running. Trying to sound sweet, she cried, "Oh, my love, you've come to save me from this brute!"

"Don't you start!" Will shouted. "Kervol, that's not happening, end of story. If you want to say you stabbed someone with that letter opener, then that's what you can tell the people back home. Who's going to tell them different? The goblins, sure, but no one's going to believe them. The only other people here are loyal to you. They'll say what you want them to say."

London got hold of the minstrel, pulled his lute away and bashed it apart on the ground. Then he kicked the man in the shin.

"You don't get it, do you?" Kervol asked. "There are protocols to follow, ways things are done around here. If people are going to take me seriously then I have to do things right. If you won't throw me a few goblins then I shall face you in battle myself! Minstrel, play a suitable tune of war. Minstrel?"

London had the minstrel in a headlock and was trying to stuff something in his mouth. "Come on, eat it! Eat the bug!"

"I don't want to! Gulp—yuck."

"That's it!" Kervol pulled the glove off his left hand and slapped Will across the face with it. "I knew you were a knave to be in charge of this filthy little kingdom—"

"Little?" Domo asked. "We've got more land than you do."

Undeterred, Kervol went on. "And I came prepared to do battle. You face an expert swordsman in the peak of human perfection." He stepped back and swung his foil around in a very showy and totally pointless fashion. "If you refuse to follow tradition then I will cut you down where you stand!"

Will rolled his eyes. "With that? Put it away before you hurt yourself."

Kervol raised his sword and declared, "As the elves say, '*vilantias keporilid viginimax!*'"

Will rubbed his eyes and asked, "Which means what, exactly?"

"Death before dishonor!" Kervol shouted. A member of his entourage hurried over and whispered into his ear. Frowning, Kervol asked, "Then what does it mean?" More whispers followed, and Kervol's face paled. "Oh."

"If you're going to insult me, do it in a language at least *one* of us understands," Will said.

Looking a bit nervous, Kervol said, "Setting aside for the moment what I just said about your mother—"

"You what?" Will shouted.

"Ooh!" the goblins chorused.

"Oh, enough of this!" Kervol lunged at Will, barely missing. For all his boasting, Kervol actually was good with his sword. Will jumped back to avoid another attack and fell over backwards. *Whoosh!* He warped to the nearest scarecrow twenty feet away.

Brandywine put her hand to her mouth in mock horror, just like her acting coach trained her. "My King, be careful!"

Kervol spotted Will and came at him again. London and all the nearby goblins were running to attack the twit. Kervol had his sword raised high to look dramatic before he attacked. This could get messy. Will needed the fight to end now. He pulled out his scepter and aimed high. "This is important. It has to be a small fire, enough to heat up the sword so he drops it and that's it. Don't burn him, please don't—"

FOOM! The white-hot blast of fire was thinner than usual but no less intense. It went over Kervol's head and melted the foil, leaving behind nothing but the handle. Kervol dropped his melted sword in shock and the goblins backed away. Then, slowly, from dozens and then hundreds of goblins came clapping and a ragged cheer.

"You idiot, do you have any idea how much these things cost?" Kervol demanded. "Blast it, I'm going to have to raise taxes again. Greta, I need the emergency speech." Kervol's entourage surrounded him, touching up his makeup and handing him another script. "Let's see, uh, where do I start?"

"You've won this day," Greta the speechwriter prompted him.

"Ah, right. *You've won this day, base villain, but I shall return, renewed and strengthened, to meet this challenge and overcome it. Mark my words.*"

"Oh for the love of God, just take the girl and leave!" Will fished through his pockets and pulled out a handful of coins. "Look, I am paying you to take her and go."

"A bribe? How much?" Kervol hurried over and looked at the pile of coins Will had got from the villagers days before. "Ha! I spend more than that getting my hair done. Talk to me when you have real money. I'm off, and you'll rue the day I return."

Princess Brandywine threw her head back and covered her eyes with a hand. "My love, I count the seconds until I am at your side."

"Just take the girl!" Will pleaded. "Please, in the name of all that's holy, take her!"

Kervol scoffed. "You don't know anything about tradition, do you?"

"I know it doesn't involve common sense," Will said. Kervol and his entourage turned around and headed south. Will pointed his scepter at them and shouted, "Hey, hey you get back here! You get back here this instant and rescue the princess. She's in danger if you don't take her. I'm a base villain; you said it yourself. Horrible things will happen to her if you leave her here!"

"That's a chance I'm willing to take," Kervol replied.

"Get back here!" Will looked at Domo and Mr. Niff, who shrugged helplessly. "Exactly how is it goblins got a reputation for stupidity and they didn't?"

Domo smiled. "It's one of life's little mysteries."

Chapter Seven

Will leaned against the tunnel wall outside his throne room. In front of him were eight goblins wearing miniature World War I German infantry uniforms. They were armed with clubs, bowling pins and rubber chickens. One goblin had the leg off a piano. They saluted him, two goblins saluting so forcefully they knocked themselves to the ground.

"Okay, now what do you do if Princess Brandywine comes looking for me?" he asked.

"Lie like a cheap rug," a pudgy goblin replied.

Will smiled. "Good. And if she tries to force her way in?"

The goblins scratched their heads and mumbled to one another. One raised his hand and tentatively said, "Invade France?"

"No. Tackle her and drag her outside. It'll be a lot more dangerous than invading France. It's very important she doesn't get inside."

"Why?" the pudgy goblin asked. The rest joined in, some jumping up and down or waving their hands. He managed to quiet them down and smiled at them.

"I'm going to play a trick on her, and I don't want her to find out."

"Ooh," they chorused.

"Keep her outside, remember," Will said. He didn't want the princess coming in while he was trying to find a way out of this mess. She was dead set on being rescued 'properly', which seemed to involve people ending up dead. The less she knew about what Will was doing, the less she could interfere.

Will left the goblins and went into his throne room, closing the door behind him. Inside this room were all the people he trusted in the screwed-up world he was trapped in. There was Gladys the magic mirror, who was currently grumbling as she added another layer of makeup to her already clownish face. Domo and Mr. Niff kept well away from Vial, the third goblin in the room. Vial was mixing some ghastly smelling chemicals in a beaker and smiling as he did it. Lastly there were the troll brothers London and Brooklyn, playing cards and standing guard for Will in the likely event that Brandywine got past the warrior goblins.

Will sat down on an empty crate, the closest thing he had to a throne, and smiled. "Thank you all for coming. Gentlemen, lady, I called this meeting because I well and truly screwed things up. Not only do I have a princess with a tongue sharp enough to cut through steel, I now have her fiancée, a king, angry with me."

"Screwing things up is a fine goblin tradition," Mr. Niff said. He patted Will on the back. "Be fair, boss, we deserve a little credit. It was me and London who started this whole mess by making King Kervol look stupid."

"He didn't need much help doing that," Will said. "The man is a certified idiot. Aren't there laws preventing people like that from coming to power?"

"Not any more than there are in your world," Gladys said sourly. "He's the oldest son of the last king, so he gets the job. And before you ask, his brothers are even bigger knuckleheads than he is."

"But they'll want his job, right?" Will asked hopefully. "Maybe I can cut a deal with them."

Domo shook his head. "We still have the princess, and whoever is in charge will want her back on their terms. Besides, getting rid of Kervol won't do any good. If something unfortunate happens to him then the next king will have to avenge him, no matter how stupid he was. It's tradition."

"I want him overthrown, not dead," Will said.

"How flexible are you about that?" London asked. "I mean, Brooklyn and me can fix things for you."

"We're real good at arranging accidents," Brooklyn added.

"No." Will paced back and forth across the throne room. "What I don't get is why he was so set on killing people today. Barbecue said he was going to chase the goblins off and that would be it. What changed?"

"What changed was that you beat him," Gladys said. A bookcase appeared next to her in the mirror's surface. She pulled a book out and opened it up. "Kervol's got a copy of *Etiquette for Royal Personages and Other Really, Really Important People*, by Yuri daFool. All the upper class twits own one. It's sort of a guide for stupid rich people."

"Why do you have one?" Will asked.

Gladys snorted. "I used to belong to people with more money than brains. They didn't feel like reading, so they put all kinds of books in here with me. I'd read them and tell them what they needed to do."

Gladys flipped through the book. "If Kervol expects to rule then he has to look like a big man to his peasants and rival kings. If he doesn't, he could face revolts, invasions or lawyers rampaging across the countryside. When he lost to Niff and London he looked weak. That's bad, but he can make up for it by going on to win a bigger victory. You know, claim the first attempt was a practice run, or say that you cheated."

"The first time he was willing to chase the goblins off and we won, somehow," Will said. "The second time he wanted bodies on the ground and I beat him. He's going to expect a bigger victory for round three, isn't he?"

"Oh yeah," Gladys said. "He's going to want a whole mess of goblins dead this time. He might settle for maiming you, seeing as you're the one who ruined his sword."

Will tapped his scepter against his palm as he paced. He stopped and smiled. "Wait, I've got it. Kervol was willing to accept a bribe to leave. He just wanted a bigger one than I had. Can we get him on that?"

Gladys flipped through her book and stopped near the end. "Nope. Hitting people up for bribes is okay. He just needs to call it tribute or a gift."

"Where I come from that's called extortion," Will said.

She smiled at him. "When rich people do it, it's called collecting taxes."

Vial stirred his concoction and cleared his throat. "Pardon the interruption, but exactly how much money would our sword-swinging monarch require to prevent another attack?"

"There's a sliding scale," Gladys said. "For making him look stupid twice in front of witnesses he's going to want something in the neighborhood of 20,000 gold coins."

Will's jaw dropped. Mr. Niff fainted. Vial dropped his beaker in surprise and was sent airborne when it hit the floor and exploded. Domo choked on his own spit and the troll brothers uttered some choice swear words in their own language.

"Twenty thousand!" Will exclaimed. "I don't have that kind of money! Domo, do we have anything like that kind of money?"

"We've got a pile of shiny rocks and a bronze statue of a wombat," Domo replied. "If we try to give it to him he'll charge us to throw it away."

Mr. Niff recovered and staggered to his feet. "The boys and I could swipe some cash from local wishing wells. We might get a few gold coins in change."

"Perhaps he would accept some form of barter," Vial said. "I have an exciting line of detonating outhouses with models for every season and occasion."

Gladys shut the book and put it back in the bookcase. "Dream on. Kervol's a king so he's going to want gold. He might not even settle for money. Face it, people, we're the weakest kingdom in all of Other Place and we beat him twice. That's a lot of humiliation to deal with. If he doesn't win big all the other kings will look down on him. There might even be a rebellion and another member of his family put on the throne."

Will slumped down on his crate and put his face into his hands. "And I thought getting out of my contract was impossible."

"Look on the bright side," Domo said. "Nobody's ever tried to get out of a king contract by getting chopped up with a sword. That could be a whole new escape route for you."

Will shot him a withering glare. "I do not want to leave here in a coffin. Okay, Gladys, I need you to look through your books and find a loophole in the rules. Niff, have the other goblins put up more scarecrows so we'll see Kervol coming and I'll have a means to escape with if he comes armed."

"You got it, boss," Mr. Niff said eagerly.

Will pointed at the troll brothers. "Brooklyn, try to keep the princess out of trouble. I know, I know, it's impossible, but please try. London, I want you with me for when Kervol shows up again."

London rubbed his hands together in eager anticipation of beating up Kervol's minstrel again. "Oh this is going to be sweet."

"Vial—" Will paused and looked at the smiling little explosives expert. "Uh, stay ready in case I need you."

"I shall have my entire stock ready for your use," Vial replied.

Will tugged on his cape. "You know, I told Kervol he should have been wearing armor, and it occurs to me I wasn't following my own advice. I didn't think he'd attack me but now I know better. Domo, I know I'm asking too much, but do I have any armor?"

"You're right, you're asking too much," Domo replied. "You're lucky you've got pants."

Outside the throne room there was a terrible noise, a mix of shrieking and whining and anguished howls. A few words came through the commotion.

"He's not here! He's, uh, he's in the bathroom!" a goblin cried.

Another squeaky voice added, "He's contemplating the mysteries of the universe!"

"He's contemplating the mysteries of the universe in the bathroom!" said the first.

The door was kicked open, and a warrior goblin flew in and slammed into Mr. Niff. Seconds later Princess Brandywine burst in with three goblins clinging desperately to her. She tossed another one aside and fixed Will with a look of pure rage.

Brandywine wasn't looking quite so pretty anymore. Her long blond hair was dirty and had twigs stuck in it. Her beautiful gown was mud-stained around the bottom. She had obviously run out of makeup a while ago. Worse than her hair or clothes was her face, twisted into a snarl that hid all her beauty.

"Twice," she said in a low, dangerous tone. "I was supposed to be married and rich and powerful days ago. I should have riches and jewels and people fawning over me, and I'm not. Why? Because *twice* you've screwed up and driven my king away!"

A warrior goblin ran into the throne room and lunged at Brandywine, screaming as he attacked. She pulled a goblin off her and batted aside the attacking goblin. With that distraction removed, she focused her attention back on Will. "I'm going to make your life utter misery every second I'm around you."

Will scratched his head. "Exactly how is that different from what you've been doing the last few days?"

Brandywine screamed and threw a goblin at him. Will ducked under the terrified screaming projectile and ran for the door with the princess in hot pursuit.

"A little help here!" Will shouted.

The trolls lunged at Brandywine, but the princess ducked under them and kept running straight at Will. Vial pulled a bottle out of a pocket and threw it in front of Brandywine. The bottle shattered and poured out a cloud of white smoke. The princess coughed and staggered, allowing Will to escape. He ran out of the tunnels and into the cool night air, putting as much distance as he could between him and the enraged princess.

Will finally stopped next to the entrance of the maze. This late at night there were no workers present, and plenty of stacks of timber and bricks he could hide behind if she found him. He leaned against the outer wall of the maze and caught his breath. Will heard someone running toward him, but thankfully it was only Mr. Niff.

"You okay, boss?"

Will thought about that for a second. "I'm stuck running a kingdom of idiots, the neighboring king wants me dead, a fire-breathing dragon is angry with me and a princess has vowed to torment me. So I guess the answer to that is no."

Mr. Niff smiled. "You make it sound like any of that is bad. Heck, since you showed up there's been more going on in a week than there was all last year. I gotta say, the boys are happy as could be."

"Really?" Will asked, his head cocked to match his confused expression.

Mr. Niff nodded. "You bet. Word was already getting around how you're doing all these big projects, and today you humiliated a king! He pulled out a sword and you pulled out a magic scepter. Talk about escalating the conflict! And what you did to his sword? I mean, wow! The boys are all talking about it. It's only been a few hours and I've already seen a big increase in recruits."

Will rubbed his forehead. "So there's going to be even more goblins coming."

Mr. Niff climbed onto a pile of bricks so he could look his king in the eye. "Lots more. Sure, this will end badly. It always does when we're involved. But think of it, the leader of the goblins humiliated a human king. It boggles the mind. Do you know how long it's been since we had a win this big? Decades! Word of this is already spreading, and soon goblins everywhere will stand a little bit taller. Well, taller until somebody stomps on them, but that's okay."

"You do know Kervol is coming back?" Will asked. "He's going to want to do a lot of damage."

Mr. Niff smiled. "Of course he's coming back. He'll shout and wreck the place, burn down buildings, throw some of us in a dungeon, maybe even salt the earth so nothing will grow. Humans and elves and dwarves have done all that to us before and we're still here. But you making a king look dumb…now that's something we have that can't be taken or burned. We'll keep that for a long time."

Will stared in disbelief at Mr. Niff. "Do you have any idea how badly this will end? I just saw one angry woman take on eight goblins and win."

"She was motivated. Don't worry about the boys. They're a little rusty, little dusty, little tarnished, little moldy. It's been a long time since they had to fight anyone. Give them a few weeks to work the kinks out and you'll be impressed."

* * * * *

Will ended up sleeping outside between two stacks of bricks, and was woken up when the goblins got back to work on the maze. Will watched them for a while, amazed how load after load of bricks, cement and timber went into the maze. The goblins worked very quickly but they weren't following any kind of plan. A lot of the time they built a new section only to find it blocked off an existing part of the maze, or didn't fit with the other new parts. They ended up having to tear out most of the new construction and rebuild. In spite of that, the maze grew hundreds of square feet each day.

Domo waddled up to him. Will pointed to the construction gangs and asked, "How much longer will this take them?"

"Days, maybe weeks," Domo said. "If you're lucky you might be able to make improving the maze a regular job for them once the major work is done. It could keep a couple hundred of them busy and out of your hair."

Will frowned. "That was my biggest concern before King Kervol and Brandywine showed up. What am I supposed to do? They're both nuts, and believe me I know loonies. I took an art appreciation class in college and my teacher could speak for hours about nothing. Half the words she used didn't exist."

“Speaking of those nutcases, we may have a problem,” Domo said. “I spoke to Gladys this morning and she said eight scarecrows are down near our border with Kervol’s land.”

“You think he’s responsible?”

Domo shrugged. “Possibly. Gladys said she wasn’t looking through them when they were pulled down, so she doesn’t know who did it. Could be gnomes, bad weather, maybe a wandering ogre (man those guys stink!), or one of Kervol’s flunkies. To be honest, I don’t think any of Kervol’s boys are smart enough to tear them down. Besides, petty vandalism is more our thing than theirs.”

Will nodded. “No scarecrows means no easy escapes for me and no way for Gladys to keep an eye on things. Is Niff setting up new scarecrows like I asked?”

“He started this morning. He may have seen what brought them down.”

“That’s what I’m hoping. Okay, I’ll get London and look into it. Check in with Gladys and see if she turned up anything new.”

Domo went back into the Goblin City. Will was glad he had Domo on his side, especially with this new craziness. He’d be at wit’s end if he had to struggle against Kervol and his own followers at the same time.

Will headed south to see what happened to his scarecrows. A few bored goblins saw him and tagged along while the rest kept working on the maze. He left behind the crumbing Goblin City and the half-finished maze, soon entering the lightly forested south part of his kingdom. The air began to tingle and ripple. Space was being charged with the goblins’ stupidity and would warp soon.

The trees and shrubs rustled as Brooklyn ambled into sight. The lanky troll saw Will and walked over. “Sir, uh, I lost the princess.”

"You did? Wonderful!" Will clasped his hands together. "Maybe she'll stay gone."

"That'd be nice," Brooklyn said. "I was kind of looking forward to roughing up that loopy king. It's no fair London gets to have all the fun."

"Tell you what, I'll let you deal with the next royal pain in the butt that shows up."

"For real?" Brooklyn asked hopefully. Will nodded. "That'll be sweet. I never roughed up a king before."

"Brooklyn, did you see any scarecrows down while you were looking for Brandywine?" Will asked.

The troll scratched his head. "Nope. Now that I think about it, I didn't see any scarecrows at all. Kind of funny."

"Okay, forget the princess and help me figure out what happened to those scarecrows. If someone is responsible I'll need your help dealing with them."

Will walked into the forest with Brooklyn and a few goblins following. There were limestone cliffs and canyons almost hidden by the growing trees, berry bushes covered with flowers, squashed pixies on the ground, but no scarecrows. Will was sure he'd seen some here the other day.

"Boss, over here," Brooklyn said. He pointed to a hole in the soft ground, the right size for a scarecrow's post. "Someone went and pulled it out."

Will didn't see footprints around the hole. He looked at Brooklyn and asked, "Do you think gnomes did it?"

The troll shook his head. "They chop them up or set them on fire. They never stole them before."

They soon found three more holes where scarecrows had been planted. London caught up with them while they were still searching. "Sorry I'm late. Gladys says she lost another five scarecrows and she can't see through any Niff put up."

"That's a lot of scarecrows gone, plus whatever Niff did," Will said. This was starting to look bad. "If he's been at this since morning he must have put up at least five more."

They heard goblins hooting and babbling in the distance. Will led the trolls and a handful of goblins toward the noise. They found Mr. Niff surrounded by a mob of fifty goblins. They were listening to him with rapt attention as he described how Will melted Kervol's sword yesterday.

"Niff, what's going on?" Will asked.

"Oh, hi boss. Everybody, this is our new king," Mr. Niff said. The goblins swarmed around him and barraged him with stupid questions. Mr. Niff shouted to be heard over the mob. "It's another bunch of recruits. They heard you went and beat up a human king, and they're here to help."

"I didn't beat him up," Will protested. "I might have humiliated him a bit, but I didn't hurt him."

The goblins cheered and clapped. One of them asked, "You're going to do it again, right? We didn't see the last time. Were there pies involved?"

"No pies," Will said. "Niff, you were supposed to be putting up more scarecrows."

"I did," Mr. Niff said proudly. "A couple of the boys and me put up twenty this morning."

"Twenty?" Will asked in dismay. Oh this was bad. Will could feel disaster looming, a talent he'd picked up fast since coming here. "Gladys says she can't see through any of them, and the trolls and I can't find a bunch that were here yesterday."

Mr. Niff's cheerful expression vanished. "That's not possible."

"You!" Making a bad situation worse, Princess Brandywine marched toward him. She was even more of a mess than when Will saw her last night, with dirt smeared on her dress and on her arms up to her elbows. She forced her way through the goblins, stepping on the smaller ones and stopped in front of him.

"She came back?" Brooklyn asked.

"I find her confusing, too," his brother said.

Brandywine pushed Will and shrieked, "You have the gall to have that scaly lummox of a troll follow me? It took an hour to get away from him. I am a princess and due all the rights and privacy that entails."

Will helped a couple of bruised goblins get off the ground after the princess trampled them. "Sorry, guys. I'm trying to get rid of her. Niff, take these guys and find out what happened to the missing scarecrows."

"You got it, boss." Mr. Niff saluted smartly. The other goblins saluted sloppily and the mob ran off into the woods.

The princess pushed Will again. She held a mud-covered hand up to her chin. "I have had it up to here with this place! I'm more important than they are or your stupid scarecrows, or you for that matter. The next time my king comes you'd better lose, or else."

"The last time he came he wanted to kill my followers," Will said.

"That's what they're for," Brandywine sneered before stomping away.

Grumbling, Will walked away. Stupid princess making all this trouble doesn't even look so good all messed up like that, Will thought. It's not like he meant to cause her any problems. Too proud to even wash her own hands, mud caked on them. He was still grumbling when he noticed something wasn't right.

"My scepter, where is it?" Will checked his belt where it normally hung. It was gone, the cloth loop holding it in place torn. "When did that happen?"

The trolls checked his belt. Brooklyn said, "You had it this morning when we met."

"Yeah, but that means…oh no. Brandywine took it when she pushed me."

"We'll get it back," London said. He and his brother ran off after Brandywine.

"Be careful!" he shouted. "This is just great! I've finally got the goblins too busy to bother me and she has to act up like this."

Will set off after Brandywine. He got three steps before he ran into a thick mass of shrubs. He was almost through when he stepped on something that snapped. Will bent down and found broken poles in the brush, the kind of poles goblins attached scarecrows to. There were more of them, and torn bits of the uniforms scarecrows wore, all ruined and hidden out of sight.

"Brandywine," he said venomously. The mud on her hands made sense now. She'd got away from Brooklyn and took out all the scarecrows she could find. She'd seen him warp between them and was making sure he couldn't do it again. That plus stealing his scepter left him helpless if Kervol showed up again.

Trumpets blared and someone strummed a lute. Will covered his face with his hand and said, "Oh no. Not now."

It was Kervol. This time he was dressed in white silk pants and a purple shirt, with black boots stained with mud. He had another bunch of roses and that same goofy smirk that suggested both a sense of superiority and absolutely no intelligence. Following him closely was his entourage, with even more people than last time. They hustled to keep up with their king while burdened with cases of wine, chocolate-covered truffles, a flagpole flying Kervol's peacock flag and sacks of rose petals they scattered on the ground before Kervol.

"*Fiend, villain, despoiler of the very world,*" Kervol announced. "*Your death at my hands will be a benefit to all creation!*"

Will smiled. Without his scepter he was helpless, and without the scarecrows he couldn't get away quickly. That left distracting Kervol as Will's best option. "You know, that is one nice shirt."

"You like it?" Kervol asked. "It's one of my favorites. The dye comes from the gland of an ocean snail. It's very expensive. It was this or a new bridge in the south of the kingdom, and the bridge can wait until next year."

Will smiled and tried not to laugh. "We have to have priorities, don't we?"

"Exactly! What's the point in collecting taxes if you don't spend them? I would have arrived sooner, but I got lost along the way," Kervol said. He held up a sheet of paper and added, "This map is worthless! I set foot in no less than five villages that don't show up anywhere on here."

Will smiled. He needed to keep the twit talking until help showed up. "Oh, you know, those places spring up like mushrooms after a rain storm."

"Really?"

"You bet. Take some good farmland, add water and stand back."

Kervol stroked his chin. "I didn't know that. I'll have to have the royal cartographer update my maps. Wait a moment, there was something I was supposed to do. Think, think, think… what was it?"

Will looked around nervously. He saw London and Brooklyn in the distance. The trolls were running to his aid. Well, actually they were lumbering to his aid. Closer to the Goblin City he saw Mr. Niff and a boatload of goblins. They saw their king in danger and were scurrying to the rescue. He needed to stall Kervol a bit longer.

"Bribes," Will said cheerfully. "You were going to ask me about bribes."

Kervol looked puzzled. "I was?"

"Oh definitely. I heard your coronation was kind of pricey." Will didn't mention the king's upcoming wedding since that might remind him of the princess he was supposed to rescue. "That must have used a lot of money and you're here looking to get some assistance."

"No, that doesn't sound right," Kervol said. "You don't have any money…do you?"

"You know, that's an interesting question," Will said cheerfully. "I've only been in office a few days, so I'm not entirely sure what I have. Tell you what, I'll go ask around and see if we have any large sacks of gold laying around."

The new goblin recruits reached them before Kervol could reply. Mr. Niff got in front of Kervol and stomped on his foot, making the king yelp and hop backwards on one foot. Mr. Niff then pulled out his knife and stood in front of Will.

"Stay away from our King," someone in the entourage yelled.

"Hey, that's my line!" Mr. Niff yelled back.

Kervol stopped rubbing his foot and snapped his fingers. "That's what I was trying to remember! Line!"

Kervol's speechwriter fumbled through her wad of papers and said, "Foul king, creature of evil—"

"*Foul king, creature of evil, you have my beloved and I have come to rescue her,*" Kervol bellowed dramatically.

"Oh just stop that," Will said. "I don't want her. I *really* don't want her, and to be honest I'm surprised you do. She vowed to make my life miserable and she's out here somewhere making trouble. Take her, please!"

The minstrel began to play his new lute. Will shouted, "Don't sing! If you open your mouth to do anything except breathe, I will hurt you." The minstrel looked nervous and backed away. The troll brothers were closing fast and he didn't want to attract their attention.

"You really don't know what you're doing, do you?" Kervol asked, his voice dripping with contempt. "We're kings! There are rules we have to follow, traditions dating back a thousand years. If following them means doing things that don't make sense, then you do them. If it means a few dozen followers get hurt, then they'd better have health insurance. No one will take you seriously if you just go and do things all willy-nilly and make it up as you go along."

Will stared at Kervol in amazement. "You'd follow the rules even when they don't make sense, and when following them makes things worse?"

"Exactly. The rules don't have to be fair or intelligent as long as they're consistent. I spoke with my advisers, and we found a way to let you out with some dignity. I'll kill twenty goblins and you can kill my hairdresser."

From back in Kervol's entourage, a frightened voice asked, "Hold on! What was that?"

"No," Will said firmly.

"Okay, I'll throw in my nail technician, but that's my final offer," Kervol replied. "Is there any way you can use your fire scepter and leave a man's skull behind? I've got this really great speech to a fallen comrade where I'm holding his skull."

Exasperated, Will said, "What is it with you and killing people? I don't want to kill anyone, and I don't want any of my goblins getting killed, either."

"Why not?" a shaggy goblin asked.

Another goblin nodded. "All our other kings would've said yes."

"Don't encourage him," Will told them. "Kervol, take your fiancée and go. Tell everyone you smashed the place up good. Tell them you killed a hundred goblins and I begged for my life. Who's going to say different? Please, take her and go."

"No, no, no, no!" Kervol shouted and stamped his foot. "*I will not be cheated out of my victory by, by*…line!"

"Honeyed words and a viper's tongue," the speechwriter prompted him.

"—By honeyed words and a viper's tongue!" he shouted. "*I challenge you to battle!*"

"You're still not wearing any armor!" Will yelled at him. He looked at Kervol more closely. Something was wrong. Will walked up to the man and checked his scabbard. "Wait a minute, you didn't even get a new sword. What are you supposed to fight me with?"

"I am a king," Kervol said haughtily. "The rules say I can order my followers to fight for me."

Kervol whistled and was answered by the thunderous pounding of hooves. Out of the forest came four knights covered head to toe in gleaming steel armor. They rode powerfully built horses wearing steel armor over their heads and sides, and saddles embossed with silver. All four knights carried large wooden shields and steel tipped lances fourteen feet long. They galloped up and stopped beside Kervol.

Will looked at Mr. Niff and said, “You don’t think it can get worse, and then it does.”

“My champions,” Kervol ordered, “attack!”

The knights charged. Will ran for his life. Will’s followers didn’t run.

Mr. Niff attacked the leading knight, his trusty knife in hand. The knight ignored the goblin and almost ran him over. Howling, Mr. Niff threw himself at the knight and grabbed the man’s leg. From there he climbed onto the saddle.

“Hey, get off there!” the knight shouted. He tried to shoo Mr. Niff off and failed. Fourteen-foot lances were good at hitting people in front of you, but terrible when dealing with someone right on top of you. Mr. Niff attacked the saddle and cut through the straps holding it onto the horse. When he cut the last strap the saddle slid off the horse and took the knight with it. The knight crashed to the ground as his horse bolted. Mr. Niff jumped off the horse and pounded on the knight’s helmet with the butt of his knife.

The next knight ran afoul of Brooklyn and London, who grabbed the horse and dragged it to a stop. The knight dropped his lance and drew a sword. He swung once and missed Brooklyn. The trolls grabbed him, threw him to the ground and kicked him a couple times.

The third knight ran past his fallen comrades and headed for Will. He didn’t reach him as scores of goblins ran straight at him. The air rippled and took on a musty smell as the goblins began to warp space. But this time something was different. All the goblins were focused on the charging knight, and they unintentionally directed the warp effect at him. The knight was almost on them when the rippling air wrapped around him. There was a *whoosh* as space warped suddenly, moving the knight and his horse one hundred feet to the west. They reappeared in a grove of trees amid a cloud of dryer lint and plaid neckties, the horse still at running at a full gallop. The knight then hit a low branch and was knocked to the ground.

That left one knight. It would take minutes for Mr. Niff or the troll brothers to catch up with Will and offer any help. It would take hours before the goblins' built up enough stupidity and craziness to warp space again. This left Will alone and unarmed to deal with the knight. He ran with the knight in hot pursuit.

The knight caught up with him and tried to stab him with the lance. Will fell down and rolled as he hit the ground, and was almost run over by the horse. He scrambled to his feet and took off as the knight came about for another charge. Will saw a small canyon with loose rocks near the entrance. With any luck the horse would slip on them. He ran toward the canyon as the knight closed in.

The plan sort of worked. The horse did start to slip, forcing the knight to slow down. Unfortunately the knight pressed his attack and herded Will into the canyon. The canyon walls were high and rough enough that Will might be able to climb them, but not quickly enough to avoid the knight. Trapped, he saw the knight circle around for another attack. Will ran down the canyon and prayed his followers would catch up in time.

The canyon was wide enough for the knight to maneuver, but slippery from water and loose rocks so that his horse couldn't go fast. Will gasped for air as he ran down the twisting canyon. Near a sharp turn he saw a wooden sign with words painted on in berry juice.

Goblins at Work

(Really, Honest)

He rounded the corner to see the canyon came to a dead end, a figurative statement that might soon become literal. Right before the canyon ended was a pit twenty feet across and deep enough that Will couldn't see the bottom. Around it were stakes driven into the rock, with ropes anchored to them trailed into the pit. Picks, hammers and wheelbarrows were scattered around the pit, all of the tools sized for Will's diminutive followers. Belatedly, Will realized this was the bottomless pit he'd ordered his goblins to dig. He could hear them chiseling away deep inside the pit.

"Uh, guys, your king could use some help up here!" he shouted into the pit. The goblins couldn't hear him over the sound of hammers and picks biting into the stone. Will heard the knight approaching, the horse's hooves clattering on the stony ground. It sounded like the horse was picking up speed. "I need help!"

The knight came around the corner and saw Will. He lowered his lance and charged. Will backed up to the edge of the pit and grabbed a pick off the ground, determined to go down fighting. The knight laughed at him and urged his horse to go faster.

Will saw a flutter of black and green out of the corner of his eye. Up against the canyon wall was a scarecrow, positioned where it could view the pit and not easily be seen. The knight charged the last fifty feet, his lance raised level with Will's heart. Will watched him charge, the horse's hooves throwing up gravel and dirt. The knight cried out in triumph. Will smiled and fell backwards. There was a *whoosh* as he traded places with the scarecrow, leaving the knight to impale an empty uniform mere feet in front of the pit. The horse skidded to a halt and stopped inches from the pit's edge. The knight wasn't so lucky and was thrown off his horse by the sudden stop. He fell in the pit, his armor and weapons clanging and clashing as he hit the bottom.

Will walked back to the pit. He looked down but couldn't see the knight or the goblins. The goblins in the pit shouted, "Quit throwing junk on us while we're working!"

"Sorry," Will called back.

Kervol Ket strolled over and looked into the pit. From inside, the knight called, "I, uh, I think I'm going to be all right."

Kervol gestured at the pit and asked Will, "I thought these things were supposed to be bottomless?"

"We're working on it. Kervol, please, this is the third time things have gone badly for you. I don't want there to be a fourth time. It wouldn't be good for either of us. Just take Brandywine and go."

Kervol's face twisted up like he'd bitten into a lemon. He wasn't aware that several goblins had caught up with them, including Vial. He didn't seem to realize how badly they could hurt him if they wanted to. It was almost like Kervol was looking through them, like they didn't even exist except when they were directly in his way.

Vial cleared his throat and said, "I suppose there's no point to it now, but Gladys sent me to tell you that she saw Brandywine uprooting a scarecrow."

The goblins encircled Kervol in case the fight continued. Vial reached into his lab coat and pulled out a glass bottle filled with a fizzing liquid bomb. He smiled and pointed at Kervol. Will shook his head and Vial reluctantly put his bomb away. Mr. Niff arrived with more goblins in tow. These goblins looked shocked by their victory, except for one goblin that was too busy petting the horse to care.

Kervol finally spoke, his voice cold and filled with scorn. "I will not lose to the likes of you. I will not tarnish the honor of my family by losing to goblins and their idiot king. If it takes all my life and all the resources of my kingdom, if I must sacrifice everything I have, I will be victorious."

"My love!" Brandywine yelled as she ran up to Kervol and threw her arms around him, unintentionally smearing mud on his shirt. "Oh the light of my life, you have come to rescue me."

"Yes, about that," Kervol said.

Brandywine looked lovingly into his eyes. "Do not fear, my King, for I have disabled the scoundrel for you."

"Really," he said dryly.

Brandywine looked around and took in the scene before her before she focused her attention on Will. She bared her teeth and demanded, "You did it again, didn't you? I'm not getting married again because you had to go and survive! I've had it. I have had enough of you and this place and your smelly, ugly monsters!"

The princess pulled Will's fire scepter out of her purse and pointed it at Will. Everyone, Kervol included, threw themselves to the ground before she could turn on the unpredictable scepter. Brandywine tried to activate it and was rewarded by a sizzling sound. She shrieked and dropped the scepter. "It burned my hand!"

Vial calmly picked up the scepter and handed it back to Will. "My dear, this is the scepter of the King of the Goblins. Did you really believe it would hurt its own master?"

Will hung the scepter from his belt, and it hummed contentedly now that it was back in his possession. "She doesn't want to be here, Kervol. If you really love her you won't make her stay another day."

Kervol glared at him, then took Brandywine's hand and scrubbed off some of the mud with a silk handkerchief. He kissed the part he'd cleaned off and said, "*I will return soon to take you away from this, this*…oh, blast it, line!"

Kervol's entourage ran to catch up with him and his speechwriter said, "This den of depravity and evil."

"*This den of depravity and evil. All your suffering shall soon be ended, forevermore replaced by a life of peace and leisure*," Kervol said theatrically. Brandywine swooned exactly like her acting coach had taught her, and Kervol caught her.

"You're making her stay?" Will demanded. "Of all the pig-headed, stubborn, half-witted—hey! Hey get back here!"

Kervol marched back toward his kingdom with his entourage and four battered knights. He was going to cause more trouble in the future. Anything Will could do to stop him—by attacking him or taking him prisoner—would only make matters worse. Will watched his rival walk away, furious that he couldn't really stop him.

Mr. Niff patted Will's hand. "He had a speech ready in case you won. That has to count for something."

Chapter Eight

"Are the ropes tight?" Will asked. He and Mr. Niff stood next to the nearly completed bottomless pit, along with close to a hundred goblins and the troll brothers. A few hours had passed since Kervol's third attempt to rescue Princess Brandywine, and the aforementioned princess' attempt to incinerate Will and many of his followers. Will had put the time to good use.

"You bet, boss," Mr. Niff said. He gave the ropes an extra tug before tying them into a knot. Goblins had made the rope, and thus it wasn't very good quality, but it was strong enough for the job at hand. "This'll hold her real good."

"You jerks!" Princess Brandywine screamed. She struggled to get out of the ropes binding her hands and feet together. Three warrior goblins stood guard around her in case she broke free, two of them carrying nets they could throw and the third armed with a lasso.

Brandywine squirmed some more and gave Will a venomous stare. "Oh you're going to pay for this! I'll see to it you spend the rest of your life in a cell, you cretin. When my fiancée rescues me, he'll burn this whole place to the ground! He'll smash and crush and burn and, and…uh, smash some more!"

Will pointed at Brandywine, and London threw her over his shoulder. "Yes, well your betrothed doesn't have a good track record destroying things. Be fair, Brandywine, you know who's fault this is."

"Yours!" she screamed.

"Not by a long shot." Will picked up Brandywine's purse and took her happily-ever-after contract out of it. "I know you didn't read this too closely, but I studied some more of it while Niff and London were tying you up. You're supposed to be rescued, princess, not sabotage your captor and try to kill him."

"I've heard about contracts for that," Domo said. "Something about liberated women."

Will held the contract up for Brandywine to see. "This clause over here says it all. You're a damsel in distress, not a damsel that causes distress. You make your future husband look weak when you play too big a role. If your plan had worked, Kervol wouldn't have thanked you for it."

Brandywine made a sour expression. "You made your point. I'll be good until my beloved King comes to smash you all. Untie me."

"Anybody trust her?" Will asked the assembled goblins.

"No!" they shouted in unison.

Will shrugged. "I don't know how these guys got a reputation for being stupid. London will take you back to the city and keep an eye on you until we get this mess cleared up."

Princess Brandywine was unceremoniously carried off, screaming abuse at everyone around her. Will headed back to the Goblin City and his throne room while Mr. Niff repaired the damage Brandywine had caused to the scarecrows. Vial followed Will back to the city.

"An astounding performance, sir," Vial said as he trotted behind Will. "Truly it was uncharacteristic of one of our leaders."

"Yeah, and hopefully what I did won't get us all killed," Will said.

"What's this? You sounded quite confident back there."

Will rubbed his eyes. "I wasn't confident, I was angry. Blast it, Vial, every time I try to do the right thing I end up in deeper trouble than before! I try to be reasonable and fair, and it always backfires."

He stopped walking and looked at Vial. "When I was back home, I did everything I was supposed to do to be taken seriously. I worked hard, I was nice to people, I studied and got good grades, and what happened? Nothing. When I tried to find work that didn't involve flipping burgers, the answer was always 'no', and now I'm stuck here."

Will bent down and looked Vial in the eyes. "Do you ever feel like you could do something amazing, something important, something that would change the world, but no one will give you the chance?"

"No," Vial said cheerful. Will grumbled and stood up, but before he could walk away Vial finished his answer. "I am a goblin. Nothing amazing, nothing important, and certainly nothing that could change my world ever came from a goblin. If no one ever gave me this chance you speak of, it's because it would be foolish to do so."

"You really believe that?" Will asked.

Vial nodded. "My King, do not be afraid that this might end badly. All your followers and I *know* it will be disastrous. There is no other way it could end. We may win a small victory here and there, as you did today, but in the end we will be defeated. After all, we are goblins."

Exasperated, Will asked, "So where does that leave us?"

"Five hundred yards from your capital city," Vial said. "That statement would be more awe-inspiring if there were other cities in your realm, but I imagine it still sounds good at parties."

Will reached the Goblin City and was heading for the gate when he heard a strange noise. It was clapping. Hundreds and hundreds of hands were clapping. Startled, Will looked for the source as even more people joined in. The noise was coming from in front of the maze.

All work on the maze had stopped and the goblin builders were gathered together where the maze pressed up against the city. There were a thousand of them in a huge unruly mob. Some carried signs saying 'William Bradshaw 2:

their guy 0', and 'Bradshaw kicks butt'. All of them were clapping, cheering and stomping their feet in unison. Over it all Will could hear them chanting.

"Will-i-am, Will-i-am, Will-i-am!"

"Kervol's coming back!" Will shouted. "He's going to try to wreck the place and hurt everybody!"

No one heard him. Their cheers drowned him out. Impromptu bands of jug players, drummers and fiddlers began to play. Will tried to be heard over the noise, but if anyone did hear him it didn't diminish their enthusiasm.

Vial walked up to Will and smiled. "You won a small victory today, My Liege. We ask for nothing more."

* * * * *

Back in his throne room, Will sat down on an empty crate. He nodded to Gladys the magic mirror. The bookcase was back behind her in the mirror's surface and Gladys' overly made-up face was deep in a book.

"You heard about the, uh—"

"You putting the smack down on four knights? I heard about it." Gladys kept paging through her book, not even bothering to look up at him. "Bravo. It didn't change anything with Kervol, but it was a good morale builder. I haven't seen the goblins so excited the whole time I've been here."

Curious, Will asked, "About that, why are you here? I figure it's pretty useful to have a magic mirror around, even with your limitations."

Gladys turned a page on her book, still not looking up. "Personality defect."

"Come again?"

"I have a personality defect," she said. "Come on, it's not like I try to hide it."

"You're not that bad. I've worked with people more difficult than you."

Gladys looked up from her book. "I'm not difficult. I tell it like it is. I don't lie, and I don't sugarcoat the truth to make people happy. When I found out my original owner was a liar and a cheat, I didn't cover for him. He took away most of my powers as punishment, and to add insult to injury he dumped me here. Can we please change the subject?"

"Oh, sorry," Will said awkwardly. "Any luck finding a way out of this mess?"

"Nope." Gladys snapped her book shut and slid it back into the bookcase behind her. "When you took down those knights you made it worse. Assaulting Kervol's followers is a minor offense, but he can make a big deal about it if he wants to. Plus the knights are more witnesses to you making a fool of him. The price of buying him off just went up to 100,000 gold coins."

"Well, I couldn't bribe him at 20,000, so 100,000 really isn't worse," Will replied in a resigned tone. "Could I get neighboring kings to help me?"

"Ha! Dream on. You're the king of a dump. If anyone was going to come to your rescue, and they aren't, they'd want lots of gold or land in return. You have no money and the land you've got sucks. Even if this place didn't suck, the contracts and spells that made the kingdom won't allow you to trade it or sell it off."

Will held up his king contract. "I know. It's spelled out here."

Article 42, subsection 2, paragraph 58, line 12: The King of the Goblins cannot sell his kingdom, because we've tried and nobody is stupid enough to buy it.

Gladys picked another book and opened it up. "On the bright side, if you can't get any help then neither can Kervol. He's nearly broke, so he can't bribe neighboring kings to help him. He won't trade off his land for favors, either, since he hasn't got much to begin with. For better or for worse, you and him will settle this alone."

Will rubbed his chin. "Hmm. This time he brought knights to help him beat me. Any suggestion what he'll try next time?"

"Don't know, but it'll be big," she replied.

"Why?"

"Come on," she chided him, "You messed things up for him three times in less than a week. His wedding has been postponed so long he'll be running out of excuses. If this drags out any longer he'll look like a fool."

"He is a fool."

Gladys nodded. "Yeah, but he's also looking like a pushover. If he doesn't get the girl on his fourth try, he'll look so weak and stupid that another member of his family might replace him. Worse, if he looks weak another king might invade his lands and try to conquer them. No, Kervol can't drag this out too much longer. Next time he comes at you he's going to do something big."

Nervous, Will asked, "How big?"

"What am I, a fortuneteller?" Gladys exclaimed. "Kervol doesn't have any wizards on his payroll, not that I know of. He hasn't got friendly monsters like ogres or griffins or walking trees working for him, either. He hasn't got any powerful magic weapons. That still leaves a lot of options open, like putting a price on your head or diverting a river so it floods us out. He's got to get it right this time, so he'll pull out all the stops."

"Lovely. Thanks for helping, Gladys. Keep checking your books for a way out of this."

As Will left his throne room, Gladys called, "Hey, thanks for putting up the extra scarecrows. I can see a lot more now."

"Not much to look at, is it?" he said bitterly.

Gladys shrugged. As her image faded from the mirror, she said, "Beats being blind."

* * * * *

Will walked through the tunnels under the Goblin City until he reached a single room at the end of a narrow tunnel. There were torches on the walls to provide light and a thick wooden door sealing the room off. The door wasn't thick enough to completely muffle the sound of someone screaming and cursing on the other side. Domo and three goblins stood guard over the horrible danger behind the door.

Will frowned as he considered going inside. "So how's the princess?"

"You have to ask?" Domo said. There was a thud as something hard hit the door. "This has been going on for hours. I think the staff at Kervol's castle would be grateful if we released her into the wild instead of returning her."

Will shook his head. "There are innocent bears and wolves out there that have done nothing to deserve that kind of abuse. Did I get here in time to help?"

"Yeah, Mr. Niff hasn't gotten back with her food yet." Cautiously, Domo asked, "You're sure you want to be the one to feed her?"

"It's my fault she's still here. I ought to do some of the work handling her."

Mr. Niff came running down the tunnel, breathing hard from exertion. He'd volunteered to bring food from the local human inn to keep his king and their unwelcome guest fed, and he carried two meals wrapped in white butcher paper.

"Here you go, boss," Mr. Niff said. He handed the two packages to Will. "Roast duck with fresh bread and apples, one for you and one for the princess. I got it here as fast as I could, so it should still be warm."

Will gratefully accepted the meal. "Thanks, Niff. I haven't had time to breathe, much less go out for food."

"I got to tell you, boss, the innkeeper isn't happy about feeding two people for free," Mr. Niff said.

"I can't blame him," Will replied. He dug through his pockets and pulled out some coins. "The next time I send you, I want you to give him this. Tell him I'm going to get rid of the princess as soon as possible."

"He won't be the only one glad to hear it," Domo added. "She bit the last guy that tried to feed her."

Will sat down and ate his lunch. "The trolls and I will deal with her from now on. I don't think she'll try anything like that with someone bigger than she is."

He stopped eating and pointed a breadstick at Domo. "I know this place isn't paradise—"

"Got that right."

"—But there's no need to make it worse than it already is." Will said as he ate. "That stuck-up snob tried to kill us all! I mean, stealing from me and ruining the scarecrows is one thing, but…hey, hold on a second." Will paused and a smile crept across his face. "I've got an idea. When I'm done here we need to go talk to Gladys. I think I might have a way to get out of this mess."

Will went into Brandywine's room and closed the door behind him. Domo and Mr. Niff waited outside in case their help was needed. Mr. Niff looked nervously at the door.

"Domo?" Mr. Niff asked.

"Yes?"

Mr. Niff fidgeted with his knife handle as he spoke. "I was wondering, about the king and Princess Brandywine. They're both human, about the same age, pretty enough the way humans judge these things. Anyway, do you think anything might happen?"

"What do you mean 'happen'?" Domo asked.

"Happen, like by being close together like this for so long they might begin to feel affection for one another. That Brandywine's exposure to other people and their difficulties might open her heart. That with time they might grow to respect one another, to recognize the value and beauty in each other's hearts, and that in time love's fragile flower might bloom."

The door next to Mr. Niff burst open as a table smashed into it. A fired clay bowl followed and shattered against the stone floor. There was the sound of furniture breaking into splinters. Over all this they could hear Brandywine's piercing shriek.

"I won't, I won't, I won't!" she cried

"It's good food!" Will shouted back. "You'll eat it if I have to pinch your nose closed until you open your mouth! Ahh! You bit me! I can't believe you did that!"

Domo closed the door and pushed the bits of broken pottery aside. Calmly, he told Mr. Niff, "No, I can't see that happening."

Mr. Niff clapped his hand over his heart. "Thank God!"

* * * * *

Hours later Will returned to his throne room. He rubbed his arm where Brandywine had bitten him, but he was excited enough that he didn't care.

Domo and Mr. Niff came next. Vial wandered in shortly thereafter, followed by London and Brooklyn. Gladys reappeared in her magic mirror, her expression betraying frustration that had almost reached homicidal levels.

"Listen, I tried, I really did, but there's no easy way out of this," Gladys said. "I can't find a way to get Kervol to accept the princess without a fight. Her contract and the rules of etiquette won't allow it."

"Forget her contract," Will said. "I want you to check the rules for issuing a formal challenge."

"What for?" she asked.

Will smiled. "I think I found a way out of this mess. Kervol challenged me to combat and sent his knights after me. What he didn't know is that our oh-so-pleasant Princess Marisa Brandywine tore down all the scarecrows around me and took my fire scepter. She did everything she could to make sure I'd lose."

"Quite true," Vial said. "There were many witnesses present when she admitted to it."

Will paced across the throne room as he spoke. "She tried to fix the fight. There's got to be some kind of rule against that, right? He issued a challenge and his fiancée, a damsel in distress no less, sabotaged me. Can we get him on that?"

Gladys smiled as the bookcase appeared next to her in the mirror. She pulled a book out and opened it with a laugh. "Why didn't I see it? We can't get Kervol for breaking the rules since he didn't order her to do it, but we've got the princess. She must be new at this to make a mistake that big."

Gladys found the page she was looking for and pressed the book up against the glass. "Here, under 'rules of engagement:' *Interfering with a formal challenge is punishable by fine, imprisonment, or exile.* Kings actually do it all the time, but they're careful not to get caught."

The goblins cheered and the trolls chuckled. Will smiled, his first genuine smile since he arrived on this crazy world. He'd found a way of getting rid of Brandywine. Now he just needed to see it through.

Will clapped his hands to get everyone's attention. "Okay, here's what we do. Domo, Niff, I need paper, pen and ink. I'm going to write out my case. Gladys, I'll need your help writing it so it's official. London, Brooklyn, first thing tomorrow morning we're taking the princess back. If I have my choice of punishments, then I'm choosing exile. Kervol's getting his fiancée whether he wants her or not."

Will slept well that night. In the morning he met London and Brooklyn outside the Goblin City. They had Brandywine, still tied up, along with a length of rope and a thick wooden stake. A few goblins were already awake and they gathered around the princess. One goblin got too close and the princess kicked him. Mr. Niff and Domo joined them, both standing clear of Brandywine.

"What am I doing out here?" Brandywine screeched. "I was trying to sleep when these clumsy oafs picked me up and carried me off. What am I, a sack of potatoes?"

"We should be so lucky," London said.

"Yeah, potatoes are way nicer than she is," his brother said.

Will smiled evilly at the princess. He took a rolled-up sheet of paper from his belt and showed it to her. "This, my dear, is a legal order of expulsion."

"What?" She stared at him, her expression changing from confusion to outrage. "You can't expel me. I'm your prisoner!"

"You interfered with a formal challenge between me and your fiancée," Will said. "So, according to the rules of engagement I am exiling you from my lands and property. You'll be happy to know I'm sending you to your beloved king."

"You can't do that!" she screamed.

Will rubbed his hands together, a gleeful look on his face, "Oh yes I can! It's all official and legal. London, if you'd do the honors?"

London picked up the princess and threw her over his shoulder. Will, London and Brooklyn headed south to the sound of cheering goblins. The three of them marched across dew-covered grass as Brandywine struggled and screamed at them.

"You're ruining everything!" she yelled at Will.

"Good."

They walked through the scrub forests filled with chirping birds and scurrying rodents.

"My happily-ever-after contract was drawn up by the law firm of Takeda Money and Runn. Do you want to get in trouble with them?" she threatened him.

"I was put in charge of the goblins by the law firm of Cickam, Wender and Downe and I'm still standing. Exactly what can your lawyers do to me that's worse than that?"

As the sun rose in the sky they marched through the village nearest to goblin lands, which didn't exist for tax reasons.

"I'll do everything I can to ruin your life!" she screamed.

"Fine, as long as you do it from somewhere else."

With the sun high overhead and beads of sweat dripping down their faces, they marched through another village that didn't exist for tax reasons. Farmers watched them pass and decided that whatever was going on was somebody else's problem. Will and his followers stopped at a fruit stand for lunch.

"I'm not eating this!" she hollered when Will offered her a plum.

"Okay." He ate it himself.

Finally, at 4 o'clock and with great difficulty, Will and the trolls found a town that did appear on the local maps, even if the inhabitants wished it didn't. Farmers and craftsmen gathered around as Will stopped next to a towering black walnut tree at the edge of town.

"What's going on here?" a farmer asked.

Will smiled. "Hi there, I'm William Bradshaw, King of the Goblins. This, uh, lady, is a princess I'm exiling from my kingdom. She's supposed to marry your king."

"Ain't never heard of goblins kidnapping a lady before," the farmer said.

"We didn't kidnap her so much as we got stuck with her," Will replied. "It's a long story. Anyway, we're returning her. We'll just dump her here and let Kervol have her."

As if on cue, Brandywine screamed every manner of curse and insult at the trolls, insulting their parents, skin color, odor and a few other things best left unwritten. The locals watched her as they might a poisonous snake that slithered into town.

"What'd we ever do to you to deserve this?" the farmer asked.

"I really am sorry," Will said. He took the rolled-up paper from his belt and handed it to the farmer. "Here, this is the formal order expelling her from my lands. Tell Kervol that she's here and he'll take her off your hands."

While London held Brandywine, Brooklyn drove the wooden stake into the ground with his bare hands. He tied the rope to it and then to the princess so she couldn't follow them back. London set her down. No sooner did her feet touch the ground then she kicked him.

Will edged away from her. "Don't get too close. She bites."

"All done, boss," London called. He and Brooklyn left the screaming princess and joined Will.

Will dug through his pocket and took out the last of the money he had. He handed it to the farmers, saying, "This won't make up for the trouble she'll cause, but it's the best I can do. Please, don't untie her. Let the king or his knights take care of her."

"Untie her?" a farmer asked. "Shoot, I'm not getting close to that one without a muzzle on her."

A second farmer watched Brandywine scream at everyone. He raised his hand and said, "I don't like the sound of her being our queen. If we gave you your money back plus some extra, would you keep her?"

Brandywine heard him. "Hey!"

"You couldn't pay me enough to make that mistake," Will said. "Again, I'm sorry about this, but it's the best of many bad options. Someday you may find it in your hearts to forgive me."

Will headed back north with the trolls, leaving Brandywine and her abuse far behind. It was dark by the time they got back to the Goblin City. Domo and Mr. Niff were waiting for them at the gatehouse. Domo had dozed off and Mr. Niff nudged him to wake him up.

"It's done?" Mr. Niff asked.

"Yeah, it's done," Will said, and stifled a yawn. "We tied her to a stake and asked the locals to tell Kervol where to find her. If Gladys and I are right, there's nothing Kervol can do but take her back."

"He'll still be angry with you," Domo cautioned.

"Let him be angry," Will said. "In a couple weeks or months I'll find a way out of my king contract and I won't even be on this planet. After that he can be as angry with me as he wants."

Will looked around. Even at this late hour the goblins were going about their business, gathering food or working on the maze. It all looked peaceful and quiet, which made him suspicious.

"What happened while I was gone?" he demanded.

Mr. Niff smiled. "More goblins came, hundreds of them. That always happens when we get a king, but never this fast. Some of them walked a hundred miles to get here."

Will tried to think, but it was hard when he was so tired. "Wait, they would have had to walk day and night to get here so quickly. Why would they do that? Most of these guys are too disorganized to wear matching socks, much less spend an entire week walking in the same direction."

"Word of your deeds travels fast," Domo said. "Goblins have been telling tales of your accomplishments ever since you arrived. And it's not just goblins doing the telling, either. Human and dwarf merchants heard how goblins drove off Kervol three times, with their new king doing the honors twice. Wherever they go they'll spread the news, which in many places is considered as valuable as the goods they sell. By morning every troll, goblin, dwarf, elf and man within five hundred miles will know about what you've done."

"How would the merchants know about us beating Kervol?" Will asked. "Nobody was there except us and him."

"They may not have seen the fight, but they saw Kervol enter the Kingdom of the Goblins with his entourage," Domo said. "They also saw him come back without the princess. That's pretty telling. Besides, do you really think all four knights and every member of his entourage kept their mouths closed? Not likely."

Will rubbed his tired eyes. "Let me guess, none of these tales will be in the least bit accurate, will they?"

Domo waved his hands. "Oh no, most of them will be honest. Merchants who tell lies upset their customers and lose business. They might not know about every little thing you did, but they'll get the parts they do know right."

Will thanked the trolls for their help and then headed to his bedroom. Something Domo had just said bothered him, but he couldn't figure out what or why. He was too sleepy to focus on anything for long.

* * * * *

The next day was bright and cheerful. Will got a quick breakfast at the human inn and headed back to face all the chaos the goblins could throw at him. He smiled nonetheless. He was getting the hang of this. Sure, his followers were loud and stupid and caused solid objects to fall from the sky without reason, but that was tame compared to what Kervol and Brandywine had been putting him through.

Most of the goblins were busy building onto the maze. Mr. Niff stopped by to tell Will the bottomless pit was finished without any goblins falling in. Will quickly talked the goblins freed up from that project into helping out with the maze. More goblins swarmed in from distant lands, and Will managed to divert most of them to the maze as well. When the innate stupidity of his followers warped space and caused pocketknives, screws and car keys to fall from the sky he took that in stride. He even managed to find time to study his contract. *Article 44, subsection 2, paragraph 15, line 12: The King cannot leave his position if he's crazy, as that makes him more qualified for the job.*

"Boss!" It was Mr. Niff, running toward Will as fast as he could. "A bunch of humans just crossed the border with Kervol's land, and they're heading this way."

"Not Kervol and his entourage again," Will groaned.

"No, it's somebody else," Niff said. "I've never seen them before. They're wearing brown uniforms and they've got oxen pulling a cart."

Will frowned. He actually knew a bit about oxen from when he worked at the petting zoo. They were very strong, and also very slow. That gave him time to think before taking action. "Get the trolls and round up some warrior goblins. We'll see what this is about."

Mr. Niff returned within minutes with the two trolls and thirty goblins. The trolls looked especially eager to throw their weight around. With as much help as he was likely to need, Will went to intercept the visitors.

He found them a few miles south of the Goblin City. There were four men, a cart pulled by two oxen, and a large wooden crate in the cart. The crate was six feet tall, three feet across and two feet deep. The men were strong and wore simple brown uniforms. When they saw Will, one of the men walked up and shook his hand.

"You're the King of the Goblins?" the man asked.

Will nodded and pointed at the cart. "Yeah. What's this about?"

"We're with Universal Packaging Supplies. I've got an overnight delivery of a letter and a package for you." The man handed him a clipboard and quill pen. "Please sign here."

Will signed and asked, “Who’s it from?”

The men took the crate off the cart and set it down gently in front of Will, while their leader took the quill and clipboard back. “The sender’s name and address are in the letter. Have a nice day.”

The men drove off, leaving Will and his followers with the crate. Will circled the crate and studied it intently. There were no markings on it except an arrow pointing up, and the words *sanitized for your protection* printed on the side. Suddenly the crate rattled. Will backed away, confused. Then he figured it out. Will dropped to his knees and covered his face with his hands.

“Oh no,” he moaned.

“What is it?” Mr. Niff asked. When Will didn’t respond, Mr. Niff took the letter from him and opened it. He read it aloud as the trolls braced themselves to attack whatever was in the crate.

“*To the foul and degenerate King of the Goblins, William Bradshaw,*” Mr. Niff began. “*Your wickedness and evil knows no bounds, and your personal hygiene leaves much to be desired. I have received your outlandish message, and I am sending you a reply more civil than you deserve.*”

The crate rattled again. Will didn’t look up. He just said, “Merciful God in heaven, please, not this.”

Mr. Niff continued to read the letter. “*For generations my family has ruled this land through a combination of good breeding and proper respect for tradition. Your vile attempt—*”

“Someone called?” Vial said as he scurried toward the band.

“No, it’s the other kind of vile, with an ‘e’,” Mr. Niff explained. He went back to reading the letter and said, “*Your vile attempt to abuse our traditions is repulsive to me and all right-thinking monarchs. Nothing better shows your base manners than your dishonest attempt to exile the beautiful and much beloved Princess Marisa Brandywine.*"

"Beloved?" London shouted. "She's meaner than a bag of rattlesnakes!"

Brooklyn watched the crate warily. "Careful, people. We're dealing with a sick mind! There could be anything in there."

"You *blame the innocent maiden for your own crimes and ill-advised deeds,*" Mr. Niff said as he continued to read. "*No one is deceived by your lies against her virtue. It is clear to all that you are a coward and seek to misuse the traditions of our land to avoid fulfilling your obligations under the law and the happily-ever-after contract to which the fair maiden is bound.*"

"I didn't see it," Will said weakly. "I thought I could keep this between me and Kervol. But if the goblins and merchants knew Kervol has been beaten, and they're telling people, then everybody knows. He's been humiliated in front of all his followers and peers."

Mr. Niff kept on reading. "*I refute your base allegations against my beloved and demand satisfaction for this indignity. I will reclaim my true love from your foul clutches by the only means left to me.*"

"But we don't have her anymore!" London protested. "We gave her back, and she's with...she's with...oh he wouldn't!"

All the goblins turned and stared in horror at the crate. It rattled again as whatever was trapped inside tried to break free.

Mr. Niff's voice lowered to a whisper as he finished the letter. "*As all lesser means of settling this dispute have been repulsed by you and your disgusting followers, I hereby declare war upon you and your kingdom. I shall rally my army and sally forth to destroy you and the hideous freaks that follow you. Sincerely and cordially yours, King Kervol Ket.*"

The crate rattled again. Will didn't look up, he couldn't. How could everything have gone so wrong? He waved to London and said, "Open it up."

Cautiously, London approached the crate and ripped it open. It was packed with straw that fell out onto the ground. Princess Marisa Brandywine also fell out of the crate. She gasped for air before screaming, "How long were you going to leave me in there?"

Chapter Nine

"Let me get this straight," Gladys said. "King Kervol stuffed his fiancée into a crate, packed it with straw and sent her to us as an overnight mail delivery. He also declared war on us."

"That's about the size of it," Will said. He was back in his throne room along with Vial, Domo and Mr. Niff. London and Brooklyn were getting Princess Brandywine back into her room and barring the door closed. Experience had taught them that this was the only way to keep her from causing trouble.

"Why didn't he send her by carriage, or at least on horseback?" Domo asked.

"Oh, oh, I know this one," Vial said. "I use Universal Packaging Supplies to get alchemy equipment sent to me, things I can't make myself. Their rates are very reasonable."

"He shipped her to us in a crate because it was cheap?" Will asked.

Domo studied an invoice that came out of the crate. "One silver coin for the crate, three for overnight delivery. You can't beat that. I imagine he had another reason for sending her economy class. She did screw things up for him by sabotaging your scarecrows and trying to kill you."

"Hold on just one second!" Gladys huffed. The bookcase reappeared in the surface of her magic mirror and she yanked a book out. She flipped through it and pressed the pages up against the mirror. "We have a cast-iron case against that snotty princess! She was caught with your fire scepter, and she admitted stealing it. He's breaking his own rules doing this."

"Yeah, he is," Will said morosely. "The problem is, I don't think he'll get in trouble for it. You said it yourself, Gladys. We don't have any friends among the other kings. If he wants to cheat, nobody's going to hold him accountable."

Will stared at the floor. He couldn't bring himself to look his followers in the eye after failing them so badly. "Face it, Kervol's hit rock bottom. We humiliated him three times. Everyone around us knows it, so they're going to look down on him for being a moron and a weakling. The only way he can get back his respect is by crushing us."

"Assuming he can crush us," Mr. Niff said proudly.

That got Will's attention. His head snapped up and he asked, "You think we have a chance?"

"Don't give the man false hope," Domo said.

"But they're the weakest of the major human kingdoms," Mr. Niff countered.

"True," Domo replied reluctantly.

Will smiled. "We're not dead?"

Domo frowned. "Niff has a point. The foot soldiers in Kervol's army are nothing to write home about. Poorly armed, lousy training, heck, no combat experience. They'd rather be home with their families than out fighting and plundering. No real threat there."

"That's great!" Will exclaimed.

Domo went on. "You already saw his knights. Two trolls, a bunch of goblins and you was all it took to beat four of them. Four knights from any other kingdom would have run right over us. They're well equipped, but there aren't enough of them, and their skills are rusty even if their armor isn't."

Will sighed in relief. “Thank God for that.”

“Of course he’s got first-rate archers, and lots of them,” Domo added.

“He does?” Will asked.

Domo nodded. “Oh yeah. His archers could pick a fly off a horse’s butt from thirty yards, and hit a man-sized target at eighty yards. They’ve got longbows, which can shoot almost as far as you can see. There’s enough power in those bows to send an arrow right through a suit of plate armor at close range.”

“Now that I think about it, Kervol’s kingdom has never been invaded,” Vial added. “I suppose that explains why.”

Domo continued. “Even the elves show them respect, and for good reason. The people of Ket train great archers. Kervol’s men win archery championships across all of Other Place. When they all shoot together they can fill the air with arrows and turn anything in the open into pincushions. One of their archers can fire thirty arrows a minute when he’s saturating a piece of ground. Their only real limitation is how many arrows they have, and arrows are cheap.”

“Why didn’t Kervol use his archers when he came to rescue Brandywine?” Will asked.

“Because they’re peasants,” Gladys said. “Knights are upper class twits with a lot of money. They look real impressive even if they can’t do the job. Archers are commoners who are really good at what they do. Which one do you think Kervol wants to be seen with?”

“But he’ll swallow his pride and use them if he has to,” Domo said. “And he has to.”

With a sinking feeling, Will asked, “How long do you think we have before Kervol comes with an army?”

"It'll be a while," Gladys replied. "It takes time to gather all the men together, collect provisions and get wagons and oxen to move everything. Plus this is Kervol we're talking about. He won't start the army moving without wine, sweets, fancy clothes and enough perfume to drown a horse. I'd say we have four weeks before Kervol and four thousand soldiers show up at the city gate."

Will stared blankly at a wall. Slowly, he said, "Um, question, if I panicked and sobbed like a little girl, no one here would be bothered by that, right?"

"Not at all," Mr. Niff said cheerfully.

"It's almost expected," Vial added.

Domo raised his walking stick. "If you don't I will."

Will smiled weakly. "Okay, I just wanted to clarify that. The weather's so nice I think I'll go outside for my nervous breakdown."

Will got up and walked out of his throne room, his face pale and expressionless. He exited the twisting tunnels underneath the Goblin City and walked out into the open countryside.

It was surprisingly peaceful considering a war was going to start. Most of the goblins were still busy working on the maze. They had to know what was coming. There'd been too many goblins present when he got the news for it to be a secret. But they weren't panicking. He'd seen them panic before, running around and screaming. Instead they showed a cheerful disinterest in the whole affair.

Will headed out to woods and marched into the canyon that led to the bottomless pit. It was quiet here. Will sat down next to the pit and pulled out his contract.

Article 45, subsection 5, paragraph 12, line 8: The King can't be removed from his position on account of embezzlement, since there's no money in the kingdom, and we would have taken it if there were. Article 45, subsection 5, paragraph 23, line 2: The King cannot be removed from office for conspiring with foreign powers, because they want nothing to do with you. Article 45, subsection 7, paragraph 2, line 41: If you've read this far you have way too much time on your hands.

"Come on, there has to be a way out of this!" he growled. Will searched through the document and its Byzantine rules. There were hundreds and hundreds of lines. Most of them made no sense. Some of them contradicted each other. Many of the rules had nothing to do with escaping the contract. Article 46 was a recipe for brownies.

Will screamed and threw the contract into the pit. It reappeared next to him seconds later and drifted to the ground. He tore it up and ate it. The contract reappeared, intact and unchewed. An army was coming to trash the place and he couldn't destroy his contract or find a loophole in it to escape it.

"This isn't fair!" he shouted.

"Tell me about it."

Will turned around to find Domo behind him. The little goblin sat down next to the pit and asked, "How did your contract taste?"

"Dry and not very filling," Will said.

"If it helps any, that was how King Arnold the Belcher got out of his contract. He served it with salsa and melted cheese. Of course he could stomach anything. That man was the only human I ever met who could eat goblin stew, even if it did give him terrible gas afterwards."

Will threw a rock into the bottomless pit. "So, I haven't been on the job a week and I've started a war."

Domo shrugged. "It happens. You're not the first king to get us invaded. We've been beat on five times since the kingdom was founded. Sometimes it was because the other side didn't like us, sometimes it was because the attacker needed a quick and easy win to boost morale. Once we were invaded because the King of the Elves thought we had the Bottle of Hope."

"What's that?"

"It's one of the fifty most powerful magic devices in all of Other Place. Of course we didn't have it, but he wasn't going to take our word for it." Domo waved his hand like he was shooing away a fly. "That's not the point. This isn't your fault. The last five invasions weren't our fault, or the fault of the kings who were in charge at the time. We're goblins, the weakest and most disorganized people in all of Other Place. The other races have beaten us through recorded history. This is just one more time."

"No one seemed too excited back by the maze," Will said.

"They aren't," Domo told him. "They're old hands at this. Kervol will come in, set some fires, tear down some buildings, collapse a few tunnels, and then he'll leave. Once he's gone we'll clean up and get back to what we were doing. It'll be fine. There are a couple of hiding places I can recommend for you."

Will didn't answer. He stared into the pit.

Will closed his eyes and tried to imagine the damage Kervol could do with an army thousands of men strong. The Goblin City would be destroyed, its buildings torn down or set on fire. It wouldn't be too hard for Kervol to do it, either. So much of the place was barely holding together as it was. The scattered goblin homes outside the city would be destroyed, too. Only the ones too well camouflaged to be discovered would survive. The maze would probably be destroyed as well.

What would happen to the goblins? Will had seen them fight when Kervol sent his knights after him. They could hold their own if they had overwhelming numbers. But Kervol was coming with thousands of men. And he had archers, good ones if Domo was right. In Will's mind he could see the goblins running for their lives, cowering and trapped in the tunnels under the Goblin City, hoping Kervol's men didn't follow them underground and finish them off.

Why shouldn't Kervol attack? The goblins had been beaten five times before. They seemed to take it for granted that they'd lose again. With so many defeats piled up over the years they'd given up all hope. It would be an easy win for that idiot. Kervol was going to come in and destroy the place. There was no telling how many goblins his men would kill. He'd do so much damage, hurt so many people, all to salvage his pride and reclaim a princess he sent bulk-rate shipping.

"Boss?" Domo asked.

"No," Will said fiercely. A terrible rage was building in his heart. It was anger formed from undeserved injury and insults, and the knowledge that throughout this mess he'd done his best to be the better man. He'd had enough.

"They're good hiding places. They don't smell or anything."

Will's eyes narrowed and he gripped his scepter hard enough that his fingers turned white. "Kervol's not getting away with this. Our guys may have started this mess, but he's the one who keeps making it worse. I tried to fix the problem and he's sending his army after us."

"Life's not fair,' Domo said.

Will stood up. "It will be when I'm done with it! Come on, Domo. If Kervol wants a war then he's getting one!"

Will marched back to the Goblin City with Domo struggling to keep up. He returned to find it pretty much as he'd left it. He spotted Mr. Niff outside talking cheerfully with the goblins working on the maze.

"Niff," Will said, "get me Vial. I have a job for him. The rest of you, stop working and gather round."

Confused, the goblins did as they were told. Some of them muttered to one another.

"He's gone bonkers. You can see it in his eyes," one goblin said.

"Lasted longer than I thought he would," another replied.

Will smiled at them and whirled his scepter around. "Okay, you probably know that we're going to be invaded. I did everything in my power to give King Kervol back his lady and he won't take yes for an answer. That half-witted, inbred bungler is determined to make a mess of things."

"Way to blame the victim!" a goblin shouted.

"He's not the victim!" Will roared. The goblins fell silent and stared at him in surprise. "God help me, we've been the reasonable ones in this mess. Kervol turned down every offer to settle this peacefully. He's going to invade us. He thinks he'll have an easy time of it. He thinks he'll destroy everything you've built. He thinks he'll walk away vindicated."

"He probably thinks that because it's going to happen," a goblin said.

Mr. Niff came back with Vial, followed by the troll brothers. Will pointed at them and said, "He won't win, not this time. You know Kervol has lost to us before. He lost to London and Mr. Niff. He lost to me. When he brought four knights, he lost again. You know he can be beaten.

"It's not just that," Will continued. "The man's a certified idiot. He can't speak straight without a speechwriter. He goes into the wilderness loaded down with fancy clothes and expensive wine. He sent his fiancée to us in a crate! Does that sound like the kind of person you should be afraid of?"

"He sounds like he'd fit right in here," Mr. Niff said.

"He does have an army," a furry goblin reminded them.

"An army is only as effective as the man commanding it," Will said. "We can beat him. I know we can. It's going to be hard and dangerous, but no more so than if we let them come in here and trash the place. I need to know if you're with me. Can I count on you?"

The goblins muttered back and forth until a lanky goblin said, "That is without question the stupidest thing I have ever heard. The chance of winning is so small you'd need a magnifying glass to see it. Only a total moron would follow you anywhere."

The lanky goblin paused, then smiled. "Lucky for you, we are morons. We're with you."

The assembled goblins cheered. Over their excited cries, Will shouted, "Niff, I'm going to need a dozen warrior goblins. Domo, tell the builders to fix up the walls around the city. Vial—"

Vial looked up at him curiously. Will smiled. "I'm going to need every bomb you have. I'm going to use them all." Vial looked shocked as Will kept speaking. "I also need you to move your lab outside the city walls. I want you to build a bomb for me, the biggest you've ever made, a weapon of unimaginable destructive power! I want it ready in time to use on Kervol's army. Can you do it?"

"I, I, yes, My Liege," Vial stammered.

"Good man," Will said. He patted Vial on the shoulder and said, "London, Brooklyn, we're going to see Gladys. Come on."

Will marched off, leaving cheering goblins behind. Vial stood where he was, too stunned to speak. One of his lab rat goblins shook him out of his reveries. With tears streaming down his face, Vial cried, "This is the happiest day of my life!"

* * * * *

Back in the throne room, they found Gladys paging through a book in her mirror. It took seconds for Will to tell her his intentions.

"We're going to do what?" Gladys asked.

"We're fighting back," Will told her. "We're going to win this."

"You're crazy," she said.

Will smiled. "Yes, but it's the good kind of crazy, not the kind where you bring a monster to life with lightning."

"Vial knows some people who could do that for you," London said.

"Thank you, but that will be for another day." Will spread sheets of paper on top of an overturned crate and then got a quill and bottle of ink. "Gladys, you have some scarecrows underground. I need you to tell me about the tunnels in front of the Goblin City. I need to know how many there are, how wide they are, and how deep they are?"

"What for?" she asked dubiously.

"Kervol has lots of archers," he said. "They'll shoot anyone who attacks them long before we could reach them. But if there are some tunnels close to the surface, we can dig up to just below the surface and have the goblins come out right on top of them. It won't matter how far the archers can shoot if there are goblins pouring out all around them and piling on them."

"It might work," she said. Her image disappeared from the mirror's surface and was replaced by pictures of the tunnel network. She went through one image after another, showing different sections of the tunnels. Finally she stopped at an image of a natural cave that had been made into a carpenter's workshop.

"This is the best one I could find. It's one hundred feet below ground, but it's in front of the city."

"It's a start," Will said. He put a few lines down on a paper, then copied the message exactly on the next one. Mr. Niff came in with the dozen warrior goblins. "Good, you're here. Guys, I know some of you have been going out and telling the other goblins what's been happening around here."

"It wasn't nothing," a goblin said bashfully.

"Can you carry a message for me?" Will asked. "I need you to find other goblins outside the kingdom and tell them something."

"Sure, what's the message?" a buck-toothed goblin asked.

Will handed a sheet to one of the warriors. "You can read, right?"

"Of course." The goblin read the message, then stared at his king in shock. It read: *The Goblin Kingdom is being invaded by King Kervol. Your King needs all goblins to come and help him drive off the invaders*. "You're kidding."

"No, I'm not." Will handed out copies to the other warriors and then wrote some more. "Tell every goblin you see. If there are places where goblins might pass through, leave the papers where they can find them."

"But, but," the goblin sputtered. "Nobody *needs* goblins!"

"I do," Will said, "every one I can get. The sooner they get here the better. Good luck, and thank you."

The warriors left, muttering and glancing back at Will. Will pointed at Mr. Niff.

"Niff, I need you to round up some more of the guys. Put up scarecrows by the border and more in the tunnels in front of the city. When you're finished, I'm going to need volunteers to spy on Kervol's army."

"I can do that," he said cheerfully, and ran off.

With that done, Will turned to the trolls. "London, Brooklyn, I'll need your help finding some digger goblins, especially their leaders."

"They don't have leaders," London said. "Just diggers who don't cause so many cave-ins."

"They'll do nicely."

Finding digger goblins proved surprisingly easy. Word had gotten around that the king had lost his marbles and actually thought he could hold off an invading army. The diggers had been too busy to watch most of what their new king had done, and they were determined not to miss out on this latest entertainment. London and Brooklyn rounded up a few diggers and brought them to the carpenter's workshop in the tunnels.

"You want what?" a digger asked. He was a tall goblin with grimy clothes, carrying a pick and a bucket. He wore a dented helmet with a lit candle on the top that offered dubious protection and little light. There were ten other diggers behind him equipped with hammers, spikes, wedges and shovels.

Will pointed at the ceiling. "I need a passage dug up to the surface from this room. It's got to be wide enough for a lot of goblins to run out from at once. If you can dig more than one passageway it would be better. And I need it done in less than a month."

"You're a loony," the goblin told Will.

"Possibly. Can you do it?"

The digger goblin frowned. "I don't know. It's an awful lot of work, and we'd need to put all the diggers on it to get it done in time. We couldn't work on anything else. Plus there's the whole issue of—"

London grabbed the digger by his shirt, lifted him up in the air and shook him. "Say yes!"

"Yes! Put me down!"

London looked at Brooklyn. "Did he sound sincere to you?"

Brooklyn rubbed his chin. "No. He sounded like he'd run off and play dice the first chance he got."

"I did not!" the digger goblin said.

London shook him again. "Say yes like you mean it!"

"Yes! We'll do it! Put me down!"

London set the digger goblin down. The goblin promptly collapsed to the floor. "Uh, not that I'm saying 'no' or anything, but that's going to be a big project. Even working hard we'll need lots of time to do it."

"I'll buy you as much time as I can," Will said. "Get the other diggers together and start as soon as you can."

The next order of business was gathering spies. Mr. Niff brought back forty goblins eager to spy for their king. They were a motley bunch. Some wore hooded cloaks and dark clothes to blend into shadows. Others were disguised as barrels, crates and haystacks, with eyeholes and openings for their legs. One goblin was dressed in a black business suit and had a big bag of candy.

"What's his story?" Will asked about the last one.

"That's Gilbert, our lobbyist," Mr. Niff said proudly. "He's a master of bribery and misinformation. Little kids see lots of stuff without anybody noticing them doing it. He pays them with candy and gets information and favors in return. He also pays them to spread information. You know, stuff we don't want traced back to us. That goblin has an intelligence network without peer."

"They all had disguises ready in advance?" Will asked Mr. Niff.

"Oh heck yeah! It's the only way we can get into the nicer towns."

Will surveyed the assembled goblins. "Okay, guys, I'm giving you a very important mission. Don't laugh, I'm being honest. I need the bravest or at least the craziest goblins to sneak into Kervol's kingdom. Your job will be to find out where his army is and how quickly it's assembling. Then you'll need to follow them as they march toward us."

"And come back and tell you what we see," a goblin in a barrel added.

"You'd think so, but no." Will handed each goblin a bundle of stakes and black and green clothes, including a hat. "These are scarecrows folded up so you can carry them. Each of you gets a scarecrow. When you find anything interesting, put your scarecrow together and point it at what we need to see. Gladys will see it and inform me."

"Ooh," they chorused.

"I don't want any heroics," Will said. "Follow Kervol's forces, watch them and nothing else. I'll send more goblins out to mess things up if you guys show me some good opportunities."

* * * * *

It was just before nightfall, and Gladys, Will, Domo and the troll brothers were in the throne room. Gladys was trying to connect to one of the bundled up scarecrows while the others watched. The spies had left hours earlier and would soon be in human controlled territory. Gladys wasn't showing anything yet. Still, a few goblins began to drift in to watch the show.

"Hold on, this could take a second," Gladys said. Her image faded from the mirror's surface and was replaced by static.

"Is there an antenna or something we can adjust?" Will asked.

"No, there isn't. Now shut up," Gladys snarled. "Give me a break. This is the first time I've tried to see through a scarecrow outside the kingdom."

"Maybe none of our spies assembled a scarecrow yet?" Domo suggested.

"Maybe they put one together, but it's too far away for her to see through," London said.

"Hold on, I'm getting something," Gladys said. The mirror clouded up and then showed the outside of the inn where Will went for his meals. A goblin walked into view, smiled and waved.

"It worked!" Domo exclaimed.

"I'm surprised, too," Gladys said.

Will smiled. "Great work, Gladys. Can we get sound with this?"

"Oh come on," Gladys snapped. "I may have been crippled by my last owner, but I'm still an Industrial Magic Corporation Magic Mirror! I've got sound in stereo, picture in picture and times 100 magnification. I also correct for red-eye."

The goblin in the mirror walked out of view and the image spun around to face a large house. There were papers pasted onto the wall and a pair of farmers reading them.

"That must be what he wanted to show us," Will said. "Zoom in and put the sound on."

The mirror crackled with the static-filled voices of the two farmers. The men were in front of the papers, so Will couldn't read them.

"The darned fool is going to ruin himself and us, too," a farmer said.

The other farmer nodded. "Yep. Don't see how he'll pay for this without raising taxes again."

"You got that right," the first one said. "And you know when the army gets here, they'll requisition all the food they need."

"What's 'requisition' mean?" the second farmer asked.

"It's a fancy way of saying steal it."

The two men walked off, clearing the view of the papers on the wall. Gladys zoomed in until they could read it.

"To arms, to arms! The noble King Kervol of the ancient line of Ket calls on all his followers and vassals to prepare for battle against a foe most foul. The Kingdom of the Goblins has dared to lay hands on our future queen, and our illustrious King is embarking on a most righteous mission to free her from their clutches.

"To all those who owe military service to their King, come post haste to the capital, Illumina, where our most magnificent army shall gather. We shall crush this terrible foe and put them in their proper place.

"P.S., the campaign against the goblins will be fully catered and troops will be paid prevailing wages. Taxes, titles and licensing fees apply. Bring your own armor and weapons. Commemorative plates, postcards, coffee mugs and souvenirs will be available for sale."

"How far away is Kervol's capital?" Will asked.

"Three days by foot," London said. "I bet an army will take twice as long to walk that far."

Will paced across the throne room, walking around the growing mob of goblins that were gathering to watch him. “How long will it take him to get his army together?”

Domo laughed. “It’ll be a while. Most of his soldiers only fight when they’re called on. They’re farmers and craftsmen the rest of the time. Getting them away from their lives will take a good two weeks. After he gets them together, he’ll need to organize them, get his siege train together and stuff like that. We’ve got a month before he shows.”

“Oh it’s going to take him a lot longer than that,” Will said menacingly. “Gentlemen, the best way to fight this war is to make sure it never starts. I’m going to need your help planning this, but from this moment on we are going to make life impossible for Kervol. When we’re done he won’t be able to go anywhere or do anything without us tripping him up. If we’re lucky, his army won’t set foot across the border.”

“You have a plan?” Domo asked.

Will smiled and swung his scepter like a golf club. “Yeah, and it goes something like this…”

Will spoke to his followers for the better part of an hour. From time to time one of them would offer a suggestion or ask for clarification, but there were no jokes and none of them laughed at him. When he finished, Will found a crowd of hundreds of goblins gathered around him, filling the throne room and backed out into the hallway. Shorter goblins were standing on the shoulders of their taller brethren.

“Well, what do you think?” he asked.

They cheered.

Chapter Ten

The next morning, Will stood outside the gates of the Goblin City. Daybreak was still hours away. The grass was wet with dew and birds sang merrily. A pixie flew overhead and got knocked out of the air by a rock, then stomped on.

"You're sure that's necessary?" Will asked Mr. Niff.

"I've been in pixie plagues before," Mr. Niff said as he wiped the squashed pixie off his boot. "It's not something you ever want to see."

"I'll take your word for it," Will replied. He paced back and forth in front of the gates, waiting along with Mr. Niff, Domo and the troll brothers. Goblins were leaving buildings and tunnels to join him, but there weren't enough to start.

"You want me to go roust them out?" London asked.

Will shook his head. Loudly, he said, "We almost have enough. If the rest don't show we'll have to start without them."

That got them moving. Dozens more goblins poured out of the city and tunnels, all of them running for the gate. Their king was planning an act of chaos and confusion the likes of which had never been seen. And it wasn't just one prank, no matter how big. Instead it was a whole series of pranks that worked together. This demanded cooperation and timing rarely seen among goblins, but the resulting madness was so enticing that they were eager to try. No goblin wanted to miss out.

Domo counted the assembled goblins. "This looks like all of the ones we'll need. We may get some volunteers if we wait."

"There's no time," Will said. "If any more want to join in they'll have to wait for the next mission."

Will walked in front of the crowd and twirled his scepter. He had some experience dealing with goblins and he knew what motivated them. They weren't going to do anything out of a genuine belief they could win this fight, but they would do a lot in the name of spreading confusion. Will just had to adjust his sales pitch accordingly.

"Gentlemen, war is upon us. Kervol Ket, our neighbor to the south, is preparing to invade us and destroy our kingdom. Who does he think he is? If anyone is going to destroy this kingdom it'll be us!"

The crowd cheered and hooted. Will let them finish before he continued. "I have a cunning plan, which may be the result of sleep deprivation or dementia of some kind. We'll leave that for history to decide. If successful, we'll cripple Kervol's army before it even enters our kingdom. Or we might just annoy him. Frankly I'm grasping at straws here."

Will pointed his scepter at Mr. Niff, the trolls and Domo. "You're going to be divided into teams, and each team has a specific mission. One of these upstanding members of our community will be in charge of each team. You'll follow their instructions as if they were my own. I know you usually talk back to me and ignore half of what I say, but if this is going to work I need your cooperation. Remember, if every team is successful we'll completely screw up Kervol's plans. As a bonus, anyone who does what they're told will be included in the next mission."

"You're planning something else?" a goblin asked.

"Oh yeah," Will said menacingly. "I'm going to send wave after wave of teams just like yours to sabotage Kervol's army. So if you want in on that, do what you're told. There's going to be plenty of opportunities to make mischief."

Domo, Mr. Niff and the trolls divided up the goblins into equal teams and ran off into the cool morning air. Will didn't know if this would work or not, but he had faith in the leaders he'd assigned, and the goblins were less likely to sabotage the mission when they liked the idea. He walked back into the city to check up on the diggers and then plan his next move.

A tiny goblin wearing a helmet that covered him down to his waist ran up to Will. "Oh no, I'm late, aren't I?"

"For this job, yes. Don't worry. There's plenty to do around here and more jobs to come."

* * * * *

Domo's team ran across the woodlands heading for the nearest village. He had 25 goblins in his team. That was more than he'd needed if everything went right, but when goblins were involved nothing went to plan. Most of these goblins had been in the throne room last night, so Domo didn't have to explain the plan to them. Well, he didn't have to explain it to most of them.

"But why do we want the war notices?" a goblin with a huge nose asked. "They'll put up more if we tear them down."

"Of course they'll put up more if they see they're gone," Domo said. "We're not just tearing them down. We're replacing them with forged notices."

Terrified, the huge-nosed goblin grabbed Domo by the arm. "Oh no, I lost the forgeries!"

Domo shook him off. "You don't have the forged notices. I do! Honestly, like I'd trust you with them."

Domo had twenty war notices that were almost identical to the one they'd seen on the magic mirror the night before. Each one had a critical difference, unnoticeable unless you knew what to look for. Two other goblins carried buckets of paste while a third goblin had brushes.

At sunrise they reached the village where Will went for his meals. The people were already up and hard at work. Domo led the goblins to a barn at the edge of the village, careful not to be seen.

"Hey, what's this town called?" a horned goblin asked.

"It doesn't have a name," Domo said. "That's one of the ways they try to avoid being noticed by the king and his tax collectors. If someone told the king they'd been in the village of Kent, he might look for it on a map or send someone there. But if someone told the king they'd been in some village and doesn't give a name, the king won't be as interested."

"That's so clever," the horned goblin said.

"Why aren't these people in charge when they're so smart?" the huge-nosed goblin asked.

Domo opened his mouth for a sharp reply, then paused. "You know, I'm not sure. I guess brains and leadership don't have anything to do with each other."

The goblins watched the townspeople go about their business. While the town had a population in the hundreds, they were soon scattered far and wide working in the fields. Domo waited until there were no more than a few people in sight.

"Remember, we can't be seen," he told the others. "The locals don't want us here to begin with, and with the war starting they might get spooked by us."

"Good!" a goblin said excitedly.

"Not good!" Domo snapped. "If they come running after us we won't finish our mission. We have to replace all the war notices in this town and the next three towns, too. Lead them away from me if you're spotted."

One of the goblins that spied on the village ran up to them. Domo hurriedly explained the plan. Once the spy stopped giggling hysterically, he agreed to help.

"How many war notices are there in the town?" Domo asked.

"Two," the spy said. "There's one on the inn and the other on a message board in the center of town."

"Only two?" Domo smiled. He had enough notices to sabotage this village and another nine, assuming they each had only two notices. "You've done good. Lead us to them, then once we're done go back to scouting. Our King will send in other groups, and they'll need your help."

"They'll need me?" the spy said in disbelief. He smiled broadly. "Somebody needs me."

"Somebody needs you to get moving," Domo prodded him. The spy nodded and led them into the village, still grinning ear to ear.

The goblins snuck into the village and hurried to the inn. They divided into three small groups and one big group with Domo. The smaller groups kept a lookout for Domo while he and the others got to work on the inn.

"Let's egg the place, too," an eager goblin said.

"No egging. They'll know we were here if we do," Domo said. "Come on, guys, if we do this right it'll be the gag of the century. Help me up."

Two goblins got down on their hands and knees and Domo climbed on top of them. There it was, the notice declaring war and summoning Kervol's followers. Domo ripped it off and ate it. He took the brush and spread paste across the wall. He handed the brush back to its owner before pressing the bogus copy of the war notice on the wall.

Before he ran off to replace the other notice, Domo took a moment to admire his work. The fake notice was identical to the original, an expert work of forgery if he did say so himself. There was one minor difference between it and the real thing. The original notice told Kervol's men to gather at the capital city, Illumina. This one told them to report to the town of Riverdale. Domo leafed through the other forgeries. Some told the men to go to the town of Sweet Water, others to Billings, and others directed them to the lair of Barbecue the dragon.

Snickering, Domo ran off with the other goblins. Kervol was declaring war, but would any of his men show up?

* * * * *

It was noon by the time Mr. Niff and his band reached the town of Sunnyvale. Sunnyvale had the bad luck of being so big that the royal mapmaker couldn't take if off the maps no matter how big a bribe he was offered. Too many kings had come through here for it to hide from their notice, and its population of 4,000 people received regular visits from tax collectors and military recruiters.

Mr. Niff's group met up with the spies and quickly recruited them into the team. Moving stealthily through the dirt streets, the goblins looked for men discussing Kervol's war. They didn't have to go far. A crowd of farmers and tradesmen were gathered next to a message board in the center of town.

"Everybody know what to do?" Mr. Niff asked. The assembled goblins smiled and nodded. Each of them had a short script filled with awkward questions about Kervol and his plans. The trick was to ask the questions without the people realizing goblins were involved. If they saw even one goblin, they'd assume this was all an attempt to distract them or ruin morale, which it was.

"It ain't fair," a farmer said in the crowd of men. "When I wanted a wife I didn't start a war to get one. I just cleaned up the house a bit and asked my girl real nice."

"Does seem like a lot of trouble," a blacksmith said. "I never heard of a goblin kidnapping a woman before, either."

A merchant raised his hand to get their attention. "Wasn't like that the way I heard it. Word is the king sent the lady to them, by mail no less."

"That is a cheap way to do it," the farmer countered. "The way he's spending money he'd better find a way to save his gold."

The goblins scattered around the crowd, hiding in houses or alleys. A goblin spy wearing an empty barrel with eyeholes cut out and openings for his feet scooted into a corner and prepared to say his lines.

"I suppose we've got no choice but to report for duty," the blacksmith said. "He is the king, after all, and if we don't show up it'll be trouble for us later on."

A goblin opened a blacksmith shop's window and said, "But we have so much work to do here." He quickly ducked back inside and closed the window.

"Yep, no two ways about that," the farmer agreed. The group was big enough that he couldn't see who was talking and assumed it was one of his fellow townspeople.

A goblin with a snorkel stuck his head out of a horse trough and added, "We'd be gone for weeks. Our families will have to do all the chores." He slipped back underwater before anyone saw him.

A carpenter nodded and said, "My wife just gave birth to a baby girl. I can't leave her like this."

The goblin in the barrel asked, "What's this part about 'prevailing wages' mean?"

"I was wondering about that, too," the blacksmith said. "Does that mean we get what we were paid last time we were called up? Merchant, what have you heard?"

The merchant shrugged. "Nobody much knows. Best guess is it means we'd be paid as much as foot soldiers and archers in other counties."

Mr. Niff stuck his head up out of a chimney. "So does that mean we get paid less or more?"

The merchant rubbed his chin. "That's a fair question. More money would be better."

The goblin in the barrel said, "That's assuming he can pay us at all. Kervol spends money like he thinks it's going to spoil."

"You're right. He's been spending a lot of money," the blacksmith said. "There was that wedding that never happened where the flowers wilted and the cake went flat, and all those extra people working in the castle. That's a good point, Hubert."

A bored-looking man yawned and said, "Wasn't me that said it. It was the talking barrel."

The goblin in the barrel panicked when he realized he'd been spotted. He tried to back up, but he was already in a corner. As he started to hyperventilate, the nearest farmer asked, "You heard he can't pay us?"

"Huh? Oh, uh, well, it just stands to reason he can't," the spy said as he fumbled through his lines. Everyone was watching him now. Mr. Niff and the other goblins were preparing a distraction so he could get away, but they needed time. The goblin spy said, "If he calls up a couple thousand soldiers, and they're paid by the month, uh, he'll need a mountain of gold to pay us all. And, uh, the way he's been spending it, where would he get it? It's not like anyone would lend it to him, right?"

"The talking barrel is right!" the blacksmith said. "I bet he'll raise taxes to pay for the war."

"Raise our taxes so he can pay us to fight for him?" a farmer asked. "That's crazy!"

The rest of the goblins watched in amazement as the townspeople kept talking to the goblin spy hiding in the barrel. Mr. Niff had been getting ready to open a chicken coop and let the hens out to cover his escape, but it didn't look like he had to do anything.

The goblin in the barrel sorted through his lines until he found a useful bit. "I bet we'll just get vouchers. He hasn't got any money, so he'll give us a piece of paper that says he'll give us our pay later."

A farmer slapped his side. "That's just what a fool like him would do. He'll spend all his money on his fairytale wedding and tell us, 'sorry, nothing left for you'. I hate it when kings spend everything they got and then cry poor!"

"We should demand to be paid up front or we won't fight," the carpenter said. He slapped the side of the barrel and asked, "What do you think?"

The barrel trembled. "Oh, uh, yeah, great idea. He, uh, he can't push us around! He can't send his army after us for asking for our money, cause we are his army, right?"

"We're a part of it, that's true," the blacksmith said.

"We should get a raise," the goblin in the barrel added, "and health insurance, a dental plan and a pension!"

“He’s right!” a farmer shouted. “If we’re going to risk our lives we ought to be properly compensated. I’m not asking for a pile of gold, but I need enough to provide for my family if I get hurt fighting. The barrel’s right!”

The townsfolk marched off, shaking their fists and shouting ‘THE BARREL’S RIGHT, THE BARREL’S RIGHT!’ Mr. Niff ran out and checked on the goblin in the barrel.

“You okay?” Mr. Niff asked.

The goblin in the barrel nearly fell over. “I think I wet myself.”

“You did good, kid,” Mr. Niff told him. “The king’s going to be real proud of you. He’ll be proud of us all. We’ve got two more places to hit tonight. Let’s move, people!”

In the distance they could hear the townspeople continue chanting ‘THE BARREL’S RIGHT!’ The crowd grew as people heard the noise and came to see what was happening. Each new man was told about the discussion, and soon enough another person was shouting ‘THE BARREL’S RIGHT!’ Mr. Niff chuckled. At least part of Kervol’s army was coming, but he didn’t think King Kervol was going to want it.

* * * * *

Miles away, London and his gang of goblins reached their first target at about the same time Mr. Niff did. They ran through pastures and woodlands around the farms, careful to avoid detection. London carried a sack filled with wooden signs and the goblins had nails, hammers and shovels. They came to the edge of a patch of woods and spotted their target next to a wide dirt road. It was a crossroad with deep wheel ruts cut into it and a signpost off to one side.

"There's our target, boys," London said. "On the count of three, we go out and rough him up. Make sure nobody sees nothing, and you lookouts warn us if witnesses are coming."

"You got it," a giggling goblin said.

London shook his fist at the goblins. "Any of you screw up and I'll rough you up when I'm done with him."

"Yes, boss," the goblins chorused.

London wasn't sure he liked the idea of using goblins for a project like this, but the king had ordered it. Grudgingly, he had to admit he needed them, if only to carry all this stuff.

London counted off his fingers. "One, two, three!"

The troll and goblins launched into action. They ran out of cover and attacked the wood signpost. The post had arrow shaped signs, each pointing to various towns, and included the name and distance to each destination. London ripped all the signs off and threw them aside. One goblin collected the signs, a second handed London new signs, and a third goblin handed the troll a hammer and nails. London nailed the new signs onto the post.

In less than a minute the signpost was totally changed. The sign directing travelers to the capital now pointed west instead of south. The sign that did point to the capital read *Terrible danger! Icky monsters this way!* A road that led dangerously close to Barbecue the dragon's lair read *Super Happy Fun Land.*

"What's this last one for?" London asked.

A goblin shrugged. "We figured if we can send some grief her way we should do it."

Two goblins back in the woods were digging a shallow pit. They'd bury the original signs before moving on to the next crossroad. Burning them wasn't an option when the smoke could be seen and might bring curious peasants. London had enough phony signs to screw up four crossroads like this. He smiled at the thought of how much trouble this would make when Kervol's soldiers tried to report in.

"Bird call! Bird call!" a voice cried out in the woods.

"No, you dummy, you're supposed to make a bird call!" a second voice said.

"I don't have tools to make anything!"

"Oh bother," the second voice muttered. "London, someone's coming!"

"Back into the woods," London ordered. The goblins ran as fast as their short legs could carry them and London brought up the rear. They had to move fast. The locals would figure out what happened and fix the sign if they were spotted in the act.

They were almost in the woods when the goblin carrying the original signs tripped and dropped them. He was struggling back to his feet and reaching for a sign when London saw a heavily loaded horse-drawn wagon with three humans riding it come into view. The rest of the goblins took cover in the woods. London grabbed the fallen goblin and hurled him into the woods, then grabbed the old signs.

"Greetings," one of the men said as he saw London. "A troll! I didn't think there were any trolls in these parts."

London quickly gathered up the old signs and lied. "Sure, there are plenty of trolls around here. We're not too far from the Troll Kingdom."

"True enough," the man said. As he came closer, London could see their wagon better. It was pulled by four horses and contained large oak barrels. "Gathering firewood, I see."

"Yep." London pointed at the barrels and asked, "What's all that stuff?"

The man smiled and patted one of the barrels. "Oil. The king of these parts, some yokel named Kervol Ket, wants oil, weapons, armor and the like. He's going to war with the goblins, if you can believe that."

"Oh, you're merchants. I can understand the weapons and armor, but what does he need oil for if he's fighting a war?" London asked.

"Boiling oil is a popular weapon and useful for starting fires," the merchant replied casually. "I daresay this king plans to make quite the mess."

"And you're supplying him?" London was proud of himself. He made that sound like a question instead of an accusation.

The merchant nodded. "There's profit to be made."

London's first thought was to rough up the merchants and trash their wagon. In some stupid way he could understand what Kervol was doing and why, but these people were going to help destroy the goblins for money. Worse, boiling oil and fire left nasty wounds that were slow to heal. These smiling merchants didn't care about that. Oh how he wanted to bust them up! But Will had said make sure nobody saw them do anything suspicious, and London was pretty sure beating up three merchants and ruining their cargo would draw attention.

London forced a smiled. "I don't think I've seen you guys before."

"We're with the Peck Merchant House, new to these parts," one of the other men said. "Do you know the fastest way to the capital?"

"Sure do." London pointed to the signpost. "This one points to the capital, but the way the road twists around you'll be lucky if you get there before the war ends. You see this one that says *Super Happy Fun Land*?"

"That way is faster?"

"Oh yeah, that'll get you where you belong a whole lot quicker. I've got to get going."

"Farewell," one of the men said.

"Good luck," London said as he walked into the woods. He waited for the merchants to leave. Once they were gone he dumped the signs into the shallow pit the goblins dug. "You heard that?"

"We heard it," a goblin said with a shudder. "Boiling oil!"

"Yeah, well, they're headed straight for Barbecue," London said. A fire-breathing dragon and a wagon carrying barrels of oil should prove to be a short if exciting encounter. "Cover up the signs and we'll move on to the next signpost."

"That was a sneaky, underhanded and very entertaining thing you did out there," one of the goblins complimented London. "You're learning so much from us."

London swatted the offending goblin.

* * * * *

Brooklyn and his goblins hurried through pastures and farmland, all of them eager to get started. They crossed one of the three bridges over the Mildly Magnificent Ket River, a muddy river named after the ruling family. Brooklyn grumbled as he ran. He didn't like his part of the plan. His brother got to destroy stuff! Why did London get to have all the fun? Oh well, orders were orders.

They passed briefly by Sunnyvale, where for reasons unknown people were shouting 'THE BARREL'S RIGHT!' That didn't make any sense, but Brooklyn had spent enough time around goblins that weirdness and stupidity didn't surprise him anymore.

"This stinks," Brooklyn said in disgust. "There's no smashing in this plan."

"But think of the chaos!" a goblin said with a gleam in his eyes.

Grudgingly, Brooklyn said, "Yeah, there's going to be a mess when we're done, but I won't get to smash anything. It's not healthy for a troll my age to go so long without committing an act of violence. I may need therapy."

It took a while, but they eventually found Gilbert the goblin lobbyist. Smartly dressed in a small black business suit, he was hiding outside a small village. Gilbert's bag of candy was almost empty from paying for information. Explaining the plan to him went quickly.

"A smear campaign?" Gilbert asked.

"Kind of," Brooklyn said. "We need to make King Kervol look dumb, but only by telling the truth. The boss says that will make it work better. And nobody can know we're doing it."

Gilbert rubbed his hands together gleefully. "So you want to spill the dirt on every stupid thing Kervol's done. Yes, plenty of material to work with."

Brooklyn handed Gilbert a grimy sheet of paper. "This is some of the stuff the boss came up with."

Gilbert took the paper and studied it. "Good. Not great, but good. There are some rhymes in here, too. That'll make it catchy so it will stick in people's minds for a while." Gilbert took out a quill and bottle of ink and scribbled on the sheet. "Better. I'm almost out of payment for my operatives."

One of Brooklyn's goblins handed Gilbert a huge sack of candy. Gilbert took one out and ate it. "Hmm, yes, raspberry cream, very good. Where did you swipe it from?"

"Kervol's entourage," a goblin said proudly. "They didn't watch their luggage the last time they were here."

"Any chance there's something here I can smash?" Brooklyn asked hopefully.

"None," Gilbert said. "Come, we must find my operatives."

A short time later they found two girls playing jump rope outside Sunnyvale. The girls were ten years old with pigtails, and dressed in well-worn and patched dresses. They saw Gilbert approaching and hurried over. "What's up, Gilbert?"

"I have a job for you, one with handsome rewards." He showed them the sheet of paper and then opened his bag of candy. "I need this recited twice today and once more every day this week when there are plenty of people watching. It's a rush job, so the pay's double normal."

"Double?" one of the girls asked suspiciously. "These aren't coconut candy, are they?"

"No, no, of course not," Gilbert assured them.

"I'll pound you good if any of these have coconut in them!" the other girl said.

Brooklyn patted the girl on the head. "I like her."

Exasperated, Gilbert said, "Please, I am a professional. I don't poison my own operatives. Are we agreed to the job and wages?"

The girls studied the paper. "Yeah, we can do this. You want a practice run?"

"If you would be so kind."

The girls tied one end of the jump rope to a fence post. One of them started swinging the rope while the other jumped. In unison they began to sing.

"Young King Kervol, clever like a fox,
shipped his wife inside a box.
He fought goblins and got beat,
three times knocked back on his seat.
Starting a war to save his pride,
taking us along for the ride.
Paying lots of soldiers we are told,
where's he getting all the gold?"

"Thank you. You were marvelous as always," Gilbert said.

"You don't want to hear the other three verses?" the first girl asked.

"That won't be necessary, or possible. I need to meet with my other operatives." Gilbert handed out the promised wages and added a warning. "If anyone asks, you heard this—"

"From an old man with a bottle of rum," the girls said together, "same as always." They left hand in hand, carrying their jump rope and candy payment.

"How many kids do we have to meet?" Brooklyn asked.

Gilbert dug through the bag of candy. "We have enough to pay another ten of my operatives. Come along. We have to hurry to get to them all tonight."

* * * * *

Hours later, the troll brothers were back together on one of the bridges over the Mildly Magnificent Ket River. Brooklyn ripped a crossbeam off the bridge and threw it into the water below, where is landed with a splash. "Now this is more like it!"

The river was named after the Ket dynasty, which had ruled these parts for centuries. The qualifier came about because the Other Place Geographical Society had decided that too many places were called 'astounding' or 'magnificent', especially when there was nothing astounding or magnificent about them. When the Society made their official maps of the world of Other Place, they'd applied rigorous standards and measurements to determine what was truly great. The Ket River was judged only Mildly Magnificent.

There were three bridges over the river, and London and Brooklyn were tearing one of them apart by hand. The trolls had already taken out a third of this bridge, leaving dangerous gaps in the floor and guardrails. The other two bridges were being taken down by the goblins. The river was fifty feet wide and eight feet at its deepest, while the three covered bridges that spanned the river were all seventy feet long and twenty feet wide. Kervol would have a hard time reaching the Kingdom of the Goblins with the bridges gone.

Smiling, Brooklyn said, "Nothing better than getting some exercise and smashing things at the same time."

"This is the good life," London agreed. He tore a floorboard off and tossed it into the water. Splash. "This king is working out okay. It's not everyone that can start a war in just a week."

"And there was that knight we beat up," Brooklyn added. He walked to an undamaged part of the bridge and started ripping it apart. It was almost midnight, but there were torches set up to provide them with light.

London chuckled. "Yeah, that was fun. Hey, Brooklyn?"

"Yeah?"

"You really think we'll win this?" London sounded genuinely curious.

Brooklyn pulled some shingles off the roof and threw them off the bridge. Splash. "Nope. We'll rough up a lot of Kervol's boys, sure, but he's got an army and we've got goblins. We'll still have lots of fun."

"Oh yeah, lots of people to pound on," London agreed.

The trolls could see the second bridge over the Ket River in the distance. There were torches illuminating the scene, and goblins in lab coats scurrying over the bridge. When all four missions were finished, Domo had gone to report to Will and bring the lab rats. London, Brooklyn, Mr. Niff and the goblins stayed behind to demolish the three bridges. Vial and his fellow alchemists came later to help with the property damage.

"We'd better hurry up and finish before Vial sets off his bomb," London said.

"I thought he was busy moving his lab outdoors," Brooklyn said.

"He was, but when the boss said he wanted the bridges down, Vial wanted to get to blow one up," London replied. "Said something about it being a learning experience. Boss probably figured it was safer to let him blow up stuff far away."

Brooklyn peered into the darkness, looking for anyone who might have been attracted by the noise they were making. But their ruckus would be nothing compared to one of Vial's larger bombs going off. "It'll bring all the locals running when they hear the boom. Hey, I think this is a support beam down here. Give me a hand with it."

The two trolls grabbed the thick oak beam and pulled. Nails popped out as they ripped it free of other beams. The bridge sagged and part of it dipped into the water.

"Sweet! One more like that and the whole thing should come down," Brooklyn said.

London looked at the second bridge and saw the lab rat goblins were running toward a patch of woods. "Vial's going to do it. Cover your ears."

The trolls ducked and slapped their hands over their ears. Seconds later there was a flash of light. The sound needed a second more to reach them.

KRACKA-BOOM!

London stood up and smiled. There was no trace of the second bridge except for a rising cloud of smoke and a rain of burning debris. London didn't like or trust alchemy. Alchemists blew themselves up too often. Still, he could appreciate destruction on that scale.

"Didn't look like Vial lost any lab rat goblins when he set it off," London remarked.

"He's getting better about that." Brooklyn looked in the opposite direction where Mr. Niff and a hundred goblins were supposed to be taking out the last bridge. "I haven't seen anything from Niff and the goblins. We may have to take that one down, too."

"It'll be good exercise," London said. He tore off a guardrail and tossed it into the water. However, instead of a splash it made a clunk as it landed.

"Watch out up there!" someone cried out from below the bridge.

London grabbed a torch and held it high. He could see something big moving under a part of the bridge that wasn't sagging. It might be a boat, but if so it was the strangest one the trolls had ever seen. It was big, maybe fifty feet long and about twenty feet wide. A pointed roof with singles covered the top. London saw goblins crawling over it, working with hammers and saws. The goblins were noisy, but the trolls hadn't heard them approach over the sound of the explosion and the noise they made ripping the bridge apart. It was strange, but the boat looked oddly familiar.

"What's going on down there?" Brooklyn demanded.

Mr. Niff climbed onto the roof of the boat and waved to them. "Hi, guys. We're just taking the bridge out."

"Taking the bridge…oh come on!" London slapped his hand over his face. The 'boat' floating down river was the third bridge. It was missing its ends, but those parts were now sealed up so it would float. "That's not what the boss meant!"

Mr. Niff smiled. "Yeah, we know. But when we sawed through the two ends and the bridge fell into the water, it floated. So the guys and me started talking about it, and we figured a bridge is basically the same as a barge, right? Both are made of wood, both have flat bottoms, and they have three of the same letters in the names. So we figured, you know, a little work and we could float the whole thing away."

"Where are you taking it?" Brooklyn asked.

Niff pointed down river. "Well, the Mildly Magnificent Ket River feeds into the Almost Magnificent Vales River, and that connects to the Actually Magnificent Thades River, and that goes out to sea. I figure we'll let the river take it out all the way. Kervol will never see this bridge again."

The barge/bridge floated gently downstream, carrying a hundred goblins with it. London shook his fist at the goblins and shouted, "Get off that thing, you little runts!"

"We will once we're done waterproofing the hull," Mr. Niff said.

A goblin with a saw asked, "Uh, wouldn't that be the floorboards?"

"Same difference," Mr. Niff replied.

Chapter Eleven

Will ate his breakfast on top of the gatehouse, the tallest structure in the Goblin City. The gatehouse was in poor shape, with the occasional missing brick and entire sections of the wall gone. There was no way it could keep out a determined toddler in its present condition, but Will had people working on that. For now he sat on a flat and intact section near the top.

He watched the sunrise as he ate, still smiling over how well things went yesterday. All the missions he'd sent his followers on had been completed. Better yet, they hadn't lost a single goblin in the process. That was important. Victories like these would build morale and show the goblins they could win. It would also slow Kervol down and buy Will the time he needed to fight off the invading army. If things continued like this they might be able to defeat Kervol's army by taking out one part at a time before it could assemble.

There was something else happening that pleased him. Will had sent messengers to ask nearby goblins to come and help. In response, hundreds more goblins were streaming into the kingdom each day. Many of them were already coming, drawn in by the contracts and spells that created the kingdom, but Will needed them here fast. He had no illusions that one goblin or even five of them could fight a man and win, so he'd decided that the key to victory in this war lay in cunning and sheer weight of numbers. If he could catch Kervol off guard and smother his army with a horde of goblins, he just might win.

"Morning," Domo said as he walked over.

"Hi. Are the others still sleeping?" Will asked.

"Yeah, they got in pretty late last night," Domo replied and sat down next to Will. "They'll be out for a few more hours."

"Excuse me," a goblin builder said as he walked by with a pile of bricks. He and hundreds of other goblins were repairing the gatehouse and city wall at Will's instruction. That was going to take a while given what poor shape the wall was in. That was yet another reason to slow down Kervol as much as possible.

"How much good do you think we did yesterday?" Will asked.

Domo shrugged. "It's hard to say. We only reached the towns closest to us, and what we did won't stop them forever. I'd say we bought ourselves three more days."

"That's it?" Will didn't try to hide his disappointment.

"What do you want me to say? We got away with it, which is more than I was expecting, but we didn't do enough to stop an army. For that matter, Kervol won't even know we did anything until he reaches the changed signs and missing bridges, so that won't deter him. It's going to take a lot more work to stop him."

"Coming through." Another goblin trotted by with a bucket of mortar. Two more goblins behind him carried trowels.

Will finished his meal and looked out over the landscape. "I'm hoping we can make things so difficult that Kervol's men will go home. If their morale fails they might give up and leave regardless of what Kervol orders them to do."

"That's a tall order," Domo said. "If anyone is going to break and run it will be us. Will, goblins haven't won a fight in recorded history. They don't mind you starting this war, what with them being idiots and all, but they don't expect to win it."

"But they've already won fights against Kervol, three of them," he protested.

Domo waved his hands dismissively. “That doesn’t count, and neither does what we did last night. Those were little victories. Goblin history is full of those. In the end they don’t change anything. When Kervol’s army shows up the goblins will try to stop him, but they’ll run for cover the second things turn sour.”

“If that happens we lose, and there’s no telling how much damage Kervol could do,” Will said. “London told me he’s buying oil for starting fires. At the very least he’ll burn everything around us. The forests, the buildings still standing, they could all go up in flames. He’ll probably tear down anything that won’t burn.”

“It’s going to be bad,” Domo agreed. “We’ve lost things we cherished before. If it helps any, the guys won’t blame you for it.”

“Duck your heads,” a builder goblin said as he came through with framing timbers. Four more goblins followed him carrying loads of bricks.

“I don’t accept that,” Will said firmly. “I’m not going to just throw up my hands and say we’ve lost before the fight even starts. We’re going to win this and that’s that. I’m going to either keep Kervol out entirely or beat him when he comes.”

“How?” Domo asked incredulously.

“I’m going to convince the goblins we can win this. I’m going to show them that the people we’re facing are incompetent and stupid enough we can trick them. I’m going to convince Kervol and his army that they can be beaten. I’m going to make them wonder if they can win this fight, and if it’s even worth the effort. Come on, Domo. If the first wave of goblins didn’t do enough, we’re sending another one.”

Will stood up and walked toward the stairs he had taken to get here. That proved harder than anticipated, as there was now a brick wall in the way. It was ten feet high, braced with framing timbers, and had wet mortar squeezing from between the bricks.

"Oh come on!" Will shouted.

"You did tell them to fix the place up," Domo reminded him.

A goblin peeked his head over the wall. "What's the matter?"

"You bricked me in!" Will said.

The builder goblin looked around. "So we did. That's the third time this morning we did that to somebody. Hold on a minute and we'll dig you out."

"Don't bother," Will grumbled. He grabbed Domo around the waist and helped him climb over the wall. Looking around, he spotted a scarecrow in the courtyard far below. "I'm going to talk to the goblins and see if they know any places we can hit. Meet me at the gate."

Whoosh! Will warped to the scarecrow, leaving his now empty uniform to drift to the floor.

* * * * *

It didn't take long to assemble a small army of goblins. Many of them had heard that last night's pranks went well and they wanted to join in. Within minutes Will had a mixed bag of warrior, builder and digger goblins, many of them new arrivals to the kingdom. The goblins provided him with a lengthy list of potential targets thanks to the years they'd spent wandering around human towns and eavesdropping on the locals. Will headed to the nearest target with his band in tow. Domo followed them, looking worried as they headed into Kervol's lands.

"This is stupid even by our standards," Domo said. "You want to launch a raid against Kervol's army?"

"Not the whole army," Will explained, "I want to hit a few of them before they can link up with Kervol's army. The men know that we beat their king three times. I want them to know that we can beat *them*, too."

"If I can't stop you," Domo said. "There's a manor house nearby run by Sir Vinders Talon. He's the knight who runs a village for the king. He collects taxes, enforces the laws, pushes people around...you know, stuff like that. Behind his back everybody calls him 'Sir Wide Bottom', even his own men."

"Wide Bottom?" Will asked.

"He earned the nickname," Domo replied. "He's got ten foot soldiers, which means we don't have enough goblins by half."

Will had two hundred eager and hopelessly incompetent goblins, an overachieving fire scepter and a rough idea where he was going. He kept telling himself this was a good idea. After all, he was at war. What would Patton do in a situation like this? Well, besides slap his own men, he'd take the fight to the enemy. Besides, with two hundred goblins against eleven men, the odds couldn't get much better.

"You guys know anything about this knight?" Will asked the goblins. "Besides the fact that he needs to cut back on fatty foods."

"He likes shouting at people," a purple goblin said.

"His horse is named Miracle, on account of the fact it can actually carry his fat butt," a tiny goblin added.

"He won the 'sniveling toady of the year' award three times," another said.

"Any advice how we can best beat him?" Will asked.

Domo said, "Don't let him fall on you, or the fight's lost for sure."

After an hour of walking they came upon Talon's manor house. It was a large brick building outside a small village, and it had an attached stable with a brown stallion that had to be the largest horse Will had ever seen. None of the farmers came near the manor house, and most wouldn't even look at it. Will heard a man shouting inside the building amid the clatter of pots and pans.

Will led his followers behind a grassy hill. He climbed to the top and studied the manor house.

"Whatcha doing?" someone behind them asked.

Will spun around and saw a farmer laying down, hidden by the tall grass. The farmer wore dusty clothes and looked bored.

"Uh, we're—" Will began.

"Oaf!" a man bellowed inside the manor. "Fool and wretch! You think these are adequate provisions for a march to the capital? Half rations! Starvation fare!"

"That's Sir Talon talking, isn't it?" Will asked.

"Yep," the farmer said. He looked down the hill and saw the crowd of goblins. "Don't suppose you're planning on doing him any harm, are you?"

"What, us?" Will asked in shock.

"No, never," Domo added.

"No, no, not us," a goblin said.

"Never even entered our—okay, be fair, maybe," Will said.

"Possibly," Domo added.

"Depends what our horoscope says," a goblin piped in.

The farmer nodded before he got up and strolled away. "Much appreciate it if you could wait a few minutes while I get my neighbors. There's a good number of people in these parts who'd like to see him get what's coming to him."

"Uh, sure, okay," Will said. "Five minutes work for you?"

"That'd be keen," the farmer said.

"Strange people around here," Will said. "We'll give him a few minutes, then go ahead with the plan."

"How do you know he's not going to bring a crowd of armed men to attack us?" Domo asked.

They heard the knight bellow from the manor house, "Blast it, my flag has mustard stains on it again! Get someone from the village to wash it. And do something about the smell."

Will looked at Domo, who shook his head and said, "Forget I asked."

Will sent the goblins around the back of the manor while he entered the stable. He found a tired-looking young man putting a saddle on the horse. Will smiled and petted the horse.

"Huh? Who are you?" the man asked.

Will smiled at him. "Hi there, William Bradshaw. Do you work for Wide Bottom, or did you get dragged in from the village to do his work for him?"

"The second one," the man said wearily. "He's the king's man, so he gets to demand labor as well as taxes."

"Bummer." Will petted the horse. "I need you to do a favor for me. Wait one minute and yell 'horse thief'. Can you do that for me?"

"Why? Hey!"

Will took Miracle by the reins and led him out. The horse was reluctant to move until Will said, "Work with me and Wide Bottom will never ride you again." That got him moving at a brisk trot. Will counted as he led the horse away from the manor. Fifty-eight, fifty-nine, sixty.

"Horse thief!" the man in the stable cried out. "Someone's stealing Sir Wide Bottom, I mean, Sir Talon's horse! Horse thief!"

Inside the manor house there were shouts and the sound of furniture being overturned. The door burst open and ten soldiers ran out wearing chain armor and carrying maces and daggers. They looked absolutely shocked. One of them spotted Will walking away and pointed a spiked mace at him.

"There he is! Get him!"

The soldiers got three steps from the manor before a wave of howling goblins came around the building and poured over them. Each soldier was attacked by twenty goblins that grabbed them, stole their weapons and pulled off their armor. Sheer weight of numbers pulled the soldiers down.

Domo watched the fight in amazement. The goblins hadn't just won; they'd won quickly and completely. Bewildered, he asked, "How?"

Wide Bottom came out next, and proved he deserved his nickname. The man had grizzly hair, greasy skin and weighed enough for two men his height. How a horse, even one as big as Miracle, could carry a man that big was a mystery. Wide Bottom wore thick plate armor, which added to his already considerable weight, and he carried a sword and shield that looked too small for him.

"What kind of madness is this?" Wide Bottom bellowed.

Domo smirked. "Goblins are involved, so it's every kind of madness."

Wide Bottom raised a meaty fist and swung at a goblin. The goblin jumped off the soldier he was grappling, leaving the unfortunate man to get knocked out by his own master. Wide Bottom waded into the mass of goblins and men, striking everyone within range. Again the goblins backed away from this moving mountain of a man, leaving his foot soldiers to get knocked around and trampled.

"Merciful God in heaven, get off me!" a soldier under Wide Bottom cried.

Wide Bottom stopped his attack and pointed an accusing finger at Will. "You wear the colors of the King of the Goblins!"

"William Bradshaw, at your service," Will said with a bow. "So sorry to bother you, but your king declared war on me, so we're staging a raid against you."

"Please move, I'm begging you," the unfortunate soldier said.

"Cur!" Wide Bottom hollered. "This is not how a war is fought. You don't hit the other man when he's not looking."

Will leaned over to Domo and asked, "You don't?"

"Apparently."

Will shrugged. "Hmm, no wonder chivalry is dead."

"I've got a wife and children," the soldier under Wide Bottom pleaded.

Wide Bottom took a step toward Will (thus sparing the life of the unfortunate foot soldier under him), and raised his sword. "So be it! This is a golden opportunity to smite you and win everlasting glory. I challenge you to a duel!"

"You and me fighting without anyone interfering?" Will asked.

"Yes!" Wide Bottom declared.

Will scratched his head. "And you've got a sword and armor, and I don't?"

"Yes!"

"Forget that," Will said. "Everybody pile on him."

Wide Bottom was a big man and fairly strong. When all two hundred goblins jumped him he managed to keep standing for five whole seconds, tottering about, completely obscured by the squirming mass of goblins. The ground shook when he fell, and goblins were thrown aside by the shock wave.

"Take their armor and weapons," Will said. "Check the house and get anything in there. Somebody get Miracle's saddle off and let him go."

Domo pointed to a speck on the horizon. "Too late for that. The horse took off when he saw Wide Bottom come outside."

The goblins piled up the weapons and armor they stole and then ran inside the manor. More weapons were thrown out the windows, mostly knives and meat cleavers, but also pieces of armor Wide Bottom had outgrown.

Will picked up a huge breastplate and held it against his chest. "Hey, Domo, is there anyone back in the Goblin City who could refit this for me?"

"You're joking. We might be able to make that fit a cow, but that's it."

A goblin stuck his head out an upstairs window of the manor and screamed, "Guys, he's got cheese!"

"Cheese!" the goblins screamed. They swarmed into the manor, tearing through the place in their excitement. The goblins came out bearing four wheels of cheese sealed in wax. They cheered and danced around the cheese wheels.

"Fiend!" Wide Bottom shouted. A man of his size could still be a threat even without armor and weapons, but he was staying well behind his disarmed foot soldiers. "King Kervol will hear of this!"

"Good," Will said.

Wide Bottom took a step back. Hesitantly, he asked, "Good?"

"Yes, it's good that you're going to tell him. I want him to know you were beaten. I want him to know your followers were beaten. His entire army will know that foot soldiers and one of their knights fought goblins and lost."

Will faced the goblins and said, "That's four times we beat them. Four times Kervol and his men fought us and lost. I know he's coming with an army, but if we're careful and we're smart, or at least cunning, we can win. Grab their weapons and armor and let's go."

The goblins looked confused. One of them raised a hand and asked, "We're taking weapons when there's cheese?"

Will grumbled and rubbed his eyes. "Take the cheese *and* the weapons and armor."

The goblins cheered and marched off with Will in the front. They carried the cheese wheels with pride and the weapons and armor reluctantly, leaving Wide Bottom and his men behind with bruised bodies and injured pride.

Wide Bottom cleared his throat and addressed his men. "We were attacked by bandits. That's our story and we're sticking to it."

* * * * *

Baron Harker struggled to keep up with King Kervol's representative, Foster Grieves, as they walked down the main road of Sunnyvale. Kervol had sent the simpering twit to make sure preparations for the coming war were complete. Harker didn't appreciate the King doubting his abilities. That the King would send this twerp, a former member of his entourage if the rumors were true, was even more galling. The baron tried desperately not to throttle Foster, but it was hard.

"Our Noble King is very anxious that all goes according to plan during this campaign," Foster said as he and Baron Harker walked down Sunnyvale's main street. Dressed in rich silks and constantly toying with his oiled locks of hair, Foster looked like a preening bird. He acted like one, too. “There has been some unpleasantness caused by his followers not living up to their responsibilities, and he doesn’t want that to happen again.”

“Yes, sir,” Harker said. Older, stronger, smarter, more experienced, and quite frankly better than Foster, Harker was an exact opposite to the King’s representative. Harker’s clothes were high quality and comfortable, but they were made from durable, well-tailored leather. Harker tried to stay upwind of Foster so he didn’t have to smell the man’s cologne. By all that’s holy, what could make such a stink?

Baron Harker was in charge of Sunnyvale, a sizable town and major source of taxes and soldiers. Sunnyvale was peaceful almost to a fault, and it should have been ludicrous to think anything could go wrong there. But there *were* problems. Almost overnight the townsfolk began demanding to be paid in advance for military service. There were also some treasonous jokes going around about the King, including an extremely nasty children’s rhyme. The whole town was in a foul mood.

As the two men walked down the street, Baron Harker saw movement in an alley. He squinted and could barely make out goblins scurrying in the shadows. There were about ten of them carrying bulging leather bags. That wasn’t unusual, as there were always goblins skulking around and snapping up garbage. The pestilent little things could even get into the center of a major city, oftentimes without being notice. People tried to stop them with locks, barred windows and even set traps. It was all to no avail. Goblins got into everything no matter how hard men tried to keep them out. Harker frowned, though, for seeing so many of them together was odd. They usually traveled alone.

“Is there a problem, baron?” Foster asked. “I don’t seem to have your full attention.”

"Nothing's wrong, sir. I was just thinking about the coming battle," Harker said. He'd just as soon not point out that there were goblins in his town when the King was going to war with them. Foster wouldn't appreciate how hard it was to keep the little pests from getting their grimy mitts into everything. Besides, the goblins saw them and ran off whispering to one another. Problem solved.

"I wouldn't describe what's coming as a battle," Foster said condescendingly. "At best this will be a chance for the army to practice. Your men will be ready, of course?"

"Hmm, oh yes, they're set to march out tomorrow. You can expect them in the town of Billings in two days."

"What? Why are they going there?" Foster demanded.

"Because that's where the war notices instructed them to go," Harker said through clenched teeth. He pointed to the message board in the center of town. Foster read the notice.

"Uh, yes, I'm sure they'll receive additional orders there," Foster replied. Harker wasn't privy to the King's battle plans, and Foster's response made it look like he wasn't, either. Harker briefly wondered if Kervol had bothered drawing up battle plans.

"Our glorious King has instructed me to check the state of your military supplies," Foster went on. "This will be the last major town he passes through, and he intends to top off his supplies before going on to victory."

"You'll find that everything is in order," Harker said. He heard some commotion down the street and saw a mob of farmers chanting 'THE BARREL'S RIGHT!' Oh, that was bad! Hurriedly, he put his arm around Foster and led him to the supply depot. "Nonperishable supplies have already been procured. My men and I will gather food, animal fodder and other perishable goods once the army begins to move."

"Excellent," Foster said. He took a scroll from his belt and handed it to Harker. "The King orders these supplies to be obtained in addition to the usual."

Harker unrolled the scroll and read it. "Wine, roses, perfume, raspberry cream candies, a wedding cake, rose scented candles."

It took a real effort for Harker not to scream, *Are you fighting a war or having a party?* at Foster. It would be disastrous for his career, but oh it was tempting! Harker gritted his teeth, counted to ten and said, "We'll have it ready."

"Good. Now, if I may inspect your supplies?"

"Very well, sir. This way."

Baron Harker led Foster to his supply depot. All the war materials were stored in an enormous warehouse normally reserved for holding the fall harvest. The building was made of thick oak boards, the doors were locked and barred, and there were soldiers guarding the place. The building also had goblin graffiti scratched into its wooden walls, including the message, *100 IQ = farmer. 50 IQ = goblin. 0 IQ = aristocrat or network television executive.*

"This is it?" Foster asked disdainfully.

"Yes, sir. There have been five men guarding the door since we filled it, and four more men patrolling the outside. The King's supplies are secure and await his arrival."

Foster snorted. "Exactly who are you keeping them safe from?"

"Bandits, thieves," Harker said, quietly adding, "their rightful owners." In war, "procure" often meant grab what you need and forget about paying for it. In enemy territory it wasn't a problem, but when you did it on your own land there could be consequences. The merchants and townspeople had lost goods worth close to a thousand gold coins, and to no one's surprise they weren't happy about it. Harker had asked for funds to compensate the owners. After all, many of these men owed military service, and having disgruntled archers who had a bone to pick with their own king wasn't a good idea. Kervol had received Harker's suggestion, considered it and wrote back that the money was needed elsewhere. Typical. Worse, when the army arrived their food and animal fodder would be obtained in exactly the same way.

"Very well," Foster said, "let's see what you have acquired for his majesty."

They marched to the warehouse, but before they could reach it a man stepped out of an alley and shook Harker's hand. "Hi there, you must be Baron Harker. Gosh it's good to see you. I've heard so much about you, and the chance to meet you in person, well, it's wonderful."

"Who are you to approach me?" Harker asked.

The stranger smiled. "You don't know me?"

Harker studied the man closely. He knew everyone in Sunnyvale, but he didn't recognize this man. The stranger wore black and green clothes, with a cape, hat, gloves and boots. He was young and had brown hair and gray eyes. The man seemed cheerful, which was surprising given how everyone else felt in Sunnyvale. Harker frowned. He was missing something, but he couldn't put his finger on it.

"You have me at a disadvantage, sir," Harker said.

Annoyed, Foster asked, "Who is this bumbling dolt?"

The man smiled at Foster. "Wow. I thought my name would have gotten around more. I know, I know, you've got your own problems to deal with, lots on your minds. But really, is it asking too much for you to keep up to date with the news?"

"News? What are you talking about?" Foster demanded.

Something was wrong here, Harker was sure of it, but what? Think, what was it? Black and green was an unusual choice of colors for clothing. Most people avoided them because they were…they were the colors of the goblin flag! Only one man would dress in those colors.

"You're the new King of the Goblins!" Harker shouted.

"He is?" Foster scrambled to get behind the baron. "Harker, call your men!"

Soldiers ran from the warehouse door and surrounded the King of the Goblins. Their enemy was still grinning, not the least bit bothered by the swords pointed at him. Instead of cowering, he smiled and said, "Yes, that's me, but I'm not a king today."

"That doesn't make sense," Baron Harker said. "How can a king not be a king?"

Down the street, a small goblin with gray skin and wearing yellow robes scurried out from an alley. "The guys are done."

"Wonderful," the King of the Goblins replied. He smiled at Harker and said, "Today I'm not a king. I'm a distraction."

With that the King of the Goblins fell over backwards. There was a *whoosh* and a rush of air as he disappeared, leaving only his clothes behind.

"Oh no," Harker said. He rushed to the warehouse and struggled to get the bar and lock off the door. Foster was shouting something at him, but Harker didn't know or care what it was. He finally got the lock off and swung the door open.

It was so quiet you could have heard a pin drop, and it would have made an echo when it did. The warehouse was empty. The mountain of supplies Harker had gathered (which sounded more polite than saying stole) was gone. The floor was covered in small footprints left in the dust, leaving no doubt who was responsible for the crime. In the center of the room was a freshly dug hole three feet across.

* * * * *

"We almost pulled it off without anyone knowing about it," Domo said as he and Will fled the town. They hurried to rejoin the rest of the goblins outside Sunnyvale.

"Yeah, but in a way it's good they saw us," Will said. "I want them to know we're responsible."

Will found the goblin horde hiding in an apple orchard with the contents of the warehouse. His followers were tired, dirty and grinning from ear to ear. They'd infiltrated the town, dug a tunnel from an abandoned house to the warehouse and emptied the place. From there they'd carried everything outside the town to a farm left empty when its owner was called up to fight. Will had stood guard outside the warehouse to distract anyone trying to get in. The goblins had almost finished looting the supplies when the baron showed up, forcing Will to slow him down.

"How about these diggers?" Will said. "This morning they showed up on our front door, I ask them to do a job the same day, and wow did they ever!"

The goblins cheered. They had a lot to cheer about. Their work had earned them a huge pile of loot. Goblins scurried over it, sorting through it for things they could use. They ate quite a bit of it, but that didn't bother Will. He didn't want the loot so much as he wanted Kervol not to have it. When the goblins were done, the remaining loot was divided into two stacks.

Domo pointed to the first stack. “We’ve got tents, rope, backpacks, lamps, torches and oil. All good stuff.”

Will pointed at the second pile. “And the rest?”

“Boots too big to fit us, saddles, riding gear and about ten thousand arrows.”

“Take as much as you can carry from the first pile,” Will told them. He grabbed a backpack and filled it with jars of oil. When they were done, the first pile was nearly gone. Once he and the goblins were loaded up he shooed them away from the remaining loot.

“So what do we do with what’s left?” Domo asked. It was a valid question. They were carrying too much to take any more with them. If they left it behind, Kervol’s followers would find it sooner or later and use it against them.

Will took out his fire scepter. He could see the fire salamander inside the scepter’s large fire opal, humming and looking hopefully at him. Tiny wisps of fire rose from the fire opals. He pointed the scepter at the remaining loot and said, “Make me proud.”

FOOM!

Chapter Twelve

A week had passed since Will led his followers out for their second wave of attacks. He didn't send out any more large-scale attacks, mostly because he'd run out of easy targets. Instead he sent out small bands of goblins to set up scarecrows and cause minor mischief. While they were doing that Will oversaw the goblins repairing the wall and digging the tunnel.

Work was going well. The wall and gatehouse weren't close to being finished, but were still coming along nicely. The diggers were half finished with their secret tunnel. Vial was busy building his bomb. Warrior goblins amassed weapons and equipment they'd need, all of it of dubious quality and origins, but better to have it than not.

Will was also keeping tabs on Kervol's war effort by means of his goblin spies and Gladys the magic mirror. Back in the throne room, Will, Mr. Niff, Domo and the troll brothers watched the magic mirror as Gladys showed them Kervol's capital city, Illumina. What they saw didn't please them.

"Look at them all," Mr. Niff said softly.

"Got to be two thousand men there," London grunted.

Illumina was a huge city and a beehive of activity. Men ran everywhere, many of them carrying weapons. There were dozens of fully loaded supply wagons outside the city and lots of empty wagons being pulled up. Over it all were huge flags bearing King Kervol's emblem of a blue peacock on a white background.

Despite everything Will and the goblins could throw at them, Kervol's soldiers were arriving at their king's command. There were foot soldiers armed with heavy iron maces and wooden shields, protected by chain armor and steel helmets. Archers wearing well-crafted leather armor came by the hundreds, each one armed with a longbow and quivers full of arrows. Off by themselves were Kervol's knights, few in number but armed with lances, swords and shields, and wearing plate armor that covered them head to toe. Their armor gleamed in the sunlight, clearly well cared for, if not brand new. Worse, more soldiers were arriving by the hour. It was not an encouraging sight.

"How did he get ready so fast?" Will asked. "I thought it would take him a month to prepare all this."

Domo frowned. "A month or longer. He must have gotten started getting his men together right after we beat him the third time."

This was disheartening. Will had begun to hope he could win the war with a string of minor victories, but Kervol wasn't giving up. Worse, he had a lot of soldiers. Sure, most of them were so dumb they didn't know their left from their right, but they were bigger and stronger than Will's goblins, and much better armed. Nothing Will had done so far had stopped them.

A worrying thought occurred to Will. "I don't have a good idea of how big Kervol's kingdom is. How many towns can he draw on for men and supplies?"

"He's got dozens of towns, most of them far enough away we can't reach them easily," Domo replied. "There are lots of small villages besides the big places. All told I figure he's got two hundred thousand people spread out over his kingdom."

Will frowned. "Then Kervol can get the men and war materials he needs from those towns and villages to replace what he lost. Kervol's resources aren't limitless, but we'll have to hit him a whole lot harder and more often to hurt him bad."

"He's still not ready to move his army," Gladys said. "This is more than I thought he'd have done by now, but he'll need at least another week before he can go anywhere."

Will rubbed his chin. "That's not a lot of time. The diggers may not be finished with their tunnel before he comes. Hey, hold up. Gladys, zoom in on those wagons near the city gate."

The image in the mirror focused on two wagons, one in front of the other. Huge timbers were lashed to the tops of the wagons, so long that two wagons were needed together to hold them. The timbers were thick and no doubt very heavy.

"What are those for?" Will asked.

"Not sure," Domo said. "Maybe they're for rebuilding the bridges we destroyed."

While they were studying the mirror, a mining cart filled with broken rocks rolled by the throne room. Two digger goblins pushed it while another riding on top of the cart shouted, "Wee!"

"How's the work coming along?" Will asked them.

The diggers stopped the cart, greatly annoying the goblin riding it. "Slow and steady. We've got enough diggers that we can replace the ones who get tired, but there's still a lot of rock to move."

"How soon until you finish?"

The goblin shrugged. "Ten days, maybe two weeks. That's not a promise, either. It's just an estimate."

The goblin riding the cart stood up and folded his arms across his chest. "I paid two snails and a small green frog for a cart ride, and we're not moving. Giddy up!"

As the cart rolled on, Will said, "We're nowhere close to being ready for this. We need to slow them up some more."

"The wall around the city isn't fixed, either," Brooklyn said.

Grinning, Mr. Niff asked, "Time to send out more goblins?"

"We have to," Will replied with a worried look at the mirror.

They left the throne room and headed outside the city. The goblins were hard at work, doing things wrong faster than ever. In spite of that, the tremendous number of goblins working meant at least some of them were doing what they were supposed to. The city wall and gatehouse were coming along nicely, and a few goblins were still working on the maze.

A new addition to the landscape was a huge pile of loose rocks generated by digging the secret tunnel. The diggers pushed filled mining carts out of the tunnels and dumped them on the ground, where builder goblins picked through the rocks and hauled away most of them to rebuild the wall.

Far away from the Goblin City were five tents, originally the property of Kervol's army before Will and the goblins stole them from a warehouse. Will and his followers approached the tents warily. They had good reason to be concerned, because this was where Vial had relocated his lab. Lab rat goblins scurried around the tents, each one bearing a bottle or beaker of gurgling chemicals.

"Has it come to this?" Domo asked.

"Yes it has," Will said. "I'm sending Mr. Niff out, too, but our chances of stopping Kervol are much better with Vial's help."

Will marched into the colony of tents while the others stayed behind. In one of these tents Vial and his followers were making their giant bomb. If all went well Will wouldn't need it, but the odds were badly in Kervol's favor. Will needed something to give him a fighting chance.

Will spotted what had to be the bomb. The largest tent contained a hollow tin cylinder three feet across. Around the cylinder were low wooden tables covered with colored glass bottles. The tent smelled of sulfur and ammonia. Lab rat goblins hammered the cylinder into shape while others mixed noxious chemicals together.

"My Liege," Vial said as he hurried into the tent. He patted the cylinder and said, "Allow me to make introductions. We're calling our masterpiece Big Bertha. We used the prototype to destroy a bridge some time ago, and it worked splendidly. Oh this is an exciting event, and most definitely a learning experience! With this experiment we will expand the working knowledge of alchemy farther than it has ever gone. Assuming we don't blow ourselves up, and probably all of you."

"Vial, the enemy is coming faster than we expected," Will said. "We need to slow them down. We also need to convince them that attacking us is going to hurt."

Vial smiled. "You have come to the right goblin. Big Bertha won't be ready for some time, I'm afraid, but the rest of my stock is at your disposal."

"Good, because I need it all."

An hour later, Will watched a crowd of goblins head into Kervol's kingdom. Mr. Niff led fifty warrior goblins, while another fifty warriors went with ten of Vial's lab rat goblins. The second group was burdened down with backpacks, boxes and crates, all filled to overflowing with Vial's hardware. This was Will's last chance to hit Kervol so hard the fool would turn back.

"You think this will work?" Domo asked.

"I hope so," Will said as the goblins disappeared over the horizon.

* * * * *

"I'm just saying this wasn't our fault," an archer said to a scout sent out by the king. The archer was the leader of a group of fifty tired and dispirited archers from the town of Billings. It was a warm and sunny day, and the dirt road was in good condition. These were the only things going in their favor since their trip to the capital started.

To either side of the road were pastures with tall grass and the occasional tree, and rolling hills to the south. Still annoyed, the archers' leader said, "The war notice said we should go to Sunnyvale, so we went to Sunnyvale!"

"I know," the scout said. Kervol had sent him to find soldiers who hadn't come to the capital, a task of mind-boggling difficulty. It took the scout days to find this group of archers wandering the countryside, and getting them moving in the right direction was hard. "There were a bunch of war notices that were messed up. It must have been some kind of printer's error."

"When we got to Sunnyvale, their war notices said we should go to Sweet Water," the archer said. "When we got to Sweet Water, *their* notices said we should got to the dragon's lair."

"Good thing I found you before you did," the scout said.

"I'm telling you, we've been marching all over the place for the last week. My men and I are tired. We've been sleeping outside all week, and we spent most of our money buying food. We've got receipts and we expect the king to cover them."

"You what?" the scout asked.

"The war notices said food and drink would be provided," the archer said forcefully, "or was that another mistake?"

The scout sighed. "No, that was real. You can talk to the king's representatives about your expenses when we get to the capital."

The last week had been impossible. A third of Kervol's men hadn't reported for duty. Scouts were sent to get them, only to find the men scattered across the kingdom. Then there was the bandit attack on Sir Vinders Talon (better known as Wide Bottom), rendering him and his men unfit for duty. To make matters worse, Barbecue the dragon sent an angry message to the king demanding to know why he'd sent soldiers to her lair. She got so angry she torched a merchant's wagon when they pestered her for directions, burning up a lot of oil.

Ahead of them was a fork in the road. There was a signpost next to the road and some of the archers walked over to read it.

"Ignore that," the scout said. "Just come with me and we'll be at the capital by nightfall."

"But it says the capital is the other way," an archer said.

"And what's this *Super Happy Funland* place?" another archer said as he pointed at the sign.

Exasperated, the scout said, "The capital is this way! Listen, I don't know what's going on, but all the signs in these parts are wrong. I've gone this way a hundred times and I know where I'm going."

"You're sure?" an archer asked.

The scout put his hand over his heart. "Positive."

"We've been getting lots of bad directions lately," the archer said.

A second archer said, "We're going to have to trust he knows what he's doing. I've never been out this way before. Have any of you?" The other archers shook their heads.

The scout pointed to the correct road. "Just keep on walking and we'll get there."

"Hey, look," an archer said. Farther up the road was an outhouse, a simple wood building with a half moon cut into the door. "Good timing. I've got to go."

The rest of the archers were close behind him. One of them shouted, "I'm next!"

"Wait a minute, this wasn't here before," the scout said. An archer ran to the outhouse and went inside while the others waited their turn. Worried, the scout said, "Hold on, something's wrong."

BOOM!

The outhouse exploded in a cloud of smoke and shattered boards. Nearby archers were thrown to the ground. The man inside was left sitting on the toilet, his face blackened, his hair scorched and frizzed out. There was a bewildered look on his face. Smoke wafted up around him as charred bits of wood rained down.

The other archers gathered around their friend. Tentatively, one asked, "Are you okay?"

The man sat for a few seconds before he looked at the others. "I'd like to go home now."

The archers glared suspiciously at the scout. He held up his hands and said, "Hey, I don't know what's going on here. Someone's trying to screw us up. There's a town just over these hills where you can get some food and use their outhouses. Just keep moving and we'll get there in time for lunch and in the capital for dinner."

BOOM! A plume of white smoke rose up over the hills. *BOOM!* A second smoke plume rose into the sky. Moments later a blackened piece of wood landed next to the scout. He picked it up and saw it had a half moon cut into it.

"Is that from this outhouse or one of those ones?" an archer asked.

One of his friends pointed at another piece of charred wood in the grass. "No, that's the door from this outhouse."

As one, the archers turned and stared hard at the scout. Desperately, he said, "This isn't my fault!"

"That's it. I'm out of here," an archer said. He turned around and headed back up the road. The rest of the archers looked at one another and then at the smoking remains of the outhouse. They turned around and left.

The scout ran after them. "You can't do this! You'll get in trouble if you don't report for duty. *I'll* get in trouble if you don't report for duty! Come back!"

The scout chased after the archers, shouting all the while. Once the men were gone, a team of warrior goblins crept out of the tall grass. Giggling, they carried off the burnt remnants of the outhouse and swept away the soot and ashes on the ground. They hurried behind a grove of trees and brought out a disassembled outhouse. Working quickly, they assembled it on the same spot as the first one. Once they were done, a lab rat goblin installed a bomb and a tripwire.

The goblins retreated back into the tall grass. The lab rat goblin shushed the giggling warriors. One of them adjusted a scarecrow hidden among the trees so it had a good view of the outhouse. In the distance they heard horses coming.

Two knights rode up and stopped by the outhouse.

"What luck!" the first knight said. "Sir Gwain, if we may stop a while?"

* * * * *

In the courtyard of the Goblin City, Will and his followers watched the magic mirror show one outhouse explode after another. With some help from the trolls, Will had brought out Gladys and set her up so the goblins could watch. Thousands of goblins watched the carnage and laughed uncontrollably as Gladys showed outhouses detonating. Even the troll brothers watched the mirror with rapt attention.

The lab rats had covered all the roads leading to the capital with Vial's exploding outhouses. They'd also rigged bombs in existing outhouses in all the towns around the capital. It got to be that a person risked his life every time he went to the bathroom.

Will chuckled and ate popcorn he'd got from the inn. Domo sat next to him, watching the mirror with a look of awe.

"My God," Domo said. "How many of these things did we put up?"

Will shrugged. "Don't know. Vial said he had fifty ready to go, but that's only the prefabricated ones. I figure if you add in the existing outhouses he rigged, then you're looking at about two hundred."

BOOM! Gladys showed another outhouse going up in smoke. A very surprised-looking man stumbled out of the smoldering wreckage. Goblins cheered and slapped each other on the back.

Will ate some more popcorn. "I've been working them pretty hard lately. I figured they needed a break and some entertainment."

"It couldn't hurt," Domo said. "How long is the show going to last?"

"Half the outhouses already went off, so I figure we're got another hour or so," Will said. "Too bad Mr. Niff isn't here to see this."

"If your plan works, he won't mind missing the show."

* * * * *

It took another eight days, but King Kervol's army finally began to move. Loaded down with ox-pulled wagons, the army made only a few miles progress each day. They traveled only eight or ten hours a day before setting up an elaborate camp including all the luxuries Kervol expected as King. Another impediment was the faulty maps the royal cartographer had made, which left out villages and sometimes rivers and hills. Half the time no one in Kervol's army knew where they were. Lastly, the farther they traveled the more incorrect signposts they found. Kervol ordered the army to stop at each signpost while he sent scouts to figure out where the roads really led. With so many delays Kervol and his army moved slower than a turtle. Still, they were moving.

On the start of the third day of marching, the sky was overcast with dark cloud that threatened rain. None of the soldiers were happy, and the possibility of being rained on didn't help. Not that this bothered the king. He was as cheerful as could be. After a hearty breakfast he went out to inspect the troops.

"Sir, a moment?" his hairdresser said. As always, Kervol went nowhere without his entourage. They took a minute to make sure he was suitably dashing before he left his opulent tent. "Very good, Sir."

"It won't be long now," Kervol said as he left his tent. "My beloved and I shall be together, and I will be recognized as a true King."

"Oh yes, Sir, the entire world will acknowledge your might and authority," his nail technician agreed.

Kervol smiled at the men as he made his inspection. Not all of his men looked fit for duty. Word had gotten out that using outhouses could be harmful to ones health and soldiers now avoided them like the plague, but the news had come too late. A fair number of men now had scorched armor and blackened hair, and they looked like they were on edge. Kervol naturally paid no attention to them.

"You're right," Kervol replied. "You know, I think this war may be just what I needed. After all, lots of kings fight dragons to get their wives. It's popular, yes, but people do it so often it's starting to go out of fashion. Now fighting a war to win your love, that's cutting edge!"

Kervol's makeup artists nodded. "Many kings will follow your example."

"That will be satisfying!" Kervol said. "Now that I think about it, it will also keep the goblins in line. I'm told one of the filthy little beasts got into the royal library a few days ago. The disgusting creature may have taken something, though it's hard to tell with the state it's in. The point is that we mustn't allow things like that to happen! I'm not just winning my bride; I'm cutting down the number of those wretched creatures. The rest will be more respectful."

"Your Highness," his publicist began, "that is the sign of a true leader! Thinking of the big picture, of the consequences. Sir, I am in awe of you!"

"You're too kind," Kervol said. He nodded to a foot soldier. The man looked frustrated with the situation, but Kervol had a real gift for seeing only what he wanted to see.

For example, Kervol wasn't paying any attention to the fact that his army was missing a thousand soldiers. Some men had gotten lost trying to reach the capital, others were sent in the wrong direction by defective war notices, and some men had never left their hometowns. Did any of this bother the King? Not unless he thought about it, so he didn't. He simply marched on with the three thousand men he had, completely confident of victory.

The break-in at his library also didn't worry Kervol. It should have. The goblins could have stolen books containing valuable information for all he knew, and if they could get into the royal library then it wasn't too hard to imagine them getting into his throne room or bedchamber. A more vindictive king than Will could easily have sent goblins in to kill Kervol while he slept.

"How many days until we reach the wretches?" Kervol asked.

"Uh, four, six at the most," his minstrel said. The minstrel was worried that the trolls would come after him again. He'd requested and received two bodyguards to protect him.

Kervol nodded enthusiastically as they walked by more demoralized soldiers. "Very good. That gives me time to prepare. Greta, how many speeches do I have to memorize?"

Greta the speechwriter shuffled through a stack of paper and handed them to the king in bunches. "There's the 'we are counting on our men' speech; the 'now we are upon the enemy' speech; the 'challenge to the enemy king' speech; and the 'thank you for your services' speech for when you're done."

More quietly, he asked, "And the others?"

She handed him two more bunches of paper. "I've got two versions. There's an 'unexpected complications' speech and a 'you'll rue the day' speech. I've got my own copy of all of them."

"Good, very good. I'll get started on them right away."

That's when he saw it, when Kervol saw something so wrong that it was impossible, even for someone as incredibly self-absorbed as he was, not to notice. He came to a dead halt, his jaw dropped, the speeches fell from his hands. At the front of the camp, where the army's oxen should he waiting to be hitched to their wagons, was an entirely empty patch of grass. They were gone, all of them.

"What's going on here!" he demanded. "Where are the oxen?"

A few bored soldiers looked over at him. "Nothing to get upset about, Sir."

"Nothing to get upset about?" Kervol ran into the field where the oxen had been last night. There were piles of dung and muddy hoof prints, but no sign of the animals. Wait! There was a note on the ground next to the men who were supposed to be watching the oxen. Kervol snatched it up. The handwriting was bad, almost childlike. It read:

We going out for beer. Will be back soon.

Signed, the cows.

"What madness is this?" Kervol demanded. "Where are my oxen?"

A soldier pointed to the note. "The note was there when we showed up this morning. Says it all right there, doesn't it?"

A second soldier nodded in agreement. "I know I'd want a beer at the end of a day if I was pulling a wagon."

Kervol crumpled up the paper and threw it away. "You fools, they were stolen! The goblins took them. Why wasn't anyone guarding them?"

"Guarding them?" a soldier asked. "But we're still in our own kingdom. Who would we be guarding them from?"

The second soldier added, "Goblins are just annoying little things. They couldn't have done this."

Furious, Kervol shouted, "Get my scouts! I want those animals found and returned immediately. We can't leave without them!"

Dozens of scouts arrived at the king's orders and found a wide trail leading out of the camp. From there, the trail separated into twenty smaller trails, each going in a different direction.

"Curse them all!" Kervol bellowed. "They're trying to slow us down by releasing our draft animals. It will take hours to find them. Go, bring them back!"

The scouts ran after the missing oxen. But after the last of them had left, Kervol saw a trail they hadn't taken. It was easy to follow since oxen were big and clumsy. Kervol snarled and followed the trail himself.

"Sir, no. Leave this to the soldiers," his publicist said.

Kervol whirled around to face the man. "Someone's trying to make me look like a fool. It's one of those goblins, I'm sure of it. I'll get to the bottom of this and skewer the little vermin myself!"

Kervol ran off with his entourage following him. He ran over pastures and through fields of wheat, shoving aside curious farmers. He lost the trail a couple of times, but always found it again. It finally led to a small village where all the people were chatting and smiling.

"What's going on here?" Kervol demanded.

"Hello," a farmer said cheerfully. He had an empty plate in one hand and a knife and fork in the other. "Oh, wait, you're the king. What are you doing in a place like this?"

"I followed this trail," he said. "A goblin came through here, don't deny it. Where is the filthy beast?"

The farmer shrugged. "He left after he gave us an ox."

"He what?" Kervol asked.

"He gave us an ox. It's a funny story. The little goblin was dressed in a gray uniform and had a helmet with a spike on top. He showed up early this morning leading an ox. He said he found it wandering in the Kingdom of the Goblins. Then he said what with the goblins being blamed for holding a princess, he didn't want his people to get blamed for stealing an ox. I can't blame him. Cattle rustling is serious business."

"So where is the ox?" Kervol demanded.

The farmer laughed. "We couldn't keep it. Sooner or later the owner could show up and ask for it back. Anyway, we talked it over and we figured there wouldn't be much of a reward for returning it. On the other hand, there's a lot of good meat on an ox, and for all the hard work we do, a free meal with that much meat would be, uh, would be…oh."

Kervol ground his teeth together so hard the farmer could hear them from ten feet away. The king balled his hands up into fists and his face turned bright red. He looked into the village and saw a pile of fresh bones next to a fire-pit and cooking pot. The villagers all had plates and knives and forks, but unlike the farmer's, not all those plates were empty. They were eating steaks.

Hesitantly, the farmer said, "There's some left over if you want."

A scout caught up to Kervol and dropped to one knee, so terrified of the King's response that he dared not look up. Before he could speak, a breeze blew over them, carrying the delicious smell of beef cooked to perfection.

"My King," the scout began nervously.

"They've all been eaten," Kervol said.

The scout nodded. "All of them have been, uh, accounted for except for four oxen whose trail leads to the dragon's lair."

It was going to take a lot longer than four to six days to reach the goblins.

* * * * *

"It was beautiful!" Mr. Niff reported to Will. He and the warrior goblins were back home celebrating their victory. Not much work got done that day with the goblins laughing and partying, but Will was willing to trade one day lost for the week or more Kervol would be delayed. Happier than words could describe, Mr. Niff said, "The farmers helped us, and they didn't even realize it until it was too late."

"You did good," Will told him. He was back in his throne room with Gladys monitoring Kervol's progress. Domo and the troll brothers soon joined them.

"Thanks, boss," Mr. Niff said. "I gave four of them to Barbecue the dragon like you told me. I even read that speech you gave me, saying we were sorry for screwing things up for her and hoping she'd accept payment. She liked the free food a lot. I don't think she's angry with you anymore."

Will smiled. "This is going great, but we've hurt Kervol's army before and he didn't stop coming. Can he find replacements for those animals?"

"Not quickly," Domo replied. "Oxen are expensive to buy, and the locals are getting upset with Kervol stealing everything that's not nailed down. They'll hide their animals from him or fight back if he tries to take them. It could take him weeks to replace those oxen."

"He's not trying to replace them," Gladys said. Her image disappeared from the magic mirror and was replaced with a view of Kervol's army. Goblin spies had been following the army for days and had planted plenty of scarecrows Gladys could see through. The picture showed Kervol's army on the move again. The wagons were moving, but hundreds of soldiers were pulling them in place of the oxen. The men looked tired and resentful, but they were still moving.

"Wow," Will said. "He's desperate."

"He's slow," London added. "You can crawl faster than that."

Will paced across the throne room. "We slowed him down some more. Kervol's men will be tired and angry with him when they get here. That works in our favor. Tomorrow we'll tell the guys they have another week to finish everything. Anything we can't finish by then won't help us, so they need to focus on completing only the most important jobs."

He stopped pacing and looked at his followers, his friends. "My first plan didn't work. I couldn't stop Kervol from coming. That means we're going to have to win this war. It's going to be hard. I know most of you don't think we can do it, but I need your help. I need you to put everything you've got into this or we'll lose for sure. Can I count on you?"

The goblins and trolls looked at one another. They surprised Will and themselves by smiling. London stepped forward and shook Will's hand. "We're in."

Chapter Thirteen

Will and Domo sat down next to the Mildly Magnificent Ket River. It was a sunny morning and a light fog hovered over the river's surface. Will ate his breakfast while they waited for Kervol and his army to arrive. It was fourteen days since they'd stolen all Kervol's draft animals and fed them to townspeople and Barbecue the dragon. According to goblin spies, Kervol's army was supposed to arrive today, but they'd been predicting that for days.

"Want a breadstick?" Will asked Domo.

"No thanks, I already ate." Domo peered over the river. "Five gets you ten he doesn't show today, either."

Will finished his food. "I'd take that bet if I wasn't flat broke. For that matter so are you."

Domo waved his walking stick. "Minor details. We waited all day yesterday and he never showed. I bet the twit ran out of wine and stopped the army until he gets more."

"Maybe," Will said. "Well, we finished all the preparations and we're as ready as we'll ever be. We even had time to leave some surprises for them."

Will and Domo looked behind them and smiled. The landscape looked peaceful enough. There was no activity except for a few goblins scurrying through the tall grass. The scene was deceptive. For the last ten days any goblin not busy rebuilding the city wall or digging the secret tunnel was put to work building traps. Working day and night, and giggling the whole time, goblins had covered the route Kervol's army was most likely to take with every kind of trap their twisted imaginations could come up with. The few goblins present were here only to add the finishing touches. Illustrating the danger, a grasshopper jumped onto a tripwire and was crushed flat when a dried out cow pie flew through the air and flattened it.

"Whoops," Will said. "That was fresh when it was set. Hey, guys, can we do something about that?" A few goblins scurried out of cover and reset the trap with fresh cow manure before disappearing back into the tall grass. "Thank you."

"I still say he doesn't get here today," Domo said.

"Hold that thought," Will said. "Someone's coming."

Will saw tiny figures in the distance wading way across a shallow spot in the river. They saw him and headed his way. Will squinted as the figures approached, then shook his head. "False alarm. It's just more recruits."

Thirty goblins climbed up the riverbank and gathered around Will. One of them shouted, "It's the King!"

"We heard you were going to fight an army," a goblin with a lopsided smile said. "Are you crazy?"

"Are you stupid?" another asked.

"What's the square root of fifty-seven?" a third asked.

Will pushed the closer goblins back and stood up. "The answers are maybe, not sure and I don't know. You guys came to help?"

A long-nosed goblin said, "You bet! It's not every day an army attacks. We want to be able to tell the next generation of goblins that we were at the sixth historic defeat of the goblins."

"I plan on winning," Will told them.

"Which gives the whole thing a bit more comedy value," the goblin said.

"Your confidence is overwhelming," Will replied. He snapped his fingers and Gilbert the goblin lobbyist came out of the tall grass. "Gilbert will take you to the city. Once you're there, the others will find a place for you to help out. Gilbert, try not to lead them into any traps."

Gilbert smiled. "I promise nothing." He set off with the new recruits following him closely.

Domo grabbed Will's sleeve and tugged. "You should have taken my bet."

"Hmm? Oh, he's here," Will said.

Kervol's army came over the horizon. There were a lot of people, including three thousand soldiers and another thousand camp followers brought along to cook and clean for the army. Behind them were dozens of wagons pulled by soldiers, moving at a snail's pace toward the river. The men kicked up a cloud of dust that hung over them and coated every exposed surface. In front of the army and moving much faster were knights riding majestic war horses and flying Kervol's peacock flag on their lances.

Will pointed his scepter at the knights. "You know, it just occurred to me that Kervol could have gotten here much faster if he used those horses to pull his wagons."

"Kervol, making pedigreed horses do work?" Domo asked incredulously.

"Sorry. I forgot who we were dealing with," Will admitted.

"Got that right. Your idea just reeks of common sense."

The army came up to the river where one of the bridges should have been, and wasn't. This particular bridge was the one Vial had blown up. Only ashes and bits of blackened wood remained. The army's advanced guard stopped at the river and looked at the place where the bridge once stood. As the men muttered to each other, Kervol and his entourage ran up.

"Impossible!" Kervol screamed. He stared in horror at the tiny remaining bits of bridge, then he saw Will. Will smiled and waved. Kervol drew his foil and pointed it at Will, screaming, "You did this!"

"Yeah, it's my fault. We were playing with matches and things got out of hand. Sorry."

Kervol shouted and stomped his foot. "You imbecile! Do you have any idea how much these things cost? You stole my supplies, you stole my draft animals, and now this."

"Don't forget the exploding outhouses," Domo added.

Surprised, Kervol asked, "That was you?"

Will rolled his eyes. "Who else would it be?"

Kervol shrugged. "I don't know. I thought they just blew up every so often. Never mind. This is just another offense against me."

"We're at war," Will reminded him. "I do things to hurt you and you do things to hurt me. That's the way it works."

"No it doesn't!" Kervol snapped. "We're supposed to rally our armies, meet on a patch of flat ground, then run right at each other. Whoever has the most men standing at the end of the day wins."

"Wow," Will said. "That's really stupid. I mean, I'm in charge of a nation of idiots and even they wouldn't do that."

"It's true," Domo said.

"It's *not* stupid!" Kervol bellowed. "All the books I read say that's the way it's done, and those books were written by educated men who watched lots of battles."

"Tell you what," Will said. "This is taking too much of my time and your money. I'm a reasonable man, so if you agree to turn around and go home, I'll give you back your princess. I can have her here by lunchtime."

The soldiers looked happy and talked excitedly to one another. Kervol saw the effect this was having on his men and gave Will a look of pure outrage. Will smiled back as Domo whispered, "Making an offer in front of his men that could let them all go home. You fight dirty."

Kervol's face turned bright red and he made a noise like steam pouring from a teapot. "You think you can brush this off with some meager offer? I cannot be so easily dissuaded from my goals, for my mind is like a steel trap!"

Will scratched his head. "You mean it's rusty and can give you tetanus?"

"No!" Kervol yelled.

Domo waved his hands. "You'll chew off your own foot to escape it?"

"It doesn't mean that, either!" Kervol yelled. "It means I won't let an idea go once I have seized upon it."

"So," Will began, "if you start doing something, and it's stupid and painful and expensive, you won't stop?"

"Exactly," Kervol said. "My honor has been tarnished by this insolent offer. I demand satisfaction!"

"I demand a cheese sandwich!" Will shouted back.

"A sandwich?" Kervol asked. "Why do you want that?"

Will shrugged. "Well, I figured as long as we were making demands, I'd ask for something I might actually get. Tell you what, it looks like you're going to be a while, so I'll go home. When you get there, if you get there, we'll settle this. I should warn you, I've made the land on this side of the river into a deathtrap. Bye."

Will and Domo turned and left. The goblins hiding in the grass got up and left with them. They walked away calmly with the goblins leading the way.

"Oh no you don't!" Kervol shouted. "You don't turn your back on me! Scouts, find a spot on the river shallow enough for the wagons to cross. As for the rest of you, whoever brings me Bradshaw's head gets a hundred gold coins!"

"Your head's worth a lot more than I figured," Domo said as they walked away.

"I'm tempted to turn it in myself," Will said. He heard men shout a battle cry and then a huge splash as the foot soldiers in Kervol's army ran into the river. Will didn't speed up. "I figure it will take them two minutes to swim across the river and five more to climb the bank. How far should we be by then?"

"We'll be inside the third layer of traps," Domo replied. "Calling them deathtraps was a bit extreme. At best they're humiliating."

"They don't need to know that." Will smiled and swung his scepter like a golf club. The splashing died down and he heard men curse as they tried to climb up the crumbling riverbank. When they got to the top he heard screams. "That must be a skunk trap."

"Those are hard to keep working," Domo said. "You have to keep feeding the skunks without getting sprayed."

As Will and his followers walked away, there were splashes followed by more screams. "Covered pits filled with raw sewage," Domo explained. "That's a favorite of mine."

Two minutes later there was a terrible noise as men cried out in disgust. One man yelled, “I don’t deserve this! No one does!”

“Which trap was that?” Will asked.

Domo smiled. “That’s a new design. You start with half a gallon of mayonnaise and leave it in the sun for three days. Then you load it into a small catapult and connect the trigger to a tripwire. If it works just right it hits them in the face.”

“That’s so wrong,” Will said. “How many did you guys set?”

A goblin scratched his head. “I lost count after thirty.”

The soldiers never got close to them. Exhausted, filthy and more than a little nauseous, they turned back and waited for the rest of the army to catch up with them. Will and his followers made their way back home, stopping briefly at the town where Will got his meals.

“You guys wait here,” he told them at the edge of town. “I need to pick up some food before Kervol shows up.”

Inside the town he found the locals gathered together near the inn. The town had a festive atmosphere, with streamers and banners hanging from the buildings. Everyone was cheerful and busy prettying up the town. When the people saw Will they smiled and waved.

Nervously, he approached them. “Uh, hi. Listen, there’s an army coming this way. My fault, really. I’m sorry about that, and I hope it doesn’t cause any trouble for you.”

“Trouble?” the mayor asked. “Nonsense! I was here the last time an army came to attack the goblins. Our town made more money that day than the rest of the year.”

Puzzled, Will asked, “How?”

"Vending," the mayor replied. Will looked more closely and saw banners that read 'Welcome Courageous Soldiers, Meat Pies for Sale' and 'Sturdy Boots, Reasonable Prices'. The streets were filled with stalls selling food, drinks and equipment. Some homes offered hot baths; sure to be popular with the soldiers when they arrived. The mayor shook Will's hand and said, "Have to tell you, we appreciate this opportunity. Any chance you could arrange an invasion next year?"

"I'll see what I can do," Will told him. "Uh, won't you get into trouble when the king realizes you're here and haven't paid him taxes all these years?"

The mayor smiled. "The royal mapmaker came by and we bribed him again. According to the new maps, we're on your side of the border."

Nervous for the people's wellbeing, Will said, "That's great, but I'm kind of worried anyway. Kervol has been grabbing anything that's not nailed down to feed and supply his army. His men might just take all this from you."

The mayor looked grim when he replied. "It took some doing, but the mayors in the surrounding towns made it clear to the king that if he keeps that up he's looking at a revolt. He won't risk fighting you and his own people at the same time. We'll be all right."

The locals cheered and thanked Will for bringing them so much opportunity for profit. Most of them gave him gifts. By the time he left, the townspeople weighed him down with free food, souvenirs and a T-shirt that read 'I Kicked Goblin Butt with Kervol'. The goblins laughed when he came back loaded with stuff.

"What did you do, rob the place?" Domo asked.

Will handed the gifts off to the goblins. "No. It seems war is good for the local economy. Everyone wanted to say thanks. I have to say I'm not sure what to do with most of this, especially the T-shirt."

"I wouldn't worry about that," Domo said. Will looked over and saw the goblins eating it.

"Mmm," one goblin said between mouthfuls, "all cotton."

* * * * *

When Will and the goblins got back to the Goblin City, the place was swarming with goblins finishing work on the defenses. The city wall and gatehouse looked terrible, but that was to be expected. After all, goblins had repaired them. Still, they were in better shape than before. Banners with a black spiral on a green background flew from the walls as eager goblins prepared for war. Over ten thousand goblins were present, armed with whatever weapons they could steal or their crude workshops could produce. Over all this chaos, the air crackled with energy as their collective stupidity and craziness began to warp space.

"Wow," Domo said, "I'm almost impressed."

"Almost?" Will asked as they walked to the gate.

"Almost. Will, we're doing better than I thought, but we're goblins. We're going to go down in flames like we always do. Expecting us to win is like asking fish to fly." The warp effect interrupted Domo's speech. The air rippled and smelled musty as small fish rained down. Goblins stopped working to eat the free food. Will smiled and Domo pointed a finger at him. "That's falling, not flying."

"It's going to be hard," Will conceded. "Kervol's too proud to give up, but I think his men aren't that stupid. His army still has to come through our traps and then get over the wall to reach us. Take that and everything we've already done to hurt them, and I think it won't take much more to convince them that they might not win, and attacking us isn't worth the trouble."

"I hope you're right," Domo said.

Will pointed to a goblin banner. "I'm curious. Is there some meaning behind that? Just thought I should know, since it seems to be the symbol of our kingdom."

"The guys were inspired to create it when they saw a flush toilet," Domo replied. "I try not to think about the symbolism involved."

"My fault for asking."

Ahead of them, the lab rat goblins were digging a large hole in the ground. Indignant digger goblins tried to push them aside and take over, but the lab rats weren't budging. More lab rat goblins brought their giant bomb to the hole, dragging it across the ground with ropes tied around it. The bomb's tin casing was polished to a shine and had the words 'This End Up' and an arrow pointing down. Vial oversaw the project, smiling ear to ear. He saw Will and hurried to join him.

"My Liege, our labors are complete! I present to you our greatest bomb ever, Big Bertha. Even if it doesn't work, or blows us all up, this is a stupendous day for alchemy and for goblins."

"You did good," Will told him. He looked at the hole and then at the Goblin City some distance off. "Why are you putting it so far from the city?"

Vial rubbed his hands together. "Based on the effect of the prototype we have to put it this far out. Any closer and it could bring down the city walls when it goes off. Mind you, that would also be interesting."

"How do you make it go boom?" Domo asked.

Vial reached into his lab coat and took out a push button attached to a cord. "This is the detonator. We'll bury the cord it's connected to underground so it can't be cut, then set the bomb off from a safe distance. I should add that 'safe' is a relative term in this matter. Big Bertha is five times larger than the prototype, but since alchemy is an inexact science the blast may be more or less than five times as big."

"Understood," Will said. "I'm going to set it off when Kervol's men get started marching toward us, but before they get in range of the blast. I figure it should scare them off."

Domo edged away from the bomb. "It scares me plenty without going off."

"A common reaction," Vial agreed. "Several goblins wet themselves when we dragged it by them."

"Kervol will be here soon," Will said, "a day at the most. Have it ready to go off by then."

Vial patted his bomb. "We will have it in place and operational by tonight."

Not far ahead was the entrance to the tunnel Will had ordered the goblins to dig. It was ten feet wide, the perfect size to let several goblins come out at a time. Builder goblins were camouflaging the entrance with fake trees and hollow rocks so no one would see it.

"Are we far enough from the bomb?" Will asked. "I don't want to collapse the tunnel on our guys."

"It might do that all on its own," Domo said. "Goblin tunnels aren't stable and this one was dug in a hurry."

Will studied the tunnel entrance. "It doesn't have to last for decades, just a few days."

A digger goblin stuck his head out of the tunnel. "If you wanted that you should have asked for our extended warranty: the tunnel's good for a week or your money back."

"I didn't spend any money on this," Will said.

The digger smiled. "Wise move."

Will took one final look at the defenses. The wall and gatehouse were in good shape, both tall enough that it would be hard to scale them with ladders or grappling hooks and ropes. The gate itself was made of oak beams bound with iron bands, so sturdy it had resisted all the damage that time, the elements and the goblins could throw at it. The goblins looked excited and had good morale. Despite Domo's warnings, Will felt confident they'd fight to defend their home.

Will and Domo went inside the city and stopped in the courtyard. Gladys the magic mirror and the troll brothers were waiting along with hundreds more goblins. Gladys showed Kervol's army inching along the road toward the Goblin City. Will and Domo joined the crowd.

"How's it going?" Will asked them.

"Slowly," Gladys answered. The surface of the mirror showed soldiers edging forward, testing the ground ahead of them with branches. One of them found a covered pit. As he went around it, he stepped onto a springboard that threw him into the pit he was trying to avoid. "Kervol just got his wagons across the river. He's got men clearing a path for the army, but for every trap they disarm they set off two more."

"Let me guess," Will said, "he's got the foot soldiers and archers removing the traps, not the knights."

"You got it," Gladys said. "They'll wait until all the hard work is done, then ride up and take the credit. Perish the thought one of them should get his hands dirty. That said, we do have a problem."

Will watched the mirror and saw the men disarm a snare. One of them looked straight into the mirror, then rushed forward and swung a mace. The image broke up and was replaced by Gladys's pouting face. "They're destroying every scarecrow they find. They've missed enough that I'm not totally blind, but if this keeps up I won't be able to show you anything outside the city."

"Once they get here it won't matter," Will said. "Thanks, Gladys. You've done really good."

"Everything's as ready as it's going to be," London said. "Niff's got the warrior goblins working hard. We can drop rocks on them when they get close to the wall, and lots of stuff worse than rocks. We even got ten goblin catapults up on top of the gatehouse."

"We have catapults?" Will asked in amazement.

"They're nothing special," Brooklyn said. "Half of them will break down on their own, and I doubt the rest will do much good."

"I'll take whatever I can get," Will said. He looked up at the gatehouse and saw goblins hurrying to finish assembling the catapults. They were small, about the size of a wagon, and had oddly large cups on the ends of the throwing arms. Will didn't know why those goblins wore aviator helmets with goggles, and to be honest he felt no great desire to find out. "How is it goblins can make catapults and bombs, but they can't fix the city on their own?"

"Fixing cities is boring," Domo said. "Now blowing them up, that gets your heart racing."

Will nodded. "Fair enough. It looks like everything's set. We just have to wait for Kervol to show up and start things."

* * * * *

Late that night, Will stood at the top of the gatehouse. There were lit torches around him providing some light. Next to Will were Domo, Gladys and Brooklyn. In the distance he could make out the campfires of Kervol's army. There were thousands of twinkling lights a few miles from the Goblin City.

"That's a lot of lights," Will said.

Gladys snorted. "It's an old trick. He's trying to make his army look bigger than it really is by lighting lots of campfires."

"That's Kervol for you," Domo said. "All style and no substance."

Will paced across the gatehouse roof, walking between the catapults. Outside the wall, Vial and his followers were placing Big Bertha. Once they were done they'd take down their tents and bring everything back inside the city. Will could hear faint noises from the enemy camp, crashes and thuds. Occasionally he heard the groan of heavy timbers bending under great weight.

"What's causing all that noise?" he asked.

"Not a clue," Gladys said. "They cut down all the scarecrows around their camp. The few I have left are too far away and it's too dark to use them."

Will shrugged. "We'll find out tomorrow. Brooklyn, take Gladys back down and check if Vial's ready."

"Can do, boss." Brooklyn picked up the mirror and headed for a flight of stairs leading down.

Domo edged toward Will. "Will, it's going to be ugly tomorrow. You might want to go into the tunnels with Gladys. It's safer there."

"I can't do that. If there's any chance we're going to win I need to be here directing things. The goblins are going to panic sooner or later, and I'll have to calm them down and get them to follow the plan."

Domo looked down. "It's not going to work. I like you. You're the only king we've had who didn't go nuts or try to burn the place down for insurance money. You actually got this mob of idiots to follow orders. I didn't think anyone could do that. But this is insane! We're going to go down like a card house in a hurricane."

Domo climbed up onto a catapult so he could look Will in the eyes. “It’s not your fault. You got saddled with an impossible job. Sit this one out. When it’s done we’ll need your help putting things back together.”

Will looked out at Kervol’s army. He couldn’t see much, just a sea of lights from countless fires. “I can’t walk away. At least some of this is my fault. This whole mess started when I agreed to help Barbecue. There were ways to stop Kervol early on, but I couldn’t find them or wouldn’t take them. When Kervol came here the first time I couldn’t let him kill anyone to satisfy his pride.”

“I was surprised by that,” Domo said. “Anyone else would have taken the easy way out.”

“I couldn’t,” Will said. “I suppose a leader should be ready to sacrifice some of his followers to prevent a disaster, but I couldn’t do it. I brought this mess on you guys. I owe it to you to see it through.”

Domo chuckled. “You’re risking your life over a bunch of goblins so stupid every time they count their fingers they come up with a different number. You’re nuts. You know that, don’t you?”

“If I’m nuts, I’ve got plenty of company.”

* * * * *

Will woke up late the next morning. He ate a quick breakfast and climbed up to the city wall to join the thousands of goblins waiting for Kervol’s attack. The goblins stood ready at the wall, gathered along a walkway and protected by a low parapet they could duck behind when the arrows started flying. They were eager and the air tingled and rippled as their collective stupidity began to build up.

“Anything happen yet?” he asked them.

"Nothing," a warrior goblin replied. "The noise died down an hour ago, but they haven't come toward us so far."

"You guys ready?" Will asked.

A warrior goblin saluted. "Revved up and ready to lose!"

The goblins around him cheered and waved makeshift weapons. They didn't expect to win this fight, but Will believed they could. There were four thousand goblins on the city wall and gatehouse to repel the attack, plus another four thousand waiting in the courtyard to counter a successful breach of the walls. Another two thousand goblins were ready to come out of the tunnel in front of the city. They were only armed with clubs and wooden shields, or baskets full of rocks. The goblins were also a lot smaller than the men they faced. Still, the goblins had the city's high wall for protection, and they outnumbered their attackers more than three to one. Scattered around the city were scarecrows allowing Will to quickly go wherever he was needed.

"Boss!" It was Mr. Niff, running as fast as he could toward Will. "The catapults are ready and Vial says the bomb is good to go. Those bums won't know what hit them!"

A warrior goblin looked at a bucket in his hands. "It looks like rocks to me. They should be able to figure out that much."

"It's a figure of speech," Mr. Niff explained.

"Good to hear," Will said. "I'm going to need you to run messages for me once the fighting starts. Think you can handle that?"

"Of course," Mr. Niff said proudly.

A group of goblins carried Princess Marisa Brandywine out from the tunnels and into the courtyard. She was gagged and tied up to keep her from causing trouble. Warily, Mr. Niff asked, "Why is she here?"

"If everything goes wrong and Kervol gets through the wall, I want him to find her right away," Will explained. "That way he might turn around and leave without wrecking anything else. It's a long shot, I know, but it's worth trying."

Domo and Vial gathered around Will and the troll brothers came carrying Gladys. Will smiled and did his best to look more confident than he felt. "Kervol's going to come at us any hour. Vial, you're with me. When I give the word you set off the bomb. London, join the goblins in the tunnel. When they go out I want you to lead the charge. Brooklyn, I'll need your help here if things go badly inside the city. Domo, I know exactly nothing about catapults, so I want you to go up there and direct things. Gladys, I'll need you to keep me posted if you see the soldiers doing something I don't notice. Questions?"

Mr. Niff raised a hand. "Why are guinea pigs called guinea pigs when they're little furry things? They don't look like pigs at all."

"I think it started as a marketing ploy," Vial said.

"Are there any questions about the battle?" Will clarified.

London raised a hand. "If we rough somebody up and they got nice things, and nobody's looking, can we mug them? I mean, we're already beating them up, why not go all the way?"

Will considered the question for a second. "I'm almost sure that's not allowed. And if they say 'stop hitting me, I give up', you have to stop hitting them."

Grumbling, Brooklyn asked, "Who comes up with these rules?"

London nodded. "Yeah, if you stop hitting a guy when he's down, he might get back up again."

Will rubbed his eyes. "Look, just do the best you can. If the soldiers in Kervol's army want to surrender or run away, then let them. Everybody go to your places."

As London and Domo were leaving, a goblin called, "Look!"

All eyes turned south, where Kervol's army finally came into sight. They were so far away the men looked like ants, but even at this distance their siege weapons were impressive. In front of the army was a siege tower, eighty feet tall and thirty feet across. Behind it and to the left was a single catapult, far bigger than the goblin catapults. The army moved toward them slowly as drummers pounded out a beat.

"Now we know what that noise was last night," Will said.

"Where did he get all that stuff from?" Mr. Niff demanded.

Gladys disappeared from the surface of the magic mirror as she looked through the remaining scarecrows outside the city. She picked one and zoomed in on Kervol's camp. The camp followers were sleeping on the ground and there wasn't a single wagon in sight. Gladys focused on woodworking tools left on the ground and piles of fresh sawdust. "I don't believe it," she said. "Those big timbers he brought with him must have been the frame for the tower and catapult. He got the rest of the wood by taking apart his wagons."

"That's…that's almost intelligent," Will said. "Kervol actually did something intelligent."

"Will wonders never cease?" Mr. Niff asked.

While Kervol's army inched toward the Goblin City, his knights rode up wearing shining armor and flying peacock flags from their lances. They paraded in front of the city, shouting taunts at the goblins.

"Cowards!" a knight shouted. "Come down from those walls and face us fairly!"

Will pointed at the knight and asked, "Brooklyn, can you do something about him?"

Brooklyn tore a brick off the wall and threw it. The knight was still shouting abuse at the goblins when the brick hit him in the head. His helmet rang like a bell and he fell to the ground. The remaining knights backed away while foot soldiers rushed up and carried off the fallen knight. Goblins on the wall jeered at them. The knight's horse took the opportunity to trot off and graze on a patch of buttercups.

"Thanks," Will said.

Brooklyn smiled. "Anytime."

The army stopped a quarter mile in front of the city. The drums stopped and the men stood at attention. The siege tower creaked as it halted. King Kervol walked out from the middle of his army, his entourage following at his heels.

"*Cur!*" Kervol shouted theatrically. "*Villain most foul! Though you think yourself safe behind these walls, surrounded by your fetid horde, I shall defeat you. I shall bring down these crumbling walls and…*uh, uh, line!" Someone in his entourage whispered to him. "*And I shall free my beloved from your clutches. Your few odiferous followers stand no chance against my mighty army.*"

"He can count, right?" Will asked. "We've got more guys just on the walls than he does down there."

"The walls aren't crumbling anymore, either," Mr. Niff added.

"Oh please," Gladys said. "You think he's going to change a speech just because it doesn't make sense?"

Will nodded. "I guess that's expecting too much."

Kervol continued to bluster. "*I have faced great peril, traversed many a mile, crossing forests deep and rivers wide, never once straying from my chosen path. I have overcome all these hardships for my radiant bride, Marisa Brandywine. (We're sure that's her name? Good) Villain! Evildoer! Behold the grandeur of my loyal followers and despair, for your fate is sealed.*"

Will looked at Gladys and Mr. Niff and asked, "There's really no chance of talking this over or reasoning with him, is there?"

"You're even asking us that?" Gladys asked in disbelief.

"What can I say, I'm an optimist," Will told her.

"I'm a realist," Gladys said.

Mr. Niff smiled. "I'm a cubist."

Will stood up and studied the opposing army. Kervol was finely dressed as always, and looked clean and well rested. His army looked tired, dirty and more than a little scared. Soldiers whispered to one another and pointed at the city wall lined with goblins. They'd been told this would be an easy victory and that they wouldn't be in danger. Now, after weeks of marching, pulling wagons and setting off hundreds of traps, they had a real fight on their hands.

Will raised his scepter and shot a blast of fire to get everyone's attention. *FOOM!* Satisfied that all eyes were on him, he shouted, "Kervol, you're as dumb as a mule and twice as stubborn! Your parents were closely, and your mother wears army boots!"

Angry, Kervol shouted, "It's not her fault! She can't find anything else in her size."

Will pointed his scepter at Kervol and yelled, "You sent me your lady in a crate and blame me for having her! I don't want her. She's loud, annoying and stuck up. That you're going to marry her shows everyone what an idiot you are.

You know what? When this is done and I drive off what's left of your army, I'll send her with you as punishment!"

Kervol's face turned red, and he fumed and shook as if he was going to explode. He finally drew his foil and screamed, "Attack!"

Chapter Fourteen

The battle began with Kervol's catapult firing a boulder a foot across and weighing a hundred pounds. The boulder overshot the city wall and came crashing down on a dilapidated house inside the city, smashing through the roof. The catapult crew hurried to reload their weapon and the siege tower began to roll toward the wall. The rest of the army stayed well back, cheering as the siege weapons did their job for them.

"Did the boulder do any damage?" Will asked.

Mr. Niff looked over the Goblin City, already ruined by years of neglect and goblin-induced damage. "You know, I'm not sure."

The siege tower rolled closer. By Will's reckoning, the tower was approaching the site of Vial's bomb. If he set off the bomb, he could disable the tower long before it reached the city. "Vial, I think it's time to set off Big Bertha."

"With pleasure, My Liege," Vial said eagerly. He smiled and held up the detonator. A horde of lab rat goblins looked on in gleeful anticipation as Vial pressed the button.

Nothing happened.

"Uh, Vial, I needed something to go boom," Will said.

Vial pressed the button again. He scratched his head and looked at his followers. "Did any of you chew on the cord?"

The catapult's arm was pulled back into position and the crew loaded another boulder. They fired again. This shot fell short, plowing into the ground in front of the city. Goblins on the wall jeered and shouted, "Air ball!"

Will watched as the siege tower came closer still. The rest of Kervol's army began to form up into ranks behind the tower. Foot soldiers were in front, followed closely by archers. Knights rode back and forth in front of the army, ready to drive off surprise attacks. The catapult's arm was pulled back down again and reloaded.

"Vial," Will said, "I don't want to pressure you, but this would be a very bad time to screw up."

Vial took the detonator apart and studied the pieces. "This looked so easy in the alchemy books. Let's see, connect the doodad to the thingamajig. Screw the thingy to the other thingy."

"I need an explosion," Will said urgently.

The catapult fired again. *Wham!* The crew finally got the distance right, and the boulder hit the wall. The wall cracked under the impact and bent backwards ever so slightly. Bricks shook loose and the goblins on the wall scurried away. Soldiers cheered and the siege tower rolled closer. The tower was well away from the bomb, rolling close to the tunnel exit.

Vial put the detonator back together and tried it again. Big Bertha still didn't go off. "I find this most curious. There weren't any parts left over when we finished. Oh, hold on. I forgot that it's equipped with a delayed detonator so everyone has time to leave the blast radius."

Will grabbed Vial's shoulder and demanded, "When is it going to go off?"

Wham! The catapult fired again and struck mere inches from the first hit, but to devastatingly greater effect. The boulder punched a hole right through the city wall and crushed a building inside the city. Goblins fled the section of wall under attack.

Vial raised one eyebrow and mumbled some numbers. "It should have gone off about half a minute ago."

KRACKA-BOOM!

The explosion rocked the entire city and left behind a pit fifty feet deep and a hundred feet across. A cloud of dirt rose up from the blast and rained down on both sides. The city wall swayed dangerously as the shock wave from the blast buffeted it, and everyone on the wall dropped to their knees and covered their heads. Kervol's men were far enough back to avoid the worst of the blast, but they were still thrown to the ground. The siege tower wasn't so lucky and fell on its side, cracking open like an egg.

Will, Brooklyn and the goblins got back up again. Vial smiled and the lab rats shook his hand. Vial cleaned dust off his glasses and said, "It wasn't magic, but still very nice! The timer does need some work."

"Look at that," Brooklyn said in awe. "What a beautiful mess!"

Will smiled. "The siege tower is out of the way. That just leaves—"

Wham! Another boulder struck the city wall a few feet from where the other two had hit. The boulder broke off a section of the wall five feet across and caused the rest to sag. Bricks fell like raindrops in a storm.

"That just leaves the catapult," Will finished. "He's taking the wall apart with that thing."

Kervol's army got to their feet. Men crawled away from the wreckage of the siege tower, more confused than hurt. The soldiers backed away from the city and stared in horror at the pit in front of them. They were spooked, and it showed. Kervol shouted at his men and pointed at the crumbling section of the city wall, trying to convince them they could still win. Illustrating his point, the catapult fired again and knocked another hole in the city wall. Foot soldiers came forward and headed to the damaged section of the wall, with the archers following closely and prepared to fire.

"They're close enough to the tunnel exit," Will said. "Niff, go tell London to start the attack."

Mr. Niff looked at the approaching army. He gulped nervously and said, "Uh, boss, the siege tower landed on top of the tunnel exit."

* * * * *

London stood at the tunnel exit, hastily put together and camouflaged to look like rocks and stunted trees. The disguise was made of flimsy bits of wood, not meant to last, but it looked convincing. Behind London was a mixed bag of two thousand warrior and digger goblins lined up in the tunnel. They were ready to go out and fight.

Maybe a little too ready. The goblins fairly bounced in their eagerness to launch the attack. London could barely keep them back.

"Come on, open the door," a goblin whined.

"We go out when we're ordered to," London told the goblins.

"How long will that take?" a bushy-tailed goblin asked.

"Can't we go now?" begged another.

London grabbed the nearest goblin and lifted him up until they saw eye to eye. "We leave when the boss says so, and not a second sooner."

The tunnel shook violently and dust rained down on them. Most of the goblins fell to the ground. The shaking was followed by a crash as the camouflaged exit buckled inwards and was crushed shut.

London dropped the goblin he'd been threatening and tried to open the door. It was jammed. He ripped it to pieces and began to panic. If he got the signal to go and the door was broken, he'd be late for the battle! London tore off the last bits of the door and was faced by a wooden wall made of thick oak planks. Near one edge of it was a wheel three feet across. He recognized it as the edge of the siege tower. He pounded on it desperately, but the oak planks resisted all his blows. He wasn't just going to be late. He was going to miss the battle entirely.

"No!" he roared. "I'm not letting down my brother and the King! We got to break through this!"

London pounded away at the barrier with his fists. Goblins gathered around him and attacked it with hammers and picks. Slowly they began to hack bits out of the oak boards.

* * * * *

Back on the surface, the situation was desperate. Kervol's catapult fired again and again, with most of the shots hitting their target. The wall on the left side of the gatehouse was crumbling apart with no less than five holes broken through it. The entire section of wall looked ready to fall.

Kervol's army gathered near the breach. Archers fired at the goblins still on the wall, forcing them to keep their heads down and their shields up. They were safe, but they couldn't do much to fight back. Hordes of foot soldiers prepared to enter the city once the wall fell, while knights patrolled the edge of the army.

"Gladys, how bad does the damage look?" Will asked the magic mirror.

Gladys showed the damaged section of the wall. There were huge holes and cracks running between them. The wall swayed back and forth even when it wasn't being hit.

"Not good," Gladys said. "One more hit like that will bring it down."

"Blast it!" Will shouted. "They're taking us apart and there's nothing we can do about it. We have to stop that catapult!"

"We still have our catapults," Mr. Niff pointed out.

Will shook his head. "It won't help. They're too small. They can't be strong enough to shoot that far."

"Not true," Mr. Niff said. "We're in range. We just have to keep their archers busy while we fire."

Will stared at Mr. Niff, not able to follow the reasoning. "Why would we need to keep their archers…never mind! If we're in range then tell Domo to fire. I'll deal with the archers."

Mr. Niff ran to the stairs leading to the top of the gatehouse. *Wham!* Another boulder crashed into the wall and brought down a rain of bricks. Cursing under his breath, Will stood up and looked around.

The archers were firing clouds of arrows, peppering the top of the wall with shots. They'd kill any target standing in the open, but with the goblins hiding behind shields and the parapet at the top of the wall, there was nothing to hit. What they were doing was forcing the goblins to keep their heads down. They couldn't fight back without being turned into pincushions by the arrow storm.

Will grabbed his fire scepter and aimed it over the heads of the archers. "You don't do small jobs well," he told it. "Well this time I need you to pull out all the stops. I need everything you have in front of the wall."

FOOM! The scepter belched out a billowing cloud of fire, a white-hot burst of flames a hundred feet across. Arrows in mid flight were swallowed up by the fire and burnt to ashes. The flames died away, leaving the goblins cheering and the archers shocked.

Thump! Thump! Will looked up at the gatehouse and saw the goblin catapults firing. All ten fired, but something was wrong. They weren't firing rocks.

"What the—" Will said as he saw what looked like small hang gliders soar off toward Kervol's catapult.

Gladys smirked. "I guess no one told you. Human catapults fire rocks. Goblin catapults fire goblins."

Sure enough, piloting the hang gliders were goblins strapped to the glider's frame, each one wearing a leather aviator's helmet, complete with goggles and scarf. They screamed in delight and glided gracefully through the air. Before the archers could recognize the threat and fire, the flying goblins swooped down on Kervol's catapult. They crashed their hang gliders into the catapult's operators and knocked them down. Quickly cutting themselves free of the straps holding them in place, the goblins raced to the catapult. Kervol's catapult was made of thick oak beams, much too tough for them to damage, but many of those beams were bound together with rope. The goblins hacked through the ropes with sharp knives until the catapult fell apart.

Goblins on the wall cheered as their fellows ran for safety. The knights rode after the goblins on the ground, shouting oaths and battle cries. The ten goblins ran to the maze and fled inside with the knights in hot pursuit.

"That was great," Will said as Mr. Niff returned. "He's lost his siege tower and the catapult. There's no way he can get through the wall now."

There was an ominous creak, followed by a cracking sound. The wall to the left of the gatehouse groaned and buckled outwards. It simply wasn't built to take the kind of damage a catapult could dish out. The gaps widened as bricks fell away. Then, with deceptive slowness, a section of the wall fifty feet across fell to the ground.

Will ran to the stairs and headed down to the courtyard. Over the panicked cries of goblins, he shouted, “Brooklyn, Niff, come on! We’ve got to hold them outside the city. If they get through, we’re done for!”

* * * * *

On top of the gatehouse, Domo and the catapult crews watched the wall come down. Foot soldiers climbed over the wreckage and into the city. A few goblins tried to stop them and were thrown aside. More goblins came, and they were forced back as well. The goblins outnumbered the soldiers, but a human soldier was worth ten to twenty goblins. Slowly, inexorably, the men forced back the defenders. Every foot of space they won made room for more men to come inside.

“Do something!” Domo shouted at the other goblins.

“We’re out of goblins to fire,” a catapult operator said. “Well, goblins with hang gliders, anyway.”

“But they’re getting through!”

The operator shrugged. “Can’t be helped.”

Domo looked around. There were buckets filled with rocks all around them. Goblins on the wall were supposed to throw rocks at the soldiers, but they were too busy hiding from the rain of arrows to throw anything. High up on the gatehouse, the catapult crews were safe from enemy fire. Domo grabbed a bucket and dumped it in a goblin catapult’s waiting basket.

“Turn half the catapult so we can fire at the soldiers inside the wall and the other half to fire at the archers,” he ordered them.

“Firing rocks?” the operator asked. “That’s not the way we do this. And who do you think you are giving me orders?”

Domo grabbed the operator and pushed him against the nearest catapult. "I'm the goblin who's going to shoot you out of this thing, minus a glider, if you don't do what I tell you to do. I refuse to lose to that pampered, self-indulgent excuse for a human. We are not going to lose after all this work!"

The other goblins looked at Domo in surprise. Domo was smaller than any of them, and they outnumbered him ten to one. But he had a crazed look in his eyes that suggested ten against one wasn't going to be enough if this turned ugly. Hesitantly, one of them said, "Okay, we'll try it."

* * * * *

Will ran into the courtyard with Mr. Niff and Brooklyn close behind. There were already a hundred men inside the wall and more coming through every minute. Goblins threw themselves at the soldiers and were beaten back every time. Some of the goblins mobbed lone soldiers or pelted them with rocks, but it wasn't enough. The goblins began to panic. They backed away from the fight and looked for hiding places, while others just ran off.

"Come on, we have to push them back," Will said. He waded into the fight with Brooklyn at his side. They knocked a few men back and Will used his scepter to turn a foot soldier's mace into molten iron. He could have used the scepter's tremendous power directly on the soldiers, but that wasn't the kind of person he was. Brooklyn picked up a foot soldier and threw him at another soldier. Mr. Niff jumped into the fight and cut an archer's bowstring.

The rank and file goblins watched in shock as Will ran into the fight. When they saw him beat back two attackers, they stopped their retreat. As Brooklyn tossed men aside and Mr. Niff tripped an archer, they began to cheer. The goblins ran toward the enemy and plowed into them.

More goblins came off the wall to help force back the soldiers, but still the men moved further into the city. The soldiers' numbers swelled to two hundred, then three hundred. When their numbers topped four hundred, King Kervol Ket himself came through the ruined wall.

"Keep moving!" Kervol shouted. "We've got them on the run!"

Thump! Thump! The catapults on top of the gatehouse fired again, but this time rocks the size of baseballs came down on the soldiers. The men cursed and raised their shields to ward off the rocks, but doing that left them open to attack by the goblins on the ground. *Thump!* More rocks came down, followed by buckets of mud, cabbages so moldy they had become liquid, and lots of spiders that looked poisonous but weren't. The soldiers were backed up against the ruined wall, preventing any more men from coming in.

Vial waddled up alongside Will and tossed a fizzing bottle into the closely packed soldiers. The explosion sent men sprawling on the ground. He tossed two more bombs, forcing Kervol's men back even further until he searched the pockets of his lab coat and came out with nothing. He smiled sheepishly and backed away. "Who would have thought I could run out of explosives? So sorry, My Liege."

The goblin catapults ran out of things to throw. Once they fell silent, Kervol and his men charged into the growing crowd of goblins. Will, Brooklyn and Mr. Niff met the charge, backed up by thousands of goblins.

It was a mess. Goblins piled onto Kervol's soldiers, with a dozen goblins attacking each man. They climbed over the soldiers, kicking, punching, stealing and occasionally biting. The first rank of soldiers was pulled to the ground and disarmed. The goblins' overwhelming numbers dragged down more men, but a stream of fresh foot soldiers and archers came into the city. Archers couldn't fire with the men and goblins packed together in the confused brawl. Doing so would hit their fellow soldiers. With few options left, they were forced to attack with their fists.

Will fought as hard as he could, forcing the soldiers back and destroying their weapons with his scepter's fire. When he saw foot soldiers breaking through the crowd of goblins, he fell backward and warped to the nearest scarecrow. *Whoosh!* He tackled one soldier, tripped a second, and used his scepter to force the rest back with blasts of fire. He traded places with another scarecrow to shore up another mob of goblins, then did it a third time. Enemy soldiers began cutting down his scarecrows until he had none left in the area. Will kept fighting.

* * * * *

London and the goblins hammered away at the fallen siege tower blocking the tunnel exit. The oak planks bent and splintered under their attack until they finally broke through. London led the goblins out of the tunnel and into the siege tower. The tower had been broken open by Big Bertha's explosion, so they had their choice of exits. London picked the biggest opening and ran into the daylight.

When London stepped out of the ruined siege tower, he saw his worst fears come true. The city wall was breached and men were pouring in. Thousands more foot soldiers and archers waited for their chance to get inside and join the fight. Goblin catapults on top of the gatehouse rained down fist-sized rocks on the waiting men, but they ran out of ammunition all too soon. The only bright spots he could find were that the enemy catapult was destroyed and Kervol's knights were nowhere to be seen.

Goblins poured out of the wrecked siege tower and gathered around London. The troll pointed at the men waiting outside the hole in the city wall. As loud as he could, he shouted, "Get 'em, boys!"

With London in front, the goblin army hit Kervol's army from behind. Most of the men still outside the wall were archers, dangerous at a great distance, but next to helpless close up. By the time the men realized they were under attack, goblins were all over them, cutting bow strings, stealing arrows and piling onto individual soldiers. Digger goblins hit men in the feet with mallets and kicked them in the shins.

Standing out above this chaos was London. He grabbed men and tossed them around like rag dolls, usually sending his human missiles into other soldiers. When a few foot soldiers tried to mob him, London grabbed one of them by the heels and used him as a club to beat the others senseless. Wherever the soldiers gathered together to mount an organized resistance, London waded through them and battered them to the ground.

A foot soldier ran away from him, followed by a second. It took London a few seconds to realize that a lot of soldiers were trying to escape but couldn't with the enraged troll and horde of goblins around them. Whenever they found an opening, frightened human soldiers ran for their lives, throwing aside their weapons and armor so they could run faster.

"Chase them out!" London shouted. "Run them all off!"

* * * * *

Inside the city the fight raged on. Foot soldiers and archers gradually forced the goblins back. King Kervol stood in the middle of his men, shouting slogans and encouragement no one could hear over the clamor of battle. Opposite him, Will led the goblins and managed to disarm a foot soldier and trip another man. Everyone in the brawl was too busy to notice that no more of Kervol's men were coming into the city.

Kervol scanned the chaotic battle until he spotted Will and forced his way through the combatants until he reached his nemesis. With a triumphant shout, Kervol attacked Will and forced him back.

Will parried the wire-thin sword with his scepter. "I'm surprised you'd get your hands dirty fighting me. Isn't that what your men are for?"

Kervol pressed his attack, forcing Will back even further. "This is how it's supposed to be done! Enemy leaders fighting man to man, hero versus villain. It's just like in the books!"

Kervol kept up his attacks and almost hit Will twice. He swung with wild abandon and ended up cutting one of his archer's bowstrings while the man was trying to shoot. All the while Kervol kept talking. "You made me look like a fool in front of the other rulers. You, a commoner, tried to stand against me. That's right, I found out about you from a lawyer I hired. You're just a bumpkin who got tricked into the job!"

"Yeah, and this bumpkin is winning," Will said. He blocked another attack and punched Kervol in the nose. "All your money and followers, and you're still losing. You lost your supplies, your siege tower, your catapult and your oxen, and you're losing the battle."

"I'm not losing!" Kervol shouted. "Kings don't lose to the likes of you!"

Will tried to use his scepter to melt Kervol's foil again, but this time the scepter only puffed out a wisp of smoke.

"Magic weapons need time to recharge after heavy use," Kervol sneered. The scepter rattled angrily, but could only generate another puff of smoke. Kervol lashed out again, forcing Will to dive to the ground. In the distance, Will heard Brooklyn and Mr. Niff shouting to him, trying to fight their way to his side. They were too far away to reach him in time. Kervol stood over Will and raised his foil high into the air, a dramatic and totally pointless gesture.

"I do believe you're out of scarecrows to escape with," Kervol declared. His entourage gathered behind him, offering encouragement and getting in the soldiers' way. "Finally, after all the cost, the wasted time, the humiliation, I win. Any last words? Try to make them memorable. My speechwriter is listening."

Will felt a tingling sensation as the air took on a musty smell. He smiled and watched as the air rippled and twisted around him. Fabric softener sheets and wads of lint fluttered to the ground as space began to warp. The goblins were focusing all their attention on the invading soldiers, and like earlier when they were fighting the four knights, they focused the space warp on their enemies even if they didn't realize it. But this time there weren't scores of goblins present but thousands of them, and their combined stupidity and craziness was that much greater.

"Last words?" Will asked. "Sure. Try to roll when you hit the ground."

Space warped around three hundred of Kervol's men, and they were thrown out through the breach in the wall, screaming as they flew through the air. When they got up they discovered that the rest of their army was on the run, and there were two thousand goblins and one very angry troll waiting for them. They ran for their lives.

Inside the city, Kervol was left with his entourage and a hundred men who'd already been disarmed and beaten up. Kervol looked around in horror as thousands of goblins surrounded him. Brooklyn helped Will up.

"Thank you, Brooklyn. I'd appreciate it if you could get princess Brandywine." The troll nodded and walked off. Will looked at Kervol and smiled. "Is your speechwriter listening? Good. You're leaving, Kervol. You're taking your fiancée and you're going to keep her. I'm sure you two will make each other miserable, and I really don't care. Most of your army is already gone. You're going to take the rest of it with you, and none of you are ever coming back."

Brooklyn came back with Brandywine, still tied up. Will dusted himself off and continued talking. "I don't care what you tell your people and other kings when you get home. You've got the girl, so I guess you can say you won. But so help me, if you send her to me again, or if you come back with your army, I will make it my life's mission to ruin you. I will leave your kingdom a smoking ruin that makes this place look like a vacation spot. Are we perfectly clear on this?"

Kervol nodded, too stunned and scared to speak.

"That's good," Will said. "Now if you'll excuse me, there's something I have to do."

Will took Kervol's foil and swung it against the city wall, bending the thin sword into a U-shape. Will handed the foil back to Kervol and said, "Brooklyn, get this guy and his lady out of here."

Smiling, Brooklyn grabbed Princess Brandywine and Kervol, and lifted them into the air before throwing them out of the city. The goblins cheered while Kervol's entourage and soldiers fled. While his entourage untied Brandywine, Kervol got up and addressed his fleeing men.

"*Soldiers who owed military service to the throne, you have failed in your patriotic duty. Oh how future generations shall shudder as they recall this infamous day!*"

Will rubbed his eyes and said, "For the love of God, somebody shut him up."

Goblins grabbed loose rocks as Kervol went on talking. "*This shall forever be remembered as a black day when the men of Ket failed to*—ouch! Who threw that? Come on, owe up or I'll—ouch!"

Kervol ran from the rock-throwing goblins, his entourage following him. Brandywine finished untying herself and ran after them, calling, “My King, beloved, it’s not my fault!”

London and the goblins with him came back to the city. “Is everybody okay?” the troll asked.

“We’re good,” Will said. “A little bruised, but okay.”

“Okay? I got to throw around a king!” Brooklyn said cheerfully. “Wait until I tell mom about this.”

The goblins gathered around Will and looked at Kervol and his fleeing army. Confused, one of them asked, “Where are they going?”

“They’re running away,” Will said.

“Are they going to regroup or something?” another goblin asked. “You know, come back later with more guys, or do a night attack?”

Will shook his head. “No, they’re gone for good. We won.”

“That can’t be right,” a goblin said. “It’s a trick.”

Will walked around the city, inspecting the damage. “Nope, he’s gone and he’s not coming back. It’s going to take a while to fix all this mess. One of the houses lost its roof.”

“No, it was like that before,” Mr. Niff told him.

The goblins hurried after Will. One of them grabbed his hand and asked, “Seriously, boss, what’s going on? We don’t win fights. It doesn’t work that way.”

Will looked at his followers. “We can win and it does work that way. You guys did it. You chased off an army.”

“We won?” a goblin asked dubiously. “Goblins, win?” He looked dumbfounded at first, but then a smile crept across his face. “We won.”

The assembled goblins cheered. Some of them ran into their houses and came out with fiddles and drums. They began to play and dance. Will almost got away before a crowd of goblins grabbed him and lifted him up. He protested, but nobody heard him over the noise. Overhead the air began to ripple and shimmer. The goblins began to chant; a few at first but it spread until they were all doing it.

"Will-i-am, Will-i-am, Will-i-am!"

Chapter Fifteen

Will woke up the following morning on top of the pile of rags he used in place of a bed. He'd been up late last night with the partying goblins, and it had taken hours to get away from the celebration. Tired and still wearing yesterday's clothes, he stumbled out of his bedroom and worked his way through the tunnels on his way to the surface.

"Breakfast," he said. "Finished up all the food, need to get something to eat."

He followed a tunnel as it made a sharp turn, bumping into the wall as he did. He began counting off fingers as he listed things he had to do that day. "Let's see, try to get the builders to fix the hole in the city wall. Maybe I can get them to patch up the buildings in the city afterwards. I need to ask the diggers to fill in the bomb crater in front of the city. I wonder if the guys like it better that way?"

He leaned against a tunnel wall and yawned. "Scarecrows, we need more of those, don't we? Yeah, we lost a bunch of them."

"Talking to yourself?" Domo asked. The little goblin walked up to Will and smirked. "I suppose it's the only intelligent conversation you'll get around here."

"Hi, Domo," he said. "Is the party over?"

"For now. Your followers are still pretty giddy, so it might start up again."

"Good for them. It might keep them out of my hair for a while." Will walked through the tunnels with Domo following him. "Is anything going on I should know about, or are the goblins still asleep?"

"There are a few things happening, but nothing serious," Domo replied. "The boys are taking the siege tower apart, or what's left of it. The builders say they've never worked with such high-quality wood. They're also salvaging wood from the catapult."

"That solves the problem of cleaning up that mess. What about all the weapons and armor we got yesterday?"

Domo smiled. "It was a good haul, wasn't it? Warrior goblins took everything small enough for them to use, so they'll be better armed than ever. Ask me later if that's a good thing or not. They're melting down armor and weapons too big for them to make new stuff."

"That's another part of the cleanup done," Will said. "Uh, Domo, I saw a bunch of knights ride into the maze during the battle. What happened to them?"

Domo shrugged. "Good question. The goblins they were chasing came out, but I haven't seen any of the knights."

Will rubbed his forehead. "We'll have to send someone in to lead them out. Once they're home maybe we can get the goblins working on the maze again to keep them busy."

Will spotted a few worried-looking goblins running down a tunnel. Puzzled, he asked Domo, "What's wrong?"

More concerned goblins hurried by before Domo could answer. "It's nothing that's going to blow up in our faces…I think."

"That doesn't fill me with confidence."

More goblins hurried by. Domo nodded and said, "I suppose not. Come on, you might as well see what the fuss is about."

Will and Domo followed the stream of goblins through the network of tunnels until they came to a large chamber. The room was empty save for a growing crowd of goblins surrounding a large stone block. The block was polished until it shined on one side and left rough on the others. Concerned goblins stood by while digger goblins prepared to work on the block with chisels and mallets.

"What's this?" Will asked Domo.

"With all the craziness going on around here I never got a chance to show you this. It's the Monument of Kings. We record the names and monikers of all our kings on this rock along with how long it took them to escape their contracts. This way when creditors come looking for a particular king we can show them that they're long gone."

Puzzled, Will asked, "So why is there a crowd here?"

"The guys decided it's time to put your name on the block," Domo said. "They came up with your official nickname last night."

"Are you sure about this?" a warrior goblin asked the diggers by the block.

"He earned it," a digger replied.

Will slipped through the goblins and studied the names on the monument. He recognized a few kings that the goblins had mentioned since his arrival, but there were a lot of others he'd never heard of, and every one of them had truly bizarre nicknames. "King Trevor the Loony, King Eliot the Other Loony, King Roland of the Missing Pants. How did you come up with these names?"

"They earned them," Domo said. "There's actually a funny story behind the last one. You see, one day—"

"I'd just as soon not know," Will told him. He saw diggers go to work chiseling a new line to the name of kings. It only took them a minute, and they stepped back for all to see what they'd done. Will leaned in closer and read his title aloud. "King Will the War Winner."

"That's not even a little insulting," a builder goblin protested. "We make fun of all our kings. It's a tradition!"

"It's earned!" a digger said fiercely. "Anybody think otherwise after yesterday?"

The goblins looked to one another before looking at Will. A reluctant warrior dressed in rags said, "We did…*win*. It feels wrong saying that."

A goblin tugged on Will's sleeve and asked, "Does this mean we have to keep winning? That sounds like a lot of work."

Will patted the goblin on the head and smiled. "You don't *have* to win, but you do have to try."

The goblins still seemed disquieted until a digger said, "Look, if he does something really stupid later on we can carve off his moniker and put on a new one."

Greatly cheered by this, a lab rat goblin asked Will, "Are you planning something embarrassingly stupid? If you are, we can help."

Will headed for the surface, but before he could leave he heard a goblin say, "He won."

"He won big," another said.

"He made it so *we* won, too," a third said. The goblins stared at the monument, momentarily awed. Some of them followed Will as he walked through the tunnels. There was a look of pride on their faces, which made Will happy.

The goblins deserved to be proud. They'd stood up against a bully and held their ground no matter what people said or thought, a first in their history. That confidence would help them to stand up again when they needed to. Maybe their victory wouldn't matter much outside the Kingdom of the Goblins, but here it made all the difference.

"Boss!" Mr. Niff yelled as he ran up to Will. "Hey, boss, the guys are wondering if it's too late for us to surrender."

"Niff, we won!"

"Yeah, and the guys are still bothered by that. I mean, losing is a fine goblin tradition. If we asked nicely, do you think Kervol would come back so we can do it right?"

Will frowned. "He'd think it's a trap. Niff, we won. Everybody did what they were supposed to do and we beat them. You're just going to have to accept it."

"That's going to take some getting used to," Mr. Niff said.

"Take your time." Will came out of the tunnels and into the courtyard of the Goblin City. The place was a mess and crowded with goblins still sleeping off last night's party. There was a lot of junk left over from the fight, loose bricks and rubble from the wall, broken bows and arrows snapped in half, all mingled in with piles of trash that had always been in the city. "We're going to have to clean this mess up, too. This is going to be a lot of work."

"You still have your king contract to work on," Domo reminded him.

Will looked down at the despicable contract, rolled up and tucked behind his belt. "Yeah, I forgot about that. Is there some way I can get people to help me with that?"

"That depends," Domo said. "Do you have money to pay them?"

Will frowned. "Not unless Kervol left behind any big bags of gold. Too much to ask for?"

Mr. Niff smiled. "He left behind bags of roses, candy, fancy clothes, bottles of wine and some other junk. We already ate most of it."

"No money, so I'm doing this on my own," Will said. "Okay, we get as many goblins as we can to fix the place up. That way they'll be too busy to bother me and I'll have some free time to work on my contract. Niff, see about replacing the scarecrows. Somebody get London and Brooklyn and have them find those knights in the maze."

"I'm on it," Mr. Niff said as he ran off.

"You've got a good day's work lined up," Domo said. "You're not doing too bad."

Will pointed a finger at Domo. "Don't get used to it. Once I have these guys out of my hair for a few hours I'm going to find a loophole in my contract. After that I'm out of here."

"Of course," Domo said with a smile.

"I'm serious! It can't be too hard. Forty other guys did it, right?"

"Forty-seven," Domo corrected him. "Of course each time a king found a new way out of his contract, the lawyers closed that loophole and made the next contract even harder to escape."

Will frowned. "What's the longest you've had a king?"

"Two years, eight months, fifteen days, seven hours, forty-two minutes and eight seconds."

"I'll be out of here a lot faster than that!" Will declared. "Give me a week to read my contract without people trying to kill me and—"

"Hey, boss." It was London and Brooklyn. The trolls were smiling, and London pointed at the city gate. "Good thing I found you. There's a minotaur outside. He wants to know if we're hiring."

"Hiring for what?" Will asked.

"For the maze," Brooklyn said. "We didn't have a minotaur before now since the maze was falling apart, but word got out you're fixing the place up and adding onto it. He says he'd like to interview for a position as 'monster in the maze'. He's got a good-looking resume."

"It's the King!" cried a squeaky voice. Will saw Mr. Niff leading a mob of goblins through the hole in the city wall. Will's brow furrowed. He didn't recognize these goblins from yesterday's battle.

"More followers, boss," Mr. Niff explained cheerfully.

One of the goblins tugged on his sleeve and asked, "We heard you won a war. Is that right?"

"Uh, yeah, we did," Will said as the goblins surrounded him.

"Astounding," another recruit said. "This has never happened before. Oh, this is stupendous! Goblins the world over will hear of this."

"Lovely," Will said in a deadpan voice.

A recruit smiled. "Once they learn of your accomplishments, they'll come by the thousands every month."

"Thousands?" Will asked. He didn't try to hide his despair. "Oh boy."

"This is exciting," another new goblin said. "What should we do now that we're here?"

"Uh, well," Will said as he wiped panic-induced sweat off his forehead. He managed a smile and asked, "You saw that big pit outside, right?"

The recruits chuckled, and one said, "Kind of hard to miss it."

"Well, we're going to need people to fill that in, maybe bury some garbage at the same time. You know what? You guys look like the right people for the job."

"Really?" asked the goblin.

* * * * *

"Really?" asked the goblin. In the law offices of Cickam, Wender and Downe, the crystal ball made the goblin's voice sound high and scratchy. Static filled the ball and Twain tapped it, trying to improve the reception. Next to his desk was a mouse hole, a pile of smashed mouse traps, and a steel bear trap twisted up like a pretzel and stained with cheese crumbs.

Twain was in a good mood. Oh sure, he still had the mouse in his office, but his newly hired king was doing well. Twain had been following Will's misadventures with breathless anticipation. There were a few spots where he'd been worried, but Twain was pleased to see things work out as well as they had. As he followed Will's conversation with the goblin, the picture turned to static again.

"Blast it, the rates for these things keep going up and the picture quality keeps getting worse," Twain said. He slapped the crystal ball, but the reception stayed bad. "Jennifer, I swear I'm going to sue the provider if this doesn't get better."

"Yes, sir," his secretary said. She peeked inside his office and asked, "How's the new guy working out?"

Twain leaned back in his chair and nodded. "Not bad, not bad at all. He's doing better than I thought he would. I'd go so far as to say he's exactly who we need for the job."

"How long do you think you can keep him there?" she asked.

Twain smiled as he put his feet up on his desk and folded his arms across his chest. “Oh he’ll be there for a while. Our friend Mr. Bradshaw is going to help us set things right.”

Printed in Great Britain
by Amazon